Going, Going, Gone!

A Nikki Carson
Auction Mystery

By

A.N. Charles

Published by A.N. Charles Enterprises
P.O. Box 1187 Hayward, WI 54843

Cover design by Dee Lindner
Cover photographs courtesy of Alexandra Charles

9 8 7 6 5 4 3 2 1

ISBN: 978-1-543070-24-8

Printed in the United States of America

For Our Lovable Felines

Chapter One

Friday

The Red Shed Auction Enterprises banner on the mobile trailer emanated a foul plastic smell in the stifling late August heat.

"Nicole Carson," I replied promptly to the young woman sitting behind the open window of the trailer. *Why does my maiden name sound so foreign to me? After all, I was Nicole Carson for twenty-four years and a Fairplay for less than four.*

Fairplay seemed such an honorable name to adopt when I married Richard. Now, the name remained a painfully ironic reminder of my failed marriage. Richard had proven himself to be a 'Dick' in every sense of the word—not once playing fair during our marriage—far from it.

"Address?" the woman asked, jolting me back to the present.

"Huh?"

"Your address, ma'am," she reiterated between loud chewing gum pops, her short-cropped red hair fluttering to the rhythmic clicking of two nearby oscillating fans, laboring to provide relief from the suffocating, torpid humidity.

"Five thirty-sev—oops! I mean six twenty-four, Campezi Lane, Hickory Grove," I answered, only to see her raise a questioning studded eyebrow. *When will I automatically remember the address of my new home, a cute bungalow in an up and coming neighborhood?* I lost count of how many times I got off work or ran errands, only to head in the wrong direction upon my return—to the house that now belonged to my ex.

"May I see your driver's license?" Red asked impatiently.

"Oh, I'm sorry," I replied, and dug into my purse—what Richard had called the 'bottomless pit,'—for my new driver's license. "Is there anything else you need?" I asked anxiously after hearing the auctioneer announce the estate auction for Clint Peterson was to begin at 10:00 a.m. sharp, and for participants to make sure to obtain a bid number at the trailer.

"I need your phone number and signature on this form, and then you're good to go. First time at an auction, ma'am?" she asked as she tugged at a fallen shoulder strap on her gauzy, bright red sun dress. The color and shape exemplified her corpulent form and highlighted her mottled cheeks, blotchy from the heat.

"No," I replied and rattled off my cell phone number, one of the few things the divorce hadn't changed. "I'm trying to make a go of it as a middleman, or is it now middlewoman?"

"Got me," Red exclaimed, pushing the form over the window counter to me. I affixed my signature on the line where her black and white polished fingernail indicated. "Here you go," Red declared, handing me my bidder's card with number eighty-two printed in large black block numbers.

"Thanks," I mumbled, and stepped aside to allow the people queued up behind me to advance.

I made my way through the throng of assembled bidders while the auctioneer, a short rotund fellow who towered over the attendees whilst perched on his platform, began his opening spiel.

"Mornin' folks, I'm Chuck Wood, or as some of the people I recognize here today know me, Woody, from Red Shed Auction Enterprises in Walnut Grove. My wife, Claire, and I are happy to be doing this auction. My father was an auctioneer for thirty-five years and I'm proud to say we've kept it in our family for over thirty-two years."

I wondered what else the Wood's had kept in the family, for Annie, my mentor, had brought me up to speed on the ins and outs of auctioneering since I was new to the trade. She told me theft, seeding, double-dealing, false recordkeeping, and more were commonplace in the industry. And Annie would know based on nearly thirty-five years of auction knowledge—hearing all the scuttlebutt from auctioneers, auction frequenters, and family estate members.

"We'll start with the tables here on the front lawn and work our way to the furniture at the side yard," Woody continued. "Now as you folks know, Clint Peterson was a collector nearly all his life. He used to be an art professor at Northern Illinois University until he retired some twenty years ago. There are hundreds of items stored in the out-building, too, and it all has to go by the end of tomorrow. We're going to stop at three today, and tomorrow we'll go as long as it takes to sell whatever remains."

I tuned out the rest of Woody's diatribe to size-up my competition. I had been attending auctions for less than a year, right after I separated from Richard, but I already recognized a few of the 'regulars.' I roughly counted a hundred and fifty people at this morning's kick-off. Experience had taught me the attendance number would spike around mid-morning and then slowly ebb from lunchtime until late afternoon.

Annie coached me to recognize familiar faces and to learn bidders' buying patterns and bidding 'tells.' In fact, she wouldn't let me attend an auction on my own until she felt confident I had established a solid foundation of information to draw upon—people, buying trends, appraisal values, you name it. Fortunately for me, the advent of technology made things much easier since Annie's buying heyday. With my trusty iPad or iPhone in hand, I was able to research items on the spot, check prices on eBay and other on-line resources, and efficiently calculate my bidding limits. Luckily, few auction goers had readily adopted technology in the way I had, a benefit derived from being younger than the average attendee demographic. For most of the people, attending auctions was a way to pass time. For me and other arbitragers, or flippers as we're known, this was business—my bread-and-butter—and I did all I could to establish a leg-up on my competition.

"Make sure and hold your number up high when you bid so I can see it and Claire can record the winning number," Woody counseled. "And don't forget folks, we've got lots of food and drinks in the food trailer. We have brats and hotdogs on the menu today, along with assorted cold drinks."

I moved nearer to the front tables and recognized Carole Winker standing to my right. She owned a house a few blocks from me on Campezi Lane. We weren't close friends, but like me she was an artist. I didn't know her to be an auction goer, but she had attended the last few auctions I had frequented. Hopefully, she wasn't becoming a regular. Competition was stiff enough without adding more flippers into the mix.

Carole rummaged through a box with rapt attention. Sidling up to the same table, I casually browsed through items until I came to the box of goods she had scrutinized a few moments earlier. The box was packed with postcards, and I immediately understood her interest. She creates and frames decoupage collages. The scenic pictures of foreign places on the postcards were a perfect fit for her work. I made a mental note to speak to her, as a few pieces of her artwork might work well in my themed-room settings at Annie's Attic, the eclectic antique and collectibles store where I worked.

Someone bumped into me and I turned to see Guy Westin stooping over a box of calendars, oblivious to his rude gesture. He was a local who hunted for items to resell at the Crane County Flea Market. He had a penchant for paper goods, especially vintage pieces. He kept a close lookout for items he could quickly turnaround and sell to buyers with whom he kept in close contact.

I could use some of the old magazines and calendars in the bin Guy was examining, but I remembered that Annie said the only time to go for paper was when Guy wasn't bidding. She also counseled me to only purchase paper goods sold by the boxful or lot. Seeing Guy took the wind out of my sails, but I was determined to make a go for the calendars. Annie's words of wisdom resonated with me: 'No one has friends at an auction, Nikki. Look out for yourself and let the chips fall where they may.'

Auctioneers often combined less desirable items with more valuable items into boxed lots. This method of combining the good with the bad had its upside by expediting the auction. The lots were often sold to bottom-fishers—those individuals, like Guy, who scooped up items nobody else wanted.

Don't misunderstand. Bottom-fishers serve a vital function at auctions. They keep the auction moving along when no one else will bid, and they clear the tables of detritus and other miscellany. Who knew what they did with the stuff they purchased. Nobody really cared as long as they didn't have to deal with it—a practice akin to waste management firms who provide garbage service. Out of sight, out of mind, as the saying goes.

Carole remained off to my right, intently digging through the contents of another box. I was curious as to what items held her interest so ardently again, but before I could make my way over to her, she became engaged in a fervent conversation with Ken Lawton and his partner, Barry Dynel. Ken and Barry run The Antique Shoppe in Walnut Grove, a neighboring burg. Ken is the owner and Barry is his right hand man. Annie considers them her competitors in a long-armed manner.

I casually sauntered over towards them. Barry saw me approach. He nudged Ken and gave a slight head motion towards me. Immediately, all three clammed up tight, making an awkward moment for all.

"Hi Carole. Hello Ken, Barry," I said as if I hadn't seen Barry's gesture. "I didn't know you two would be here today. Are you buying for the store?"

"Yes," Barry replied laconically, nervously shifting from foot to foot. I looked to Carole for a kindly word to bridge the awkward silence as Ken abruptly turned his back to me, but she, too, was cool and aloof. Thinking their behavior ill-mannered, I awkwardly stepped away to examine items perched atop the nearby row of tables.

Not many people cared for Ken, including Annie and me, but we tolerated him like the common cold. At one time, Ken had done a bit of appraising for Annie. Several times after she had marked items according to his appraised values, strangers would come in to her store and buy the pieces—too quickly to her way of thinking. She told me she had once mentioned the oddity of it to Jenny O'Hara, a Hickory Grove native who tended bar at the Shamrock. Jenny had attended high school with Ken and warned Annie not to trust him. According to Jenny, 'If you shake hands with him, you better check to see if you have all your fingers afterwards.' Annie hadn't enlisted Ken's appraisal services since; even though she knew Jenny didn't always back up what she said with facts.

Nevertheless, Barry frequented Annie's Attic to sell items on occasion, but Annie suspected his visits were at Ken's prompting to spy on her inventory and to size up their competition more than anything else. Few, if any people, could pull the wool over Annie's eyes as she knew her business inside and out—she was not one to be taken. Lately, Barry's visits had diminished, perhaps due to his over-inflated wholesale prices. Why they felt they had to gouge business associates and make for bad relations was beyond us. Maybe there was truth to the rumor they were going to retire soon and no longer cared about maintaining valuable business relationships.

I glanced over at the trio again. Carole was fervently nodding her head while Ken vigorously shook his back and forth. *I wonder what that's about?* I wanted to move closer to overhear what had them so animated, but Ken clutched Carole's arm and pulled her roughly away from the assembled bidders. Barry moved to his side, ever silent and watchful.

Annie had informed me that besides being in business together, Ken and Barry were also life partners. Ken, the brains behind the business, knew his antiques. He was also aggressive and liked to push his considerable weight, about three hundred pounds of it, around. Barry, on the other hand, was passive. Slim with a pale complexion, he was in his early forties, at least a good ten years younger than Ken.

Barry glanced about furtively as Ken grasped Carole's upper arms and shook her violently. Her face contorted in rage and she lashed out at him with a sharp kick to his shin. Ken howled in pain, released his grip on her, and limply hopped on one foot. Barry observed me watching them, touched Ken's arm, and said something quietly to him. Ken growled something in hushed tones and pointedly shook his finger at Carole who reacted with a sneer, said something in return, and stalked off. Although I didn't know Carole well, her actions startled me.

Clearly Ken was not happy. He waved his hands with small jerky motions as he spoke to his partner. To judge by Barry's ashen countenance, Ken was taking things out on him. He finished scolding his partner, did an about face, and returned to a chair placed next to the trailer where Woody's helpers had set a table. Ken, his face flushed, reached in his pants pocket, extracted a handkerchief, and studiously wiped spittle from his chin and sweat from his brow and neck. Barry meandered over to where bidders, in anticipation of the auction start, were gathered either sitting in chairs or standing next to the auctioneer's trailer.

Besides the confrontation itself, something else struck me odd about the scene I had just observed. Ken had been his usual pushy self, but it was the haughty look on Carole's face when she kicked him that stuck in my mind. I never knew her to be violent, but then Ken had become physical and all she did was act in defense. Regardless, her actions were so out of character from the woman I thought I knew, I decided to see if I might be of help to her.

"How's it going, Carole?"

"Good, Nicole. How are you?"

"Great, except for this heat."

"Yeah, it's going to be a scorcher."

"I'm not sure I'm going to make it through the whole day," I lamented. "Hey, I couldn't help but see you having words with Ken. What's he all steamed up about?"

She flashed me a brief hard look before resuming an innocent countenance. "It was nothing. He got mad when I told him I thought his appraisals were too high."

"You mean he appraised the items for this auction?"

"Yeah, and inflated all the prices which means Woody will begin the bidding higher than usual."

"Don't let what Ken does intimidate you—he's a known bully. If I can help, let me know, Carole."

She answered my offer of assistance with a harsh, mocking laugh. "Don't worry, I can handle him. He doesn't frighten me."

"You're braver than I am. I don't know what I'd do if he started to push me around," I admitted.

"Just give him a swift kick in the balls," she said with another laugh. "That works on most of 'em."

Carole's gruff, unexpected statement left me momentarily taken aback. Obviously, the impression I had formed regarding her from our previous encounters required a serious reappraisal. I tried to make light of the matter by replying, "I should have tried it with my ex."

She acknowledged my capricious statement with a wry grin.

"How did you make out at the Krieger auction?" I asked, changing the subject to assuage my tension.

"I couldn't make it," she said, her previous intensity returning to her countenance.

"The auction last week," I clarified, "you know, the one in Walnut Grove?"

"Uh-uh. I wasn't there. I was out of town. Must have been somebody else," she declared emphatically, turned and walked away.

Stunned, I stood transfixed, eyes agape. I was not mistaken. Carole had been at the Krieger auction, for I distinctly remembered her buying an antique music cabinet I had my eye on. *Why did she lie and tell me she wasn't there?*

With a little time to spare, I tried to digest Carole's strange behavior and sauntered over to a big white, sleek credenza and two maple display cases set amongst other furniture arranged on the side lawn. Looking close, the workmanship and details appeared to be identical for all three pieces. *Are they a set and someone decided to paint the credenza, but left the other cases natural?*

Two men were in a heated discussion near the credenza. I brushed by them to get a closer look at the big white beast. The paint greatly reduced the credenza's appeal and monetary value to my way of thinking. Also, it was large and unwieldy. As an individual piece it didn't look like much, but if it was stripped, and proved a match for the two maple cases, the trio held great promise. I knelt down and examined the back. A slight indentation was in the center, six inches above the base. I scraped at it with my nails— flicking off paint in small chips. Checking to see no one was watching me, I worked away at the spot until the words 'Made in France' were barely legible.

"Bingo," I said under my breath, my pulse racing. Standing up, I brushed off my jeans and hoped my excitement wasn't noticeable to any onlookers. If I wasn't mistaken, the credenza was truly an Art Deco era piece. Clint Peterson had an affinity for collecting pieces from the 1920s to judge by other items scattered throughout the auction. Art Deco pieces never went out of favor, and lately they were commanding all-time high prices. The credenza might easily be worth two thousand dollars or more once restored to its original condition.

The two men standing nearby remained engrossed in discussion and seemed oblivious to my presence. When I bent over again to examine the underside of the credenza for possible water damage, I couldn't help but overhear part of their conversation. "He'd make a great acupuncturist— he's been sticking it to people for years." *Why are people so cranky today? The heat and humidity must be bringing out the worst in people.* Tempers were flaring and would only worsen as it was only ten-thirty.

I walked away so as not to show my enthusiasm to others mingling nearby. With a final glance at the credenza, I said a silent prayer. I decided to bid up to six hundred dollars for all three pieces—surely, that would suffice—at least I hoped so. In the past, I had seen many an instance where the heat of competition spurred bidders to pay outrageous prices for items over the going prices on eBay. An auction was no place for emotions to take over.

If I do win the pieces, how will I move them? They were much too big for my SUV, and the credenza alone would easily tip the scales at well over a hundred pounds, making a truck necessary to convey the pieces to the shop. I usually relied on Annie's husband, Burton, to lend me a hand and the use of his truck to move large pieces, but he and Annie were spending a long weekend up at Lake Geneva, a resort town in southern Wisconsin. I noticed Ken and Barry drove a new truck. *Will they help me if I win the pieces?* I asked myself before I regained my senses. Ken would never agree to do me or anyone a favor.

It was time to rejoin the auction to see how far Woody had progressed. A quick reexamination of the items remaining on the tables assured me I hadn't missed anything of interest, except an odd looking pipe caught my attention at the far end of the table. Stepping sidewise, my purse banged into a woman squatting down, looking through a box of unframed art. She was dressed all in black, including her black fringed leather fanny pack.

"Oh, I'm so sorry. I didn't see you," I apologized, noting that even her shoulder length hair, tied in a ponytail, was black.

She gave me a nasty look. "Why don't you look where you're going?"

"I said I was sorry," I replied defensively.

She airily waved me off with a curt hand motion and returned to study the box's contents. I could feel my own temperature rise at her abrupt dismissal—as if I was nothing more to her than an annoying insect. Exasperated by her attitude, I bit my tongue. This auction wasn't boding well for me. *Should I call it a day and just go home?*

Chapter Two

The woman-in-black spent an inordinate amount of time looking through a few select boxes. When she finally moved on down the row of tables, I assumed her spot and began to browse through the containers. Most of the art pieces were of good quality, perhaps a treasure or two were hidden amongst the items. I reached in my purse for my iPad, but when I finished my hasty research, I determined none of the artist names would put substantial cha-ching in my cash drawer. I didn't expect to find a Renoir, but I was surprised Clint Peterson hadn't collected something of greater value. Maybe the woman-in-black had the same thought and that was why she had studied the boxes' contents so thoroughly. As far as I could tell, Peterson collected pieces he liked and didn't care about their investment potential. In a way, I was glad I hadn't found anything—Miss Snippy looked like she could be a formidable adversary.

At least two hundred people were now in attendance, making it hard for me to do any item research unnoticed, so I surreptitiously tucked my iPad back into my purse. An expensive gadget, I liked to keep it out of sight, away from prying eyes. I didn't want one of my most valuable tools to illicit the curiosity of my competitors, nor for them to think I was well-off. I wasn't. Impressions can be everything. Annie instructed me to always keep a low profile, and I abided by her wisdom, even down to the old t-shirt and jeans I wore so people wouldn't bid me up thinking I had money to burn.

Many of the attendees, probably collectors like the late owner, swarmed about the tables, checking out the goods. Annie had warned me to arrive early, but unfortunately, my two cats, Inky and Dinky, had other ideas for me this morning.

Inky had found a loose lower corner edge on the rear screened door and had pushed her way through to the outside. I spent a frenzied half-hour trying to coax her out from under the porch, while her sister Dinky, the more timid of the two, watched on from the doorway. By the time I retrieved Inky, barely enough time remained for me to clean up and make the start of today's auction. Without having proper time to do any research in advance, I now had to wing it to stay one step ahead of the auctioneer, and more importantly, the other bidders.

I quickly perused the figurines and glassware on the first row of tables, and determined it was going to be difficult to make much money flipping them on eBay or selling them through the antique store for many of the items had passed their heyday of desire in the marketplace. Everybody and their uncle were now selling their parents' and grandparents' precious heirlooms on-line. Vintage goods, once scarce due to the limited means of reaching the buying public, now flooded the market. Goods like Japanese occupied-era salt and pepper shakers, milk glass, hand-made quilts, figurines, collector plates, and silver-plated tea sets, had become anathema for flippers and antique dealers alike. Easy availability, made possible through technological advances, had caused the bottom to fall out for many items that once commanded respectable prices. Nonetheless, savvy buyers could still earn double or treble their investment if they were choosy and bought the right items at the right prices.

A table full of Art Deco era clocks and other miscellaneous items were coming up next for bid. *Okay, Nikki, this is it—dog-eat-dog competition. If you want to make a go of it without anyone's help, steel yourself for the competition. Go get 'em girl!*

"Folks, this table of items will be sold as 'bidder's choice,'" Woody announced. "When the bidding ends, the top bidder has a choice of what to buy and how many to buy."

The bidding started at ten and quickly moved to twenty. Carole jumped in, and she and another bidder quickly ran the bid up to fifty. After she stopped bidding, she withdrew an iPad from her purse and moved off to the side. *I'm not the only one to incorporate today's technology in this business.* It was only a matter of time before a majority of auction goers would jump on the technology bandwagon, especially with the recent influx of young people like me entering the business.

"Seventy-five," a woman shouted from my right. I glanced over to see who the competition was and spotted Crazy Mary.

"Ma'am, you're already the high bidder," Woody announced to the delight of the crowd.

"What's up for bid?" she asked.

"It's for choice on the table, ma'am."

"Don't you know what you're bidding on?" a woman standing next to Crazy Mary asked incredulously.

"I don't need to know. If someone else is bidding the price up, it must have value, but I'm the one who's going to win it—not that it's any of your business," Mary said defiantly. Her declaration left more than a few people within hearing range wagging their heads in disbelief. Mary won the bid and I crossed my fingers hoping she wouldn't select one of the Smith Sentric clocks. She stepped forward and claimed a large mantel clock made of chromium and black Bakelite.

"Figures," I mumbled under my breath as I saw she had gone for size, granting me my wish. She hadn't a clue as to where the real value resided.

Crazy Mary was one of the regulars. She obtained her moniker because she became easily confused at auctions with uncanny constancy. Granted, even for the initiated, auctioneers' patter is often difficult to understand.

Auctioneers' bid calling, or what some refer to as their 'cattle-rattle,' required one's full attention, but she made a regular habit of not following the bidding process.

Throwing prudence aside, Crazy Mary's bids often exceeded the average retail prices for items. When she wanted a particular item, she didn't care how much it cost. She was a private collector, not in the reselling business. Someone once told me she was a hoarder; her house packed to the rafters with her *treasures*, and I believed them to judge from her irrational behavior. On numerous occasions, I heard her bidding against herself. Today's example was just one more reflection of her impulsive, rapacious character. I just hoped she didn't bid on anything else I wanted. While she added local color to auctions, she was also an extremely uncouth individual, and I made every effort to avoid crossing her path.

After Crazy Mary claimed her prize, the auctioneer began the bidding process again for the next choice. The bidding stalled at twenty-five until Carole jumped in. The remaining two Sentric clocks were perfect for my Art Deco living room ensemble, but I hesitated to up the bid because little profit existed for reselling the remaining clocks on a stand-alone basis. If I won them, I'd have to rely on my room's aggregate value. Trusting the value would be there, I flagged my number at the auctioneer. Woody was ready to bang down the figurative gavel with my bid in the lead at thirty dollars when I spied Ken giving Barry an almost indiscernible nod. Barry held up his bidding number and shouted, "Thirty-five."

How can this be? The estate appraiser has an advantage over everyone else, and for Barry to bid on Ken's behalf seems an obvious conflict of interest. Outraged, I wagged my number to Woody and immediately turned my attention back to the pair. Barry was watching Ken like a hawk, earnestly waiting for another bid signal. Ken gave me a disdainful look and ever so slightly nodded his head back and forth to his partner.

Pressing forward, I seized the two Smith clocks I had won at forty dollars. One was a chrome and blue glass beauty and the other was made of brass with chromium adornments—pieces that would really bring sparkle to my display. In my previous haste, I had failed to notice that the letter 'T' on one of the clocks was larger than the other letters in its marking. This small difference made the clock more valuable to collectors and helped assuage my buyer's remorse for the price I paid. I was elated with my discovery, not to mention the pleasure I felt in beating Ken at his own game.

While Woody resumed the bidding for the remaining clocks, I went to my car to unburden myself of my winnings. By the time I returned, Woody had progressed to the next table where two of his helpers were unpacking a large boxful of Fiesta dinnerware.

"This is choice per set, not per box," Woody announced.

I groaned audibly, for I had hoped to buy the entire box as one lot. An array of colorful dishware, complimented by table linens, glasses, and vases would make an ideal table display in my staged kitchen ensemble. I should have known Woody was no fool. He knew by selling the sets individually, each would command a higher price. The unpacked tableware looked so cheery and attractive in their bright cobalt blue, red, light green and yellow colors that everyone would want them. As I scanned the assembled crowd, there was no sign of Crazy Mary—her absence a positive sign. *Did she take a lunch break?*

Bidding opened at twenty, but no one started the action. Woody tried for fifteen, but still no one bit. With a scowl, he lowered the bid to ten and someone countered with five dollars. I became excited to see so little interest, but my enthusiasm was short-lived. The woman-in-black stepped forward and bid ten. I upped the bid to fifteen and she immediately countered with twenty. If I went higher, it would be a chancy break-even at best for me.

"Twenty-two fifty," I shouted, setting the pace at a smaller increment level.

"Twenty-five," she countered without hesitation.

I shook my head from side to side to let Woody know I was out. Much to my surprise, the woman-in-black only selected the yellow and red sets which left one more red set, a green set, and two blue sets.

"Anyone else for twenty-five?" Woody asked as he surveyed the crowd.

Thankfully, no one accepted his offer and the bidding restarted. I kicked it off at five dollars again. This time an elderly man to my right bid seven-and-a-half. I edged over to him, thinking about a side-deal. "Are you bidding on a particular color?" I was ready for any response ranging from stony silence to outright hostility.

To my delight, he gave me a smile and said, "One of the blue sets."

Something about his manner made me feel he was trustworthy. "It's yours," I said and waved off my bid to Woody.

Now came the moment of truth to see if my trust was well-placed. The gent, true to his word, claimed only one of the blue sets. He gave me an encouraging nod of thanks as he carried his dishes away.

"Anyone else for seven-fifty?" Woody solicited.

This was the risky part. If anyone else claimed one of the sets, I was screwed. Auctions are a funny competition. I've seen them bring out the best in people and the worst. More times than not, it was the worst. Biting my lip, Woody worked the crowd and I waited anxiously to see if my bet paid off.

Yes! No one bid and Woody restarted the bidding. After no one picked up his opening of five dollars, he declared, "All three sets for ten."

I vigorously wagged my number. "Do I have fifteen?" he asked.

He worked the crowd for what seemed an eternity before he announced, "Sold, ten dollars."

Wow! Like I said, you never know how bidding will go. The frequently illogical nature of live auctions made them both exciting and stressful. Often I had won the top bid for a choice of items, like the woman-in-black, only to see the bidding drop off dramatically during the ensuing round for the remaining lot items.

There was risk involved in 'choice' bidding and auctioneers relied on it. They knew that by creating anxiety, people often bid more than they normally would under less stressful circumstances. The stress factor was also one of the reasons why auctioneers don't make their ramblings more intelligible—their slurring patter put people on edge, adding to bidder anxiousness.

A helper packed the dishes into two boxes, and I happily hefted my winnings to my SUV, while Woody moved on to a row of boxes filled with books. After safely stowing the dinnerware, I climbed in the driver's seat and opened my freezer pack. I doused my hands with sanitizer I kept handy before I wolfed down a peanut butter and jelly sandwich I had hurriedly made this morning. I replenished my fluids with a half bottle of water, toweled the dirt and grime off my sticky arms, and relocked my vehicle.

When I returned to the action, Woody had reached the outdoor holiday decorations lined up on the sun-kissed lawn. The temperature had risen into the nineties and the humidity was off the charts. The blistering heat was continuing to have a noticeable effect on those present. The crowd had thinned out and those who remained looked drained. My hair was matted to my forehead and neck. Thankfully, I had it cut into a bob for the summer—a style Richard didn't like, but one my beautician and I thought best highlighted my facial structure.

I listened attentively to Woody's cadence still going strong. As much as I often questioned the integrity of auctioneers, I did admire their ability to work long hours, especially when conditions were far from optimal, like today. I knew I couldn't do it. They must have vocal chords like a mastodon to unceasingly speak their mumble-jumble for hours on end.

A sheet-music cabinet that had caught my eye earlier was next up for bid. I surveyed the crowd for potential competition. The woman-in-black stood near one of Woody's helpers, Carole sat nearby, animatedly entering something into her iPad, and Crazy Mary rested in a stadium chair, near the smelly privy of all places, her winnings stashed under her chair. Ken, seated by Woody, was dabbing at the sweat on his brow, and looked like he might succumb to heat stroke at any minute. He eyed the crowd with displeasure and I followed his gaze. When I did not see Barry standing at his post by the auction trailer, I figured his absence was the cause of Ken's obvious annoyance.

Similar music cabinets retailed for around a hundred-and-fifty dollars. Woody opened the bid at fifty and I raised my number. Ken hiked the bid to sixty, acting irritated that he had to personally bid rather than do so surreptitiously through Barry. I would have gone up to a hundred since I knew someone I could sell it to for a fast turnaround, but thankfully Ken stopped bidding at seventy-five dollars.

Ken turned to the auctioneer and told him to sell the credenza and cabinets next and then stop for the day. *That's odd. I never knew an appraiser to instruct the auctioneer on how to conduct his auction. The auctioneer is always the person in charge.*

"All right folks, these pieces are the last items of the day," Woody said, giving Ken a reproachful look. His announcement caused nearly all of the remaining attendees to take their leave. "Don't forget folks, tomorrow we're selling the rest of the goods out here and all the items in the storage building. Get here early for a preview. We kick off at nine. The shed is packed with goodies, hundreds of unique items and collectibles, so be sure to tell your friends," he shouted to the retreating bidders.

"What'll I hear for an opening bid?" Woody asked. "Do I have two hundred?" My heart leapt with joy when no one showed the slightest interest in bidding for the credenza. Woody cajoled the crowd to elicit a favorable response, but the few remaining attendees were tired. It had been a hot, draining day, exacerbated by the necessity to mostly stand to bid on items strewn about the grounds. Tomorrow would be much more comfortable, as most of the bidding would take place at one location and bidders could rest comfortably in chairs.

I opened the bid at a paltry twenty-five dollars. I could hardly hide my enthusiasm and my heart began to pound like a heavy-metal drummer. To my chagrin, Woody did his best to solicit bids from the meager bunch, teasing and wheedling them, but try as he might he received no takers. Incredibly, my bid of twenty-five dollars stood. I figured I had practically stolen the piece because few people wanted to deal with something so bulky on such an uncomfortable day. I snatched up the matching side cabinets, too, for twenty each, but my elation at having won the three pieces was temporarily mitigated when I reconsidered the problem I now faced. *How am I going to move them?*

When one of the auction helpers brushed by me, I reached out and grabbed his arm. "Excuse me. I just bought those pieces," I said waving my arm at the furniture that grew in enormity every time I looked at the pieces. Do you know of anyone with a pickup truck or trailer who would help me move them? Of course, I'll pay for it," I added giving him my best damsel-in-distress look.

"Sorry, I can't help you," he replied brusquely and strode off.

A feeling of helplessness, followed by dejection, settled on me. Someone lightly touched my left arm, and a deep stentorian voice said, "I couldn't help but overhear, miss. I have a truck and would be glad to help you move the furniture."

I turned and looked up into a pair of vivid blue-green eyes. It was like staring into the depths of the ocean. I judged my savior to be in his early fifties. He had curly brown hair turning to gray at the temples and a deep bronze tan. His faced was lined with character, as if he had worked on a horse or cattle ranch his whole life. A big smile, highlighted by even rows of white teeth, was offset by a thick bushy mustache. He was a rangy character, raw-boned, a little over six feet tall, and I guessed he weighed about a hundred and eighty pounds.

A warm happy feeling came over me as I studied his face. "Thank you, so much. You're a lifesaver. I insist on paying whatever you think is reasonable."

He considered my offer for a second. "How far away do you live?"

"Actually, I want the pieces taken to my workplace in downtown Hickory Grove."

"Hmm, that's about three miles from here. How does ten bucks sound?"

"That works for me if it works for you. I'll settle up and see if I can get one of the workers to help with loading the pieces into your truck."

"You look fit. Are you sure we need help?"

I wasn't sure he was teasing me until I took in his grin. "Thanks for the compliment . . . I think. I'm Nikki," I said and held out my hand.

"Brett," he returned and shook my hand with a firm grip. "I'll back my truck over and meet you here after you settle with the man."

"Sounds good."

I was fifth in line at the trailer and two women in front of me were grumbling about Woody stopping for the day. "It's only two o'clock," I heard one of them say. "He said it would go until three."

"It's because of the heat; he was losing too many people. Tomorrow's supposed to be cooler," the other replied.

"But I can't come tomorrow. I've got to take my kid to soccer practice."

"Too bad. I overheard one of the workers say the really good stuff is in the shed."

After the two women paid their accounts, I handed my bidder's number to Red, and said, "I'll need some help moving some of the furniture I bought."

"Sure thing, ma'am. I'll get one of the boys to help as soon as you're done here."

Red looked drained from spending the day in the hot-house trailer. She wasn't nearly as ebullient as she had been earlier, hardly saying a word as she added up the cost of my purchases. Her hair was in matted strings, sticking to the sides of her face and neck. I knew I had to look as bad as she—my hair was wet like a mop, my eyes stung, and the little make-up I had applied earlier had to be long gone.

"Do I need a new number for tomorrow?"

"Yeah, unless you want me to reserve the same number for you," she replied wearily.

"No, I can't imagine why I'd want it."

"You'd be surprised, honey. Sometimes people want their favorite number, they think it's lucky."

"Takes all kinds," I replied with a shake of my head.

"And I meet 'em all. Makes the world go 'round they tell me," she added with a sigh.

Red definitely wasn't the same person I had met at the start of the day. She shoved the calculator ticket over to me. Following Annie's sage advice, I checked Red's numbers against the figures I had noted in my iPad. Everything matched. *Good.* More times than not, I discovered discrepancies—a common occurrence as whoever was responsible for recording the sales prices often became distracted during the auction. They frequently lost the monetary point where bidding stopped, or worse, noted the number of the wrong bidder. After I settled my account, Red picked up her walkie-talkie and summoned aid. About a minute later, a young man appeared at my side, sweat dripping from the tip of his nose.

"She bought the white credenza and cabinets," Red told him.

"I've got a truck and another fellow to help load them," I offered as an appeasement to his drained countenance.

He merely nodded. His *War Against the Machine* t-shirt, soaked with sweat, clung to his body outlining his wiry, lean muscular frame. I led the way to Brett who was securing a couple of blankets around the credenza with bungee cords.

The two men made short shrift of lifting the credenza and side pieces into Brett's truck bed. The young helper returned my thanks with a quick smile and curt nod before another bidder shanghaied him to assist with a refrigerator. I grabbed the kid's hand and stuffed a five dollar bill into it as he turned to leave. He gave me a smile, nodded his thanks, and hurried away to catch up with the other customer.

"Oops. I forgot. I also bought that music cabinet," I said pointing at my prize.

"Looks light enough for the two of us to handle," Brett said pleasantly and strode over to the stand to test its weight.

He was right. The two of us easily lifted the cabinet into the truck bed and secured it beside the credenza. Brett checked to ensure all pieces were safe against movement and gave me a thumbs-up sign.

"Follow me. I'm driving a silver GMC SUV," I told him and walked off to fetch my vehicle.

At *Annie's Attic*, I pulled around into the alleyway behind the store and Brett angled his truck toward the rear entrance to make unloading easier.

"I'll fetch a handcart," I offered, while Brett readied the pieces for unloading.

First, we unloaded the music cabinet and set it off to the side. Then we pulled the blanket the credenza laid on to the edge of the truck's tailgate. Carefully, we eased the credenza to the ground, an end partly resting on the handcart. Both of us tilted the cabinet over until its full weight rested on the cart before Brett maneuvered the piece through the store's extra-wide back door. After twenty minutes of moving items here and there, we finally had all the furniture positioned to my liking. Brett busied himself with his blankets and cords while I easily wheeled the music cabinet into another corner of my room.

Fishing a twenty dollar bill out of my purse, I handed it to him and said, "You earned it."

"I'll owe you one then."

"Oh, do you work for Red Shed Auction Enterprises?"

"No, I'm a retired carpenter. I mainly do odd jobs now. I go to most of the auctions in the area to buy beat up old furniture to restore for resale. I'm sure we'll run into each other again. I've seen you at the last couple of auctions."

"Really?"

"You're hard to miss, Nikki," he said with a grin.

I actually blushed like a school girl. I was embarrassed and flattered at the same time. "I'll send whatever business I can your way. Do you have a card?"

He reached into his back jeans' pocket, took out his wallet and fished out a card. "Excuse the condition," he said handing me a damp, wilted card. "This humidity is a killer."

"It sure is. Would you be willing to restore the credenza for me?"

"Yeah, that shouldn't be too hard. It looks to be in good condition. I would have bid on it myself except I got to talking to a fella I know and it was gone before I noticed it."

"Lucky for me. I'll call you if I decide to strip it, okay?"

"We *are* talking about the credenza, aren't we?"

There I was blushing, again. "Y-yeah," I stammered. "Thanks again for all your help, Brett. I don't know what I would have done without you."

"The pleasure's all mine. Call me anytime. Be seeing you around," he said as he climbed in his truck and drove away.

"They don't make 'em like that anymore," I said aloud and instantly regretted saying so when I realized Denise was standing behind me.

"Too bad he isn't younger," she ruminated.

"I didn't mean it that way."

"I did," she said with a laugh. "He looked sexy sweaty."

"He's a retired carpenter. Say the word and I'll introduce you."

"Naw, I try not to date guys old enough to be my father."

"C'mere and look what I bought today at the Peterson auction," I said, grabbing her arm and pulling her into my staging room.

"Wow, those are some pieces," she exclaimed as she stepped over to the credenza for a closer inspection.

"Wait till you see the Fiesta dinnerware I scooped today."

After I carried the boxes from my car into the back room, Denise helped me unpack the plate settings. "Wow, these are in mint condition, Nikki. Do you know how long I've looked for a set in this condition?" she moaned admiringly. "Amazing—there aren't any chips or crazing," she said as she gave the pieces a closer inspection. "Will you sell me a set?"

"Sure. I'm only going to use two of the settings. How about twenty?"

"Deal," she quickly agreed.

"Okay, pick whatever set you want." *Life is good.* I had just doubled my money on the Fiesta dinnerware and still had two complete sets to use in my staged kitchen setting.

Denise stacked up the orange set. Gushing, she declared, "These are the real finds from the thirties. They're too good to use—I'm just going to display them," she added before she rushed off with her prize while I repacked the remaining dishes.

Afterwards, I slid the music cabinet out from the wall to examine it more closely. A stamp on the rear panel revealed *Larkin Furniture Company Buffalo, New York*, as the manufacturer. Printed underneath the stamp, in faint lettering, was *Inspected March 30, 1911.*

"Yes!" Not only was the cabinet in perfect condition, it was a genuine antique, over one-hundred years old, and easily worth twice what I paid for it. "Thank you, Clint Peterson," I murmured, looking skyward, "for having good taste and taking care of your stuff."

I couldn't wait to call my friend, the music teacher, who had expressed an interest to me months ago in purchasing such a piece. When she answered my call, I excitedly told her about the cabinet. "There's an exquisite lute and piece of sheet music painted on the front door. It's from 1911 and in excellent condition."

She picked up on my excitement and said she'd stop by the store tomorrow to examine the piece. I told her I'd be attending an auction, but if the piece met with her approval, to leave a check at the shop for me. I was in a super mood as I drove home. What started out dubiously, turned out to be one of my better days of auctioneering, and to think I almost let the woman-in-black chase me away.

Inky and Dinky immediately greeted me when I unlocked my abode's back door, rubbing against my legs and crying for food. I popped open a can of wet food and put a heaping tablespoon of savory chicken feast on each of their plates. As usual, Dinky marched over to Inky's plate and I had to gently nudge her back to her own. She watched me to see if I was going to leave, and when she realized I was staying to monitor her activity, she capitulated and hurriedly ate her own food allotment, voraciously gnawing the meaty bits in between loud purrs.

I couldn't wait to peel off my dirty, sticky clothes. After a nice long cool shower, I threw on a pair of jeans and a light blue silk top with white lace edging. I added veggies to some leftover nachos and plunked down on my sofa to watch TV while I nibbled. My cell phone vibrated in my pocket as I downed the last chip. It was Annie.

"How did it go today?" she inquired.

"Great." I filled her in on Ken's antics and how Guy bought his usual truckload of items. Almost as an afterthought, I said, "Ken and Carole Winker had a little tête-à-tête. She actually kicked Ken in the shins."

"Damn, I wish I was there for that one. What happened?"

"I don't know. They went off to the side and had one heck of an argument over something. I asked Carole about it later, but she blew me off."

"That *is* odd. I wonder what they're up to," she mused.

"And another strange thing happened. When I talked with Carole, I asked her if she bought anything at last week's auction and she disavowed ever being there. Annie, I know she was there. Why would she lie to me?"

"I don't have the slightest idea, sweetie."

"You know, something's funny, Annie. When I asked her what she and Ken were arguing about, she said his appraisals were too high and had told him so. Now that doesn't make sense unless he works on a percentage basis of the total appraised value. And how would she know what his appraisal values were, and why would she give a hoot?"

"Maybe Ken is in league with Woody for a percentage of the take," Annie volunteered.

"That would explain their interaction today. Ken acted like he was Woody's boss. He'd only act that way if he had a stake in the auction and was trying to protect his interest."

"Yeah, I wouldn't be surprised if they were in cahoots. Ken would work a deal with the devil for an extra buck," she ruminated.

"I saw Ken direct Barry on what to bid on, too—seems so unfair."

"There's no law against it as far as I know, Nikki. Better keep an eye out for Ken and Barry, though. When Ken's done an appraisal for an auction house, he's got a leg up on everybody else. He's a shrewd buyer, but remember he won't bid above half the amount he's appraised an item to be worth," Annie counseled. "He's got to turn it around and make a buck."

"And that's not all, Annie. There was a mysterious woman all dressed in black who exchanged words with me. She's about my age, wears her black hair tied back into a ponytail and uses dark eye make-up. She's attractive, in a severe looking way—in really good physical shape, too. Ring a bell?"

"I can't place her. She sounds like a Goth-doll."

"Yeah, sort of, but she's a bit city chic with a pompous air about her. I accidently bumped into her and she nearly tore my head off. The heat was getting to people today. It was a real scorcher at the auction and everybody was on edge."

"Regardless, don't let people run over you, sweetie. The hot spell doesn't excuse bad behavior."

"Don't worry, Annie. I'll stand up for myself. Are you having a nice time in Lake Geneva?"

"It's okay, but there are too darn many people around. Good luck at tomorrow's auction, and remember what I taught you."

"I will. Hugs and kisses to you and Burton."

"Goodnight, sweetie. Love you."

Talking to Annie always calmed me. I turned off the light and snuggled in with Inky and Dinky, ready for whatever the new day would bring. Or so I thought!

Chapter Three

Saturday

I awoke to a dull irregular thumping sound—Inky batting one of her sparkle balls around the bedroom with her paws. She had managed to swat the ball under my wardrobe cabinet, the opening underneath too narrow for her to do anything but flop down and stretch a forelimb in a vain attempt to retrieve her lost toy. Dinky used the moment to straddle Inky and sit down on her. Inky howled and batted at Dinky in an effort to force her off.

"None of that, now," I scolded Dinky.

Dinky backed off her sister and gave me an innocent look, her eyes a gleaming brilliant blue. I shook my head and looked at my clock. Ten minutes to seven. I turned off the alarm on my iPad, donned my slippers and robe, and went to the kitchen. After making a cup of coffee, I peeled a banana and sliced it over some instant oatmeal. For added energy, I scooped my usual big dollop of peanut butter on top and returned to the bedroom with my breakfast.

The weather forecast was for ninety-one degrees according to the weather app—a little cooler than yesterday, but not much. Finished with breakfast, I returned to the kitchen where I made another cup of coffee and prepared a quick lunch for the auction—a vegetable wrap stuffed with arugula, olives, sun-dried tomatoes, and a pesto spread. I placed an ice pack on top of the wrap in my small cooler and added a couple bottles of water. Even though it was to be less humid today, the heat index would be high, so I put a wet washcloth in a baggie and added it to the thermal pack. Lastly, I donned a loose fitting green cotton sundress, a straw sunhat, and a pair of sandals in preparation for another arduous auction day.

During the drive, I reflected on my relationship with Annie and last night's conversation. She was like a mother hen toward me, but I appreciated her looking out for me—especially considering I had only lived in the area for four years—since marrying Richard. Not being born in Hickory Grove, I was considered an outsider. Even Annie, who was born here, told me she was often treated like a tourist because she had relocated to the big city for a few years before returning. *The ins and outs of small town living are the same everywhere*, I mused.

Annie's reasons for nurturing me weren't altogether altruistic, I reminded myself. She was ready to retire to Florida for the winters and was banking on turning the business over to me as part of her retirement plans. And truth be told, I was looking forward to becoming a full-fledged entrepreneur. The items I managed to score at yesterday's auction marked significant progress toward achieving my goal.

Smiling at Annie's faith in me, I nevertheless felt nervous and a bit frightened when I contemplated the considerable risk involved in owning and operating Annie's Attic. The future seemed so uncertain in the antique and collectibles world. Today's society increasingly trended away from placing value on goods that were once stylish—the latest and greatest of past eras. Now everything was disposable. The key was for me to take things at my own pace and not be pressured into something I wasn't ready to tackle. "Just do your best," my father used to say, "and you'll have no regrets."

"I miss you dad," I said aloud as I pulled into a parking spot at the auction. Shrugging off the momentary loss I felt at my parents' passing, I tucked my thermal pack behind the seat, out of the sun's fiercely penetrating rays, and locked up. It was odd, but the sad remembrance of my parents gave me a strange feeling of foreboding—as if I was going to a funeral instead of an auction. *Snap out of it. You need to get out more, girl, and make new memories.*

Today, I arrived at the auction with time to spare. A quick look around showed the auction staffers busily setting up, and Woody, with a helper, was setting a table and chair atop a large, wide, flat moving trailer. Boxes of goods had been placed on the trailer surrounding Woody's to-be auction station. Behind the trailer, glass cases lined the entrance to the big sliding-door of the storage shed that was actually a pole-barn building. They weren't letting anyone into the storage building yet, but a quick look inside revealed rows of tables filled with items. A long day awaited me, especially if they sold each item by choice and not by boxed lots.

I perused the contents of the glass cases, securely locked to prevent handling of the items but at the same time denying anyone a closer inspection of the pieces. Undoubtedly, the contents would be the target of Ken's interest since he alone had examined them during his appraisal. Several Lalique statuettes and three ornate oriental daggers were amongst the enclosed items.

Red, bare-shouldered in a gauzy red tube-top, had resumed her position in the trailer issuing numbers to today's bidders. I went to hand her my license, but she waved me off saying, "You're already in the system, ma'am. I just need you to verify nothing has changed. I know it sounds crazy, but you'd be surprised at how many changes I get from one day to the next."

After signing for my new card, she tore off my number, and handed it to me. "How'd you make out yesterday?"

"Okay, I guess. I'll know better when I turn the goods around."

"Check out the Lalique today," she whispered. "Look them over real close, dear—there are a few that are genuine and some that aren't. Don't get stuck with the knockoffs."

"Thanks for the advice." *Why is she befriending me? She certainly knows a lot about the crystal. Is she Woody's shill, trying to drive up prices?* I wasn't used to people I didn't know doing me favors, but then I thought about Brett's exhibition of unsolicited generosity yesterday. Maybe I was too judgmental. *Not everyone is like my ex, Richard.*

Walking to the pole barn, I spotted Cyndi Comings, a single mom who waitressed at the Fire Sign, a quaint restaurant that was a favorite to both locals and tourists alike. She had been very sympathetic towards me when she had first learned of my impending divorce. We were on friendly speaking terms and through numerous conversations, she appeared to have a strange respect for me, saying she admired the strength I had exhibited in leaving Richard. Although we were close in age, she looked up to me, often asking my advice regarding personal matters.

"Hi Cyndi. Didn't expect to see you here today."

"I love auctions, they're so exciting! I try to attend whenever I can," she said from under a big brightly colored sun hat. "I buy stuff to help save for my son's college fund. He's turning three next week and tuition is so expensive, I figure I can't start saving too soon. I miss seeing you at the restaurant."

"Yeah, I'm on a strict diet and budget these days. I'm saving every cent I can for business."

"Tell me about it," she agreed effusively. "Being a single mom is rough."

I gave her a big hug. "If you ever need help, call me."

"I appreciate the offer, but it's not that bad. Hey, they've finally opened up the barn. Let's go see what we can't live without," she giggled with an effervescent glow, possessing a naturally ebullient attitude that was contagious.

Walking toward the building, I surveyed the items outside. "I'll be damned. They're gone."

"What's gone?" queried Cyndi.

"Two toy soldier lawn ornaments—they were here yesterday and now they're gone."

"They must have 'walked-off' during the night. I've seen it happen a few times, sometimes during the day, too."

A man's voice boomed nearby, interrupting our conversation.

"Be careful and move it by the other display cases up front."

It was Ken giving orders to two auction workers who were setting a big upright case where ordered. Ever at Ken's beckoning, Barry stood by.

"You two are busy with auctions these days," Cyndi commented to Ken and Barry.

Barry started to say something, but Ken stopped him short, said something inaudible, and led him away by the arm.

"Friendly, isn't he?"

"Yeah," Cyndi snorted, "a real asshole. I don't know how Barry puts up with him. Ken keeps him on such a tight leash."

"I'll say. Ken signaled Barry yesterday whenever he wanted him to bid on items."

"Yeah, I've seen him do that, too. Hey, what's this?" she asked holding up a piece of carved wood. "It looks like a bottle stopper, except the shaft is too narrow."

"Beats me, but there's more of them in this box. Ee-yikes! There's a mouse in here," I yelled and dropped the box back onto the table.

Cyndi laughed. "You'd think the auctioneer would at least clean up this stuff before selling it."

It took a few seconds for my heartbeat to return to normal, before I could respond. "Everything that was sold yesterday was clean. They must have run out of time to care for the items here in the shed."

"Look at it all," she exclaimed with a wave of her arm. "When I die, I want all my stuff burned so people can't rifle through it and comment about it."

Chuckling, I rejoined, "I don't care what happens to my stuff when I die. I always thought it would pass on to my kids one day, but that doesn't seem very likely anymore."

"Today's younger generations don't appreciate older things anyway," Cyndi replied consolingly. "My niece, who's only seven, already told my sister she doesn't want any of our 'old lady stuff.'"

Good grief! Cyndi's younger than me, and her sister's daughter thinks she's an 'old lady!' Hell, I still feel like I'm eighteen.

To change the subject, I asked, "How are you doing with your son's college fund?"

"Not bad. I've already saved enough for his first semester. But it's getting harder and harder. Things have changed a lot in the last five years. The deals aren't there like they used to be. And people, like Ken and Barry, have deep pockets and make it tough on ones who don't."

"Funny, Ken and Barry didn't seem to bid on many items yesterday. In fact, I outbid them for a music cabinet."

"Good for you. I'll let you in on a little secret," she said sotto voce. She looked around to make sure no one was within hearing range before she continued, "Sometimes, I bid them up just for the heck of it."

"Give 'em a taste of their own medicine, eh?"

"Yeah, Ken deserves it. What kind of things do you buy, Nikki?"

"Mostly furniture and decorative pieces—stuff I can put together into ensembles and sell as complete sets. What about you?"

"I like vintage clothes, purses, jewelry—small things I can easily resell on-line that don't weigh much. My trouble is I only buy things I like, and then I have a hard time parting with them," she admitted.

Ken, his pudgy legs doing double time, suddenly scrambled past us yelling, "Stop! Stop!" at the top of his lungs. "Hey, you two, come back here!"

Everyone turned to see who Ken was addressing. A young couple who were retreating to the parking lot, turned to see what the ruckus was all about. The boy gave the girl a questioning look and said something to her before they walked back towards the shed.

"Where are you going with that?" Ken asked the pair accusingly.

"What? This?" the young man asked holding up a carrying case. "It's our lunch," he said, unzipping the case to reveal the inside.

Everyone laughed and Ken's face turned a bright crimson. "I thought you were walking off with something," he mumbled in way of explanation without an apology.

The girl shook her head in disbelief. Her companion retorted, "What an asshole."

His character assessment of Ken was met with another round of laughter. The couple turned and walked away while Ken began to berate the workers for their rough handling of another display case.

"Serves him right," Cyndi said. I nodded agreement and we began to examine the multitude of items that filled the rows of tables in the storage building.

When we reached the end of the first row, Ken's voice boomed out, "That's not acceptable." His admonition was directed to Woody. Barry, ever by Ken's side, looked embarrassed when he observed Cyndi and me watching them. He murmured something to Ken who said abruptly, "This isn't over," and stalked off with Barry in tow.

"Sheesh, he never stops does he? I'm amazed he hasn't given himself a heart attack by now. I saw him arguing with a woman yesterday, too."

"Probably that time of month," Cyndi giggled.

Unable to suppress a laugh, I kidded jovially, "You're awful."

Before moving to a new row of items, I took a moment to scan the assembled mass of people and spotted the woman-in-black again. She stood out like a sore thumb, wearing satiny black slacks, a matching silk top, and a broad patent leather belt that gathered her long blouse against her slim waistline. She certainly didn't heed Annie's advice about dressing inconspicuously. She stepped over to Ken and started to give him an earful to judge from her animated gestures and his taciturn look.

Curiosity overcame me. Pushing my way through the crowd, I approached the couple and overheard her say, "I saw them in the glass case yesterday before you closed the shed doors. Now, they aren't here. Where are they?"

Ken's face flushed as he mopped at his brow, "They must have been moved during set-up. I'm sure they're here somewhere."

"They better be. I have a picture of them on my cell phone, and if they don't come up for bid today somebody's going to answer for it. And that's not all that's disappeared," she continued vociferously while poking him in the chest. "You're lucky I don't care about the other things, but if you know what's good for you, you'll remember what I said."

Her voice's edginess matched her appearance. She was one tough character. As gruff as she was towards me yesterday, I admired her spirit in calling Ken on the carpet. It never crossed my mind to call him to task over the missing toy soldier decorations. I had to hand it to her; she certainly had chutzpah.

Ken looked like he had just eaten a moldy piece of lettuce and had tried to wash the taste out of his mouth with lemon juice. The bully didn't like getting a dose of his own medicine. He vigorously waved Barry over and briefly said something to him before Barry dutifully hurried off.

I wonder what missing items have them in such a tizzy?

Woody's voice reverberated through the loud speaker system. "Ten minutes to go folks! Only ten minutes. If you don't have your number, hurry and get one at the trailer. We're going to begin by finishing the yard items over here to my right. Then, we'll start with the items on the trailer. We'll be closing up the storage shed now and no one will be allowed inside except for the workers. When the items on the trailer are sold, we'll replenish them with the goods from the shed. Set your chairs up right in front here, but leave an aisle way for the workers."

The selling order was exactly opposite what one of the auction workers had told me earlier when I had inquired. A quick double-check confirmed the toy soldiers remained missing-in-action. I shrugged off the loss and returned to the trailer for a last look through the boxes stacked around Woody's table and chair. Cyndi, having the same idea, was already pulling items out of a nearby box to see what treasures were hidden underneath.

"They told me they were going to auction the art items first," I complained to her.

"That's not unusual, Nikki. I think they forget what they've said half the time. They get too caught up in things."

"Yeah, either that, or they're doing somebody with money a favor."

She nodded in agreement as she continued to rummage.

"Look at this," I exclaimed, holding open a large manila envelope I had extracted from a box in front of me. "Have you ever seen anything like this before?" Inside were pressed flowers that a very skilled hand had painstakingly painted pictures onto their dried leaves. The numerous details were incredibly intricate and so small that the painter must have used a magnifying lens during their creation. I heard the person next to me suck in their breath, and when I turned to see who it was; the woman-in-black was staring at the flowers I had removed from the envelope.

Am I a dolt or what? I had just committed one of Annie's cardinal sins and allowed a potential bidder to discover an item of interest to me. By her reaction, the woman obviously knew something about the painted articles and their worth. Thankfully, my self-effacement was short lived, for Woody began his auction spiel.

Woody's minions unpacked the contents of a box onto the table in front of him, his throne atop the trailer, while others unpacked boxes and arranged pieces in a staging area at one end of the bidding table. I shuffled down a row of chairs until I came to mine, next to Cyndi's. She already had a few wins by her side.

I spied a set of Art Deco cocktail glasses on the table for the next round of bidding. They'd make a perfect addition to one of my exhibitions.

I remembered what Annie had told me about watching Ken closely. When I looked at him, he had a faraway look in his eyes and nodded ever so slightly toward Barry who flashed his number at Woody.

"I have ten dollars—do I hear fifteen for choice?"

No one accepted Woody's offer. Barry had won. To my amazement, Ken leaned over and scooped up the cocktail glasses I had planned to bid on in the next round.

"Did you see that?" I asked Cyndi. "Those glasses weren't sitting in the for-choice lot when Woody began the bid. Wow, what a slick move that was by Ken. I was going to bid on those."

"Hey," a woman's voice shouted from the rear. All heads turned. "Can you not add more items once bidding begins?" the woman-in-black asked.

Woody seemed at a loss. He turned to one of the worker's and asked what the woman was asking about. Ken said something I couldn't quite make out. I only caught the big "B" word. His use of the word in public startled me.

"Those glasses he chose were placed on the table after you started the bid. How are we supposed to know what is being auctioned off if you add items after the bidding starts?" she protested voluminously.

"It's for the items I said before I started the bid," Woody answered weakly, still unsure as to what the woman's complaint was about.

"No, you're not getting it," she cried in consternation.

I decided to jump into the fracas and shouted, "She's right. The cocktail glasses Ken just claimed were added to the bid table after you began the bidding process. They weren't part of the original lot." I turned to look at the woman-in-black. She gave me a self-satisfied nod, while other bidders shouted their agreement with our assessment of the incident.

Woody and Ken exchanged words. Woody, obviously unnerved, announced in a shaky voice the glasses were going to be resold. Bidding began again. I dropped out at twenty. The woman-in-blacked upped her bid over Ken's bid and won the glasses. Ken returned her triumphant grin with a sneer when she strode forth and claimed her winnings.

A quick glance at the next staged lot, a sundry of items such as fountain pens and old cigarette rollers, revealed nothing of interest. I asked Cyndi to hold down the fort while I retired to my SUV for a quick bite to eat. The inside of my car was like an oven from the heat and blazing sunshine. I lowered the windows to let the smoldering air escape before I poured ice water onto my washcloth and wiped my face and neck. Leaning back in the driver's seat, I slowly ate my sandwich and thought about Ken's behavior.

He has a temper, no doubt about it. In fact, it seems like he argues with everyone he speaks to. I reminded myself he was a bully and bullies were blusterous and overbearing, a behavior used to intimidate people in order to get their way.

With smug satisfaction, I thought about the woman-in-black putting Ken in his place. *Has Ken met his match?* This woman intrigued me. I was definitely going to have to learn more about her.

I returned to the auction and discovered the storage building had been reopened to the public. I was eager to see what items were likely to be next up for bid. As I made my way into the shed, someone bumped into me and rushed off without so much as an 'excuse me.' I turned and saw Barry's retreating form before he was enveloped within the crowd. His rude jostling was another sign of the steamy conditions taking their toll on manners. I shrugged it off and began to search through the items.

"Look at these glasses. Anything this beautiful has got to be old," Crazy Mary declared as she held up an Art Deco cocktail glass to the woman standing next to her. With a groan, frustration overcame me knowing Mary was going to bid on the set just because she liked how they looked without knowing a thing about them. Suddenly, inspiration befell me. I rushed back to the table of goods I had examined previously. The furry field mouse I had discovered earlier scampered to safety inside a coffee mug lying on its side on the bottom of the box as I moved items aside. I picked up the mug, placed my purse over the top, and casually carried it over to where Mary, bent over, was peering intently into a box of items sitting on the floor beneath the table. I glanced around to make sure no one was watching me, slid my purse aside and tilted the mug over her open purse. The mouse desperately tried to gain a foot hold before sliding out of the mug plummeting into her purse.

Replacing the mug on top of the table in front of me, I turned to Mary, and asked, "Excuse me. Do you happen to have a tissue I can borrow? These boxes are filthy."

"Aren't they though?" she agreed and dug into her purse to satisfy my request.

"Aaaaiii," she screamed, dropping her purse as if it was suddenly on fire.

Acting as though her sudden outburst had scared me, and in truth her shrill screech did startle me, I kicked her purse, shooting its contents willy-nilly about the floor.

"Oh, I'm so sorry," I said contritely.

While Mary bent over to retrieve the scattered contents of her purse, I snatched up the box of glassware, dashed to a middle-aged female worker at the entranceway, and declared, "Can you auction this off next? I've been waiting all morning for these to come up—I don't think I'll be staying much longer."

She hesitated, but eventually conceded, "I guess it'll be okay." Taking the box, she carried it to the front of the trailer and passed it to a worker who immediately unpacked its contents onto the end of the bidding table.

Luck was with me as seconds later the last of the previous items being auctioned were swept from the table in one lot and the glasses set in their place. Woody announced, "What do I hear for this fine set of glasses? Do I hear twenty?"

I nervously looked for Crazy Mary and opened the bid at five. A young guy in his early twenties upped the bid to ten. Without hesitating, I raised it to fifteen. The other bidder went to seventeen-fifty and I raised it to twenty. The guy hemmed and hawed for a few seconds before dropping out.

"Going, going, gone," Woody announced.

With a small sense of pride and a mischievous guilty feeling, I claimed the set of glasses. Like Annie always said, 'All's fair in love, war, and auctions.'

Cyndi was folding her chair and readying the boxes of items she had purchased when I returned to my chair. She appeared agitated.

"Leaving already?"

"Uh-huh," she replied in distress.

"What's wrong?"

"Nothing," she snapped at me.

"Do you need help with your boxes?"

"NO! I have them all," she shouted brusquely and hurried off.

Now what the hell did I do? Did I win something she wanted? If I did, I didn't have a clue what it was. Has to be this heat!

Next up for bidding were the three ornate daggers I had seen in the tall upright display case at the start of the day. I had no idea of their worth since they were kept locked up and I hadn't researched them. The woman-in-black won the bid at a hundred-and-thirty dollars. She picked all three of the daggers as her choice and carried them gingerly towards the parking area.

As the afternoon wore on, the temperature began to sap my remaining reserves of energy. Two days of auctioning in the hot, steamy sun would tax anyone. I decided to give the remaining items in the shed one last perusal and call it a day when someone nearby exclaimed, "Look! Somebody pulled the sheets off those furniture pieces. The auctioneer must have forgotten about them." I looked toward the corner where the voice had emanated from and bumped into Carole Winker.

"Carole! I'm sorry. Hey, I'm glad I ran into you. Excuse the pun, but I've been wondering if you would show me some of your artwork. It might be just the thing—"

Cutting me off, she replied, "Yeah, sure. Give me a call," in a strained voice before she raced away like she was going to a fire.

Why is everyone acting so weird lately?

I spied two heavy, claw-footed pieces of furniture made of tiger oak that had been covered earlier, but now showed their glorious stripes. "What's with these pieces," I asked the nearest auction worker as I stood admiring them.

"They're not for sale. They're reserved for a family member," she informed me as she tugged on one of the sheets to recover the furniture. "Can you give me a hand? This cover is stuck on something."

I walked around to the back of the furniture. Dark in the corner, my foot struck what felt like a rolled rug. Bending over, I grabbed the sheet and gave it a tug. It held fast, so I pulled harder. The sheet suddenly came free and I almost lost my balance. I looked down to see what had held it so firmly and found myself staring into Ken's sightless eyes, an ornate dagger stuck in his throat.

Chapter Four

"Aaaaiii," I screamed at the top of my lungs stumbling backwards and reflexively pointing at Ken's lifeless form.

The auction helper darted around the furniture and looked to where my shaking hand pointed. "Mother of God," she said and shouted to one of her coworkers.

My legs folded from under me and I collapsed with a violent lurch onto the shed's cement floor. I didn't want to look again, but morbid curiosity took hold. In the dark corner, Ken's head lay in a pool of blood that looked like used car oil. Although there wasn't much light, the dagger looked identical to one of the three auctioned off earlier— those won by the woman-in-black.

Somebody shouted for everyone to clear out of the pole barn, but my legs weren't having any of it. I tried to stand, but shook so badly, I gave up. Dizzy, my nausea exacerbated by the heat and stuffy air in the barn, I crouched somewhat below one of the display tables and lost my lunch.

"Give me your hand," someone nearby said.

Weakly, I reached out and the woman who I had tried to help with the sheets firmly gripped my hand and tugged. Putting my other hand on the table, I managed to unsteadily gain my feet. I reached down, retrieved my hat, and straightened out my sundress. She put an arm around my waist, and together we stumbled outside.

Trembling, I told her uncertainly, "I'll b-b-be alright, now. Just let me sit a bit and get some fresh air."

"Nobody leave!" Woody ordered. He took immediate charge of the situation instructing his assistants to clear the shed and to block both ends of the circular driveway. His presence of mind astounded me.

Word spread like wildfire. Everyone milled around, talking about the murder. In no time, sirens blared in the distance and police squad cars began to arrive. The steady hum of conversation was drowned out by a policeman speaking from atop Woody's chair.

"Please give me your attention. I'm Dwayne Andersen, Hickory Grove's Chief-of-Police. If everyone will give us their full cooperation, we'll try to get you on your way as soon as possible. Lieutenant Corso and Sergeant Reilly will take down your information. If you saw anything or heard anything you think will help us in our investigation, see Lieutenant Corso or me personally. Anything at all," he urged.

Dread overwhelmed me as I kept seeing Ken in my mind's eye—the sheet clutched desperately in his hand— his face a distorted death mask of horror. I didn't want to talk to anyone. I wanted to run home to the comfort of Inky and Dinky and safety of my little abode.

Someone shook me by the shoulder. I turned and looked up into a pair of dark eyes—the darkest orbs I had ever seen. Huge black irises surrounded the pupils and devoured me. I couldn't stop sinking into them, each a bottomless abyss.

"Are you the woman who found the body?" the policeman asked, shaking me from my numbed state.

"Uh-huh," I said fighting off another round of nausea. "I think I'm going to be sick again," I managed weakly.

"Here, let me help you," he said, holding out his hand and pulling me up. Standing up did help to clear my head. I remained a bit woozy as he led me by the arm to one of the police cars and started the engine. The air-conditioning vanquished my nausea, but I soon became chilled. He took notice of my condition, turned the a/c down, and asked, "Do you feel good enough to talk?"

"I g-guess so."

"I'm Lieutenant Corso, Jake Corso. Call me Jake. What's your name?"

"Nicole Carson," I answered dully.

"I'm going to record our conversation. Is that all right with you, Ms. Carson?"

"Nikki."

"All right—Nikki. Do I have your permission to record our conversation?" he reiterated.

"I guess so," I replied numbly.

"Are you married, Nikki?"

"No, I'm recently divorced."

"Is there anyone I should contact to help you?"

"N-n-no."

"Tell me why you were at the auction today, Ms. Carson? Was there a special reason why you came to this auction?"

"Yeah, I make my living buying and reselling goods I purchase at auctions, estate sales—that sort of thing."

"Do you live in Hickory Grove?"

"Six-twenty-four Campezi Lane. I work at Annie's Attic," I answered in anticipation of his next question.

"Now take your time and tell me what happened."

Hesitantly, I began from the time I walked into the pole barn until I discovered Ken's body. When I reached the part about finding Ken, the picture of his face frozen in death's grip returned to me and I started trembling. Jake lowered the windows to warm the car's interior and handed me a bottle of water.

I took small sips slowly until I was confident my stomach could handle it, and then rinsed out my mouth to rid myself of its sour taste. Jake must have read my mind, because he popped the tab on a can of diet coke and handed it to me. "Here, this should help clear the bitter taste away. Water won't do it."

"Thanks." I took a big swallow and swished the cool liquid around in my mouth. I opened the door and spat out the foamy swill, repeating the process until the stale taste was dispelled. "Sorry," I said a bit embarrassed. "I couldn't stand the taste. I haven't thrown up since I was a kid."

"I understand. You've experienced quite a shock."

"You can say that again."

"When was the last time you saw the deceased alive?"

"About two hours ago—maybe longer. I don't know. It had to be before I ate lunch because I bid on something I was sure Ken and his partner wanted and Ken wasn't in his usual chair beside the trailer—by where the auctioneer stood."

"How long were you in the building before you found the body?"

"Maybe ten minutes."

"Can you identify anyone who was in the shed from the time you found the body, going backward to the time you entered it?"

"Crazy Mary—"

"Who?" he interrupted.

"I'm sorry. It's what everyone calls her. I don't know her last name."

"Why do people call her crazy?"

"It's not because she's really crazy. I mean, she is, sort of. No, that's not fair. She's called that by regular auction-goers because of the way she bids at auctions. She gets easily confused during bidding and she'll pay anything to win something she likes. She's idiosyncratic, not really crazy, if you know what I mean. I don't want you thinking she's unbalanced or anything."

"All right. Who else?"

"Carole Winker was in the shed. I spoke briefly to her as I went inside. She was coming out and acted like she was in a hurry."

"You say she was in the shed when you talked to her?"

"Uh-huh."

"Keep going," he prodded.

"There were other people, but I couldn't tell you who they were. I don't know them by name and I can't say with certainty when they were in the shed. It's all a blur."

"What about the woman whom you were helping when you found the deceased?"

"Oh yeah, I forgot about her. She just asked me to help her cover the furniture with the sheet. There was another auction worker inside there, too—a man. I don't know either of their names."

"Did you know the deceased?"

The suddenness of his question caught me by surprise. Blood rushed to my head and my ears became hot. *This is crazy. I'm not guilty of anything, so why do I feel so nervous under his unflinching scrutiny?*

"Y-yes, I know Ken and his partner, Barry. Rather, I should say I know *of* them. I've only briefly spoken to either of them a few times here and there. Mostly I know about them from what Annie, the lady who owns the store where I work, has told me."

"Have you ever done business with them?"

"No."

"Do you know of any reason why someone would have killed him?"

"Not specifically."

"What do you mean by 'not specifically'?"

"I mean, Ken was generally known to be nasty. I don't know anyone who liked him. He was a bully," I added weightily.

"I see," he replied and took a few seconds to contemplate my answer. "Who knew him to be a bully?"

A warning alarm went off in my head in response to his question. I didn't want to name specific people and implicate them simply because of hearsay. "Anybody who had any dealings with him," I answered vaguely. "He was pushy, rude, and arrogant to auction goers, and even people who visited his store."

"Uh-huh," he replied with weary sarcasm. "Did you see anything odd or different with Ken and his partner today?"

"Nothing out of the usual."

He kept up a stream of questions, although I couldn't make out much rhyme or reason to them, and they quickly became a jumbled mess in my mind. He jumped from one area to another and then back again. I assumed it was normal police procedure—a tried and true technique to check and double-check the validity of my answers. Whatever the purpose behind his methodology, he abruptly ceased asking me questions and switched off his recorder. He jotted down my phone number, work number, and checked my driver's license information.

"Do you feel well enough to go home now?"

"Yeah, I suppose so," I replied a bit uncertainly.

"I'll have someone drive you home. I'm also going to have a counselor come by your house. She has a lot of experience with trauma victims and she'll help you deal with what you've experienced today. Is that okay?"

"No. I'm fine. I only need a little time to myself," I asserted.

"I really think you should talk to her. There's often a delayed reaction to witnessing traumatic events."

"I didn't witness anything," I said, wondering if the way he had phrased his statement was intended to trap me into divulging the fact I had actually seen Ken killed. Anger flared within me at such a thought. Taking a few deep breaths to steady my nerves, I said, "I only found his body. Really. I'm okay," and thrust open the squad door.

"Wait," he ordered, and busily jotted something onto the back of a business card. "This is my card. If you change your mind, the counselor's name and number is on the back. Call me if you think of anything else that might be important. Come to the station Monday morning and make a statement."

I told him I understood and assured him another half-dozen times I felt good enough to drive home on my own.

"Show the card I gave you to the officer at the entranceway and he'll let you drive through, Ms. Carson," he said and thanked me for my assistance before I walked away.

I returned to the auction area. The crowd had thinned out to a couple dozen people resting in their chairs and a few individuals sprawled under the shade of nearby trees. Barry, his countenance bearing a white, distraught look, was speaking to the auctioneer whose mouth was tightly shut in a grimace. *Isn't it odd how Woody doesn't seem to be comforting Barry in his hour of need? I guess men handle tragedy differently than women. Maybe they aren't friends—only business acquaintances.* Then I remembered the way Ken had angrily spoken to Woody earlier. *Or maybe there's more to it . . .*

I retrieved my chair, folded it, placed it in its bag, and walked towards my car. My thoughts were racing with everything that had transpired during the last two days. There was so much more I could have said—should have said—to Lieutenant Corso, but all I wanted to do was go home to Inky and Dinky and get as far away from the auction grounds as possible.

Midway to my car, I spotted the woman-in-black standing next to a silver BMW with a police officer. The trunk was open, and as I walked by I heard her say, "I told you, Sergeant Reilly, the daggers were in the back seat, not the trunk. I must have forgotten to lock my car because they're not there now."

"Is anything else missing?"

"No."

"You'll have to come down to the station for more questioning."

"But I've told you everything I know."

"You'll have to tell it to my boss."

"This is ridiculous. I don't even know the guy's name. Why would I kill him?"

"I didn't accuse you of killing him, Miss North. It's police procedure. We want to clear this up as fast as you do and the sooner we have your statement the sooner we can put all this behind us."

So her last name is North, and she's single. In all the excitement, I had completely forgotten about the daggers and the woman-in-black. *Was she telling the truth about not knowing Ken? What if she's the killer, the murderess?* My curiosity began to kick in—a sign that I was already getting over the shock of discovering Ken's body.

I made a mental note to ask Denise about Miss North at my first opportunity. Denise knows everything about everybody in Hickory Grove, as she makes it her business to pump anyone for information who visits Annie's shop. But it was a one-way street with her. She intensely disliked anyone to know anything about her personal life. So much so that she lived in a secluded house on property completely enveloped by pine trees and overgrown hedges thusly preventing a view of her house from the street or neighboring houses.

I tried to heed Lieutenant Corso's advice and concentrate on my driving, but the events of the last two days overwhelmed me. All the odd things—the arguments, the strange behaviors—rushed through my mind in a swirling kaleidoscope. He had been easy to talk to, but for some reason, I had felt reluctant to share everything I knew with him. There were so many things I hadn't told him. *I need to talk to Annie. She is always so level-headed. She'd know how to handle things.*

My cell phone rang as I pulled into my garage. When I answered, a woman's muffled voice said, "Keep your mouth shut if you know what's good for you," and the connection disconnected.

Chapter Five

"What? What the hell!" I cried, staring at the phone in my hand. "This is unreal." Instead of being scared I was angry, outraged, mystified—my thoughts and emotions a jumbled, tangled mess. I stayed in my car until my heart stopped racing. With my emotions somewhat under control, I searched in my purse for Lieutenant Corso's card and entered his number into my phone.

"Hello. Lieutenant Corso? This is Nicole Carson—the— eh—the woman who discovered the body at the auction," I explained clumsily, not able to come up with a more pleasant way of introducing myself on the spur of the moment.

"Yes, Ms. Carson."

"I just received an anonymous threatening phone call. The caller told me I'd better keep my mouth shut if I know what's good for me."

"Did the person say anything else?"

"No, that's all they said and then disconnected. It was a woman's voice."

"Are you sure about that?"

"Absolutely."

"Do you have caller ID?"

In the heat of the moment, it completely slipped my mind to look up the number. "Wait till I look up the number," I told him, embarrassed by my mental error.

After I recited the number to him, he said, "Probably a public phone, but we'll run it down. Make sure you mention the phone number in your statement Monday."

"I will," I promised before hanging up. I'm not sure what I expected by reporting the incident, but the conversation left me feeling insufficient and vulnerable. *Something more needs to be done on my behalf, but what? It's only a phone call. What more can Lieutenant Corso do?* I reasoned the police might be able to trace the number, but like the Lieutenant more or less said, the caller would be stupid to have used a private phone.

I mulled this fact over in my mind as I entered my bungalow where persistent "meows" greeted me. Inky and Dinky were excited by my return and at the same time a trifle upset at my tardiness. Their displeasure was quickly overcome by carnivorous anticipation when they heard the can opener. I figured they had earned a special treat for my extended absences over the last two days. Inky couldn't wait for me to spoon out the salmon. She jumped up on the kitchen counter and I had to clumsily hold her at bay with my elbow as I placed a heaping tablespoon of deboned fish on each of their plates.

Observing their feeding frenzy, my own hunger surfaced as I had only half-digested my lunch before giving it up earlier. Too drained to cook, I called the local pizzeria and ordered a large vegetarian pizza for delivery. My diet would be blown all to hell, but what-the-hey—it's not every day you become embroiled in a murder. Grabbing a diet soda from the refrigerator, I slipped off my shoes and sprawled out on my sofa where Dinky soon joined me. Together we watched Inky play with one of her toys, a small cloth fish stuffed with catnip I had suspended with a piece of rubber string from the top of an archway.

I felt Dinky's body suddenly tense, and I lay still as she re-positioned her body into a crouch and sprung off my thighs like a shot from a sling. She landed on top of Inky, who, blind-sided by her sister's whirling mass of fur, howled and batted at Dinky. Dinky, ears back and eyes frenzied, took off for a game of tag with Inky following in hot pursuit.

Dinky had a tendency to dominate her sister, especially when Inky was enjoying a special moment of her own— with me, basking in the sun, or enjoying a favorite toy.

There had been many a time when I had seen Dinky carry a sparkle ball of Inky's in her mouth and push it under the closed door to roll down the basement stairs leaving Inky batting at the door.

I listened to make sure Inky was holding her own with Dinky before I tackled my feelings. While the anonymous phone caller had upset me, I was more rankled than scared.

Who would dare call me and leave such a menacing message? I don't know people who would do stuff like that—or do I? My thoughts then segued over to Ken's death and a shiver ran up my spine. *Did I rub elbows with the killer at the auction? Will I be looking at others from now on at the auctions and think that the person standing next to me could be the murderer or murderess? Would they be thinking the same thing about me?* The more I thought about it, the more I realized Ken's murder needed to be solved quickly—before suspicions got out of control. Maybe I could unscramble this mess myself—after all, I was there, and saw and heard plenty.

I was amazed about how the shock at my finding Ken's dead body had abated and was now supplanted by an overwhelming desire to unravel the mystery behind his murder. Obviously, the prime suspect had to be the woman-in-black, Miss North. After all, she was the one who had won the three daggers. *Even though she told the policeman the daggers had been stolen from her vehicle, what else could she say to claim her innocence? On the other hand, what motive did she have for killing Ken?*

She and Ken didn't appear to personally know each other when she had complained to Woody at the auction about Ken's fast one with the cocktail glasses. On the other hand, I recalled how Ken had referred to her as a 'bitch' when he stepped in to explain to Woody what the fuss was all about. His crass remark was so outside the bounds of normal auction decorum that I, along with a number of other bidders, had been shocked by his outburst.

Would Ken have called the woman a bitch if he didn't know her? Would the mysterious Miss North kill Ken for calling her a derogatory name? Granted it had been a stifling hot and muggy day, and the auction attendees had reacted with discomfort—angers had run high and tempers were short-fused, but to kill someone over name calling seemed an unlikely happenstance to me. North struck me as a strong woman who wouldn't take guff off of anyone— she was someone who would give back twice as much as she was given—she'd fight fire with fire, but she was not a murderess. *On second thought, she is someone who would call and threaten me to keep quiet. But keep quiet about what? What did I know that was so important?*

Suddenly I recalled the confrontation I had seen between her and Ken before the start of bidding. The woman-in-black, a more fitting name than Miss North, had held Ken accountable for removing articles from one of the glass cases. Articles she wanted to bid on. And she had said, 'they,' referring to more than one item being missing from the cases. Had she been referring to the daggers? If so, someone had returned them because she had won them later.

Thinking back, I tried to piece the sequence of events together in chronological order. But the more I tried, the more I became confused and uncertain of my efforts. My thinking was too helter-skelter to calmly arrange the events in a timely order. There were just too many items to account for in relation to what I had observed and at what time.

What if Ken and Barry are pilfering items and fear the woman is wise to their scheme? If that was the instance, Ken may have confronted her and attempted to bully her into disavowing her earlier claim. So confronted, she could have lashed out to counter his physical advances, striking back blindly with one of the daggers she had won. No, if it were me, I'd have simply walked away or kicked him like

Carole had—not stab him. But North was a hard cookie, and I distinctly remembered her carrying the daggers to her car after she had won them. Of course, she may have later put the daggers in her waist pack.

Then there's Carole. *Is she as bold as the woman-in-black? Didn't she say a swift kick you-know-where usually took care of most aggressive males?* I had seen Carole, on two different occasions in heated discussions with Ken. There was definitely some bad blood between the two. *And what do I really know about Carole?* Like me, she was an artist who sold her artwork through the local galleries. She lived on the same street as me, and is unmarried—like me now, but she has a boyfriend and has lived in Hickory Grove her entire life according to what Denise had told me.

Carole was becoming a regular auction goer, but she didn't buy items for outright resale. Instead, she purchased items to reuse in her artwork. *So why was she arguing with Ken? Does she suspect him of questionable practices like the woman-in-black?* My thinking returned full circle to the same place my earlier cogitations about Miss North had taken me.

The caller could have been Carole instead of the woman-in-black. *But why would Carole threaten me? I don't know anything—wait a minute! Carole had been at last week's auction and she denied being there when I mentioned it to her. Sure. That's it. She doesn't want me to tell anyone about her whereabouts last week. But that's silly. How could her attending a past auction correlate with Ken's murder?*

And what about Cyndi? I had never known her to act strangely, apart from normal youthful folly, but today she had been downright rude towards me. The Cyndi I knew was always cordial, even upbeat, and treated me like an older sister whenever we had run into each other. Yet, she had acted nervous and short with me— practically running to her car—abruptly leaving the auction around the time

Ken had been killed. This latest rumination made me sit up with excitement. The timing was right. Cyndi left right around the time Ken had disappeared. *Did she flee because she had discovered Ken's body and didn't want to become involved? Or was she making a getaway after killing him?*

My mental machinations were sharply halted by a knock on the door. The pizza deliveryman had arrived. I checked first on Inky and Dinky's whereabouts to make sure it was safe to open the front door. Seeing them enthralled with a chipmunk who had ventured close to the shrubs by the back porch, I unbolted the lock.

Before I could open the door, the handle turned in my grasp and someone wearing a dark green ski mask shoved their way inside. My assailant grabbed me by the shoulders and roughly thrust me back. I lost my balance, tripped, and fell unceremoniously landing with a loud thump on my derriere.

Wearing scuffed black boots, worn blue jeans, and a black t-shirt, the man towered ominously over me. What was happening was so surreal—I froze, I couldn't move. My hearing, suddenly acute in my helplessness, heard heavy bass reverberations penetrate the night air down the block moments before a car's brakes squealed loudly. The invader whipped his head around at the noise, and said, "Shit." Returning his gaze to me, he shouted hoarsely, "Keep your trap shut. If you don't, I'll be back to shut it permanently for you," and dashed out the front door.

Moments later there was a knock at the screen door. A teenager stood looking inside at me, holding a pizza box in hand. "Come in," I rasped breathlessly, kneeling, putting a hand on the living room table and pushing myself to my feet. He opened the door and stood obediently inside the entryway. "Did you see the guy who was just here?"

"You mean the guy who ran down the street?"

"Uh-huh. Hold on a minute," I said and grabbed my phone to dial Jake. "Lieutenant, this is Nicole Carson

58

again," I blurted out before he could say hello. "A guy wearing a ski mask just forced his way into my home and threatened me. A pizza delivery driver interrupted him and he ran away."

"Are you okay?"

"I'm fine, a little shaken up is all. The pizza guy is still here. What should I do?"

"Keep him there until I get there. Give me your address again," he ordered. He said he was on his way and disconnected.

"What's your name?"

"Jon. Jon Lee."

"Jon, that was the police. The guy you saw running away just broke into my house. The police want you to stay here until they arrive and ask you some questions."

"Geez, lady, all I saw was the backside of some guy—I didn't see his face."

"Then tell the police that."

"But I got three more pizzas to deliver. If I don't deliver them on time, my boss will fire me."

"I'll speak with your boss and it'll be all right," I assured him and called the pizza parlor's number. After the manager came on the line, I told him what had happened, and added, "I'll make good for the other pizzas Jon was supposed to deliver. Can you can make three new ones and have somebody else deliver them to your patrons?"

"I suppose," he agreed, somewhat appeased by making three additional sales.

"Here," I said handing Jon my phone. "Talk to him to make sure everything's all right."

Assured he wasn't going to lose his job, Jon handed me back my phone and asked, "Was that guy tryin' to rob you or somethin'?"

"Or somethin'," I allowed. "Would you like somethin' to drink while we wait?"

My small imitative joke went unacknowledged as he asked, "You got any Mountain Dew?"

"No, but I have Coke and Diet Coke."

"I've got a bottle of Mountain Dew in my car," he said suggestively.

With a chuckle, I said, "All right. I'll buy the pop, too. Get the other pizzas and help yourself while we wait."

He bolted out the front door and for a moment, I considered how foolish I had been to trust him, but to my relief he returned a few seconds later with his precious Mountain Dew and pizzas in hand. He opened one of the boxes, took out a slice, and to my surprise began to eat as if it was his last meal. I went to the kitchen to fetch him a glass and some paper plates and napkins. When I returned, he was already finishing off his second slice.

"Don't they feed you?"

"When it's slow," he replied between mouthfuls.

"How much do I owe you?"

Jon added the three pizzas and a Mountain Dew to my tab and said, "$73.37."

He was a good looking oriental kid—probably of Chinese descent to judge from his bone structure. He wore his hair over his ears, cut in a zig-zag pattern along the neck-line. It must have taken his stylist a long time to get the design so meticulous and even. Suppressing a smile at his 'do', I counted out four twenties and told him to keep the change.

"Hey, you're all right, lady," he exclaimed while reaching for another piece of pizza.

"What's on that pizza you're eating?" I asked, suspiciously eyeing the toppings.

"Anchovy, broccoli, garlic, and Canadian bacon."

"Tell you what, Jon, after the cops go, you can take that one with you."

"Really?"

"Yep."

"You live here all alone?"

"Yeah, I just got divorced."

"Why would a guy toss off a good-looking chick like you?" he asked as he reached for another slice.

His back-handed compliment felt good. At least I wasn't so old he hadn't recognized my female charms. He finished off the slice with gusto and immediately picked up another helping. I watched him devour two more pieces and wash them down with pop. *Does this guy have a hollow leg or what?*

The front doorbell rang, sending Inky and Dinky galloping into the living room—half in curiosity and half in fright. They crawled to safety under the couch and peeked out with big shining eyes.

The caller was Lieutenant Corso wearing tan chinos, a white shirt, and a pair of Nike sneakers. He was accompanied by a uniformed policeman who he introduced as Sergeant Reilly. I invited them in, and after everyone was seated, offered them pizza. "Anything to drink?" I asked, playing the perfect hostess.

Jake asked for water while Sergeant Reilly took me up on a Coke. When I returned from the kitchen with their drinks, I saw Inky and Dinky working their noses overtime from under the couch, smelling the pizzas and newfound company from the comfort of their hiding spot. I set the tray down onto the coffee table, and listened to Jake questioning Jon. "You didn't see his face at all?"

"Uh-uh. All I could see was the guy's back—he was tearing down the street."

"Where did he go?"

"I dunno. He ran around the corner and disappeared."

"How do you know it was a man?"

"Cause he looked like a guy and ran like one," Jon answered with a sarcastic overtone, as if it was the dumbest question he ever heard.

"All right, you can go," Jake told him curtly after Sergeant Reilly noted his contact information.

"Don't forget your pizza," I reminded Jon.

With a smile he folded the top over on the box, thanked me, and dashed out the door carrying the pizza in one hand and the near empty bottle of Mountain Dew in the other.

"Were you expecting someone," Jake asked, motioning towards the remaining three partially eaten pizzas.

"No. I felt sorry for the kid. He said he'd get fired for not delivering the pizzas to the other customers in time. So to make amends with his boss, I bought all the pizzas he was to deliver."

At my pronouncement, Jake gave me a quizzical look. "If you're hungry fellows, help yourself. But I warn you. I have no idea what the toppings are except for this one—it's vegetarian."

"You don't appear too upset after somebody just broke into your house," Jake said.

"I don't think the reality has fully hit me yet."

He nodded his head slightly in understanding. "Can you describe anything identifiable about the man?"

For the next few minutes, I told him everything I remembered regarding the intruder. His partner entered notes into a tablet PC while Jake listened intently to my recap. When I had finished, Jake said, "The pizza kid said the guy had run quickly. He must be somewhere between his teens to thirties. What do you think?"

"He was awfully big to be a teen. And his voice sounded more mature, too. I'd say the guy was in his late twenties or early thirties."

Let me get this straight, "First, you get a phone call from a woman telling you to keep quiet. Then some guy breaks into your house and threatens you to keep still. Somebody must be scared of something. What do you know that would make the perpetrators feel threatened?" he asked, eyes narrowed.

In all the commotion at the auction, I had failed to fully take in Jake's appearance. My previous impression was one

of an amorphous, nondescript form with big, dark eyes—
like remembering a mannequin's features. Now, when I
studied his face, piercing dark eyes stared back at me from
a handsome face. Enormously long eyelashes softened his
penetrating stare. Somewhat rugged in cut, he looked to be
in his early thirties, solidly built, muscular. His dark brown
hair, closely cropped, highlighted a strong jawline, with
high pronounced cheekbones. My gaze wandered to his
hand where I looked for a ring and observed he didn't wear
one.

Jake must have followed my glance, because when I
looked up, his eyes held me in a steady, unwavering gaze
that seemed to see through me. Slightly blushing at my
school-girl curiosity, I answered him, "I don't really know,
but after the phone call I ran through things in my mind
trying to figure what I knew and came up with a few
ideas."

Jake prodded me to share my thoughts. I told him and the
sergeant everything I could recall from the two days at the
auction that might be relevant.

"Why didn't you tell me all this before?" Jake chided.

"I guess I was too shaken up. Besides, you told me I
would have to come down to the station and make a
statement tomorrow," I added defensively. "Do you know
what I think, Lieutenant?"

Jake gave his partner a questioning look and cocked one
eyebrow. "What?"

"I think the woman-in-black did it."

"Who?" Jake asked.

"Miss North," I answered.

"Why do you think she did it?" Sergeant Reilly asked
excitedly while Jake gave him a baleful look.

"It's simple. Like I told you at the auction right after the
murder," I said looking at Jake, "she made a small scene
with Ken and practically accused him of stealing items that
were supposed to be auctioned. Then she confronted him

during the auction in front of everyone, and accused him of underhanded dealing—which, by the way, he was guilty of as I observed it, too. He called her a bitch in return—loud enough for her and others to hear it.

"Believe me, she's not the type to take something like that lying down. I accidentally bumped into her before the auction began and I thought she was going to rip into me. She's one tough cookie. Look at how she dresses—all in black, and look at how she wears her makeup," I attested. "She won the murder weapon at the auction and pretended to lock the daggers in her car. Did you discover any evidence of her car being broken into?"

Sergeant Reilly intently followed my discourse, a look of concentration on his face. Jake, on the other hand, looked amused. His face bore a small grin. "No, we didn't," he answered. "Her car was unlocked when Sergeant Reilly checked."

"See? Everything points to Ken's murder as a crime of passion. Nobody in their right mind would plan to stab somebody to death with one of those little daggers, let alone do it at a public auction with a bunch of people around. So who's the only person likely to have become mad enough to kill him on the spot?" I asked portentously.

"North?" Jake replied with a supercilious look as if he was playing along to appease me.

I ignored his patronizing countenance, and said, "Right! Who else could it be?"

"Any of the people who were in the shed at the time," Jake replied with a knowing look. "Your Miss North wasn't one of them."

"What? How do you know she wasn't in there?"

"Because no one saw her there and we have reports from three witnesses who say she was sitting out front during that part of the day."

"Except when she won something, like the set of daggers, and then she took them to her vehicle. I've read many mysteries and I know how inaccurate eye witness testimony can be," I asserted. "I just proved she wasn't sitting out front every minute. When she went to her car she could have easily circled back and slipped into the shed. Maybe she wore all black on purpose. It was pretty dark in the back of that storage shed where Ken was killed."

Jake grimaced at my amateur sleuthing, but let it pass with a small shake of his head back and forth.

Inky, followed by Dinky, finally decided to brave the strange company and emerged from under the couch in hopes of receiving a cheesy treat. I quickly flipped the pizza box lids closed to prevent them access, and they moved on to sniff and rub against the pant legs of the two officers who didn't seem to mind.

After the three of us discussed the pros and cons of my assertions, the atmosphere became more relaxed and we settled into a question and answer routine while we worked on the pizzas. I re-stated the facts thoroughly—what I had seen and experienced firsthand, leaving out any of my further suspicions. The pair stayed for almost an hour before Jake told his partner to pack up. He assured me everything I told him would be held in the strictest confidence, but I had my doubts from what I'd read.

"Well, I hope I've helped solve the murder," I said, thinking they probably wished everyone was as helpful as me.

Jake ignored my prideful boast. "Keep your doors and windows locked, and don't answer the door for anybody until you first check who it is. It's unlikely your intruder will return. He's delivered his message. Don't forget to come down to the station Monday for your statement."

"I have to go to work at ten."

"Come down at eight and ask for me," he said matter-of-factly. "And one other thing, do you own a gun?"

His question left me momentarily speechless, "Uh, no. Why?"

"It's probably better that you don't. I was worried you might try to use it if your intruder returned."

"Gosh, no. But maybe a baseball bat or something would be good, huh?"

"All a bat is going to do is piss off the guy who'll probably take it away and use it against you. Use your wits; they're your most powerful weapon."

"My wits? Yeah, all right. If I have any left after this thing is through," I agreed sardonically.

"Or try some of your logic on them. That should confuse them long enough for you to run to safety."

"Very funny, Lieutenant. See if I help you anymore," I admonished to his retreating back.

After they left, I locked the screen and front door, checked all the windows, and locked the back door as Jake had advised. The living room looked like I had hosted a pizza party for a dozen people as I surveyed the aftermath—three boxes of partially eaten pizzas, dishes, glasses, and empty pop cans. After straightening up, I poured myself a glass of red wine, and searched for Inky and Dinky. I found them nestled next to each other on top of my bed sound asleep.

"Some watch kitties you are."

Jake's parting comment made me want to redouble my efforts to solve Ken's murder. Nothing would bring me greater pleasure than to bring the killer to justice and wipe that smug look from his face.

I returned to the living room and considered all the questions Jake had asked. He gave nothing away, no hint as to whom the police suspected. Everything I told him about Carole, Cyndi, and the woman-in-black, he accepted with professional indifference. I was on my second glass of wine when my phone rang. A glance at the caller's number told me it was Denise.

I was all talked out, so I let it ring. She must have heard about Ken's demise and was undoubtedly calling to pump me for information. A few seconds after it stopped ringing, my phone beeped letting me know my caller had left a voice message. As I suspected, it was Denise. She sounded all out of breath with excitement and asked me to call her as soon as possible. I decided to wait until Monday, when I'd see her at work. That way I'd only have to tell the story once to her and Annie.

I corked the bottle of wine, washed up, brushed my teeth, and crawled into bed, careful not to disturb the two princesses sprawled atop the bedspread. I checked my phone for calls and listened to a message from Annie. "Denise called and told me about Ken. Call me." I groaned audibly. I should have known Denise would report in for business and speak to Annie over the weekend. *What was I thinking?* A glance at the clock showed me it was too late to call Annie now. I did the next best thing and sent her a text message. "I'll call you tomorrow. I'm OK. Just need some ZZ's. Hugs, Nikki."

Exhausted, I finally fell asleep. My last waking thoughts were about the unknown woman who had called and the intruder who threatened me. *Could the two incidents be related in some way?*

Chapter Six

Sunday

A crash, followed by crackling noises, awoke me. I laid still and intently listened to the odd sounds stirring from the kitchen. *The kitties are up to something, but what? Did I leave anything on the kitchen counter last night for them to get into?* There it was again—but this time the noise sounded like the crinkling of a bag. *What could that rustling noise be?* Then it came to me and I smiled. *Dinky is in the garbage again.* This would be the third time she'd been naughty and I only had myself to blame. A solution was to buy a small trash receptacle I could place under the kitchen sink, but I hadn't gotten around to buying one yet. I sat up in bed, turned my alarm off, and wondered what emanating odor had enticed her this time.

Richard had never wanted pets. He argued their care would take time away from us. What he meant was that I should be there for him and him alone. He admittedly said he was selfish in that manner, constantly wanting me by his side, but I learned what he was really saying was he wanted me to wait on him hand and foot—picking up his dirty socks, washing his laundry, cleaning house, and making his dinners—because when we were together, we rarely did anything outside of play house.

The situation might have been tolerable if everything had been equitable in our marriage, but he lived by a double standard. When he was not at work for long hours, he played poker with the boys on Fridays nights and golfed on weekends, leaving little time for us to spend any quality time together. After we separated, I visited the local Humane Society and adopted Inky and Dinky, sisters that were now nine months old. On many a lonely night, they kept me company and gave me something to love, and returned my affections.

Drawing open my bedroom blinds, a grey cloudy day stared back at me. Groggy eyed, and with a slight headache, I slid my feet into my slippers and shuffled into the kitchen to see what all the racket was about that had stirred me from my sleep. Sure enough, Dinky had tipped over the garbage receptacle and was now trying to crawl into an empty Cheetos bag. Inky, sitting on the kitchen counter, watched her sister's every move with big round green eyes.

Dinky is crazy over Cheetos. I periodically buy them as a special treat for her. Inky is less enthused about them, and eats about one to every three pieces Dinky devours. Inky heard me and meowed loudly as a warning to her sister when I entered the kitchen. Dinky instantly stopped tackling the bag and gave me her big-eyed innocent look. *Who me?*

I picked up the spilled refuse and fed the little beasties a can of food—tuna for Inky and chicken for Dinky. Although they were from the same litter, they had different fathers, which explained their strikingly different characteristics and tastes in food. Inky, as was logical, was entirely black with relatively short hair. She was sleek and smaller than Dinky. Dinky was not so aptly named. Dinky's father must have been a Himalayan tom, because Dinky had long silky cream-colored fur with grey paws. Dark grey fur highlighted the area around her nose, eyes, forehead, and ears. Her most striking feature was her eyes—enormous sky-blue orbs that often portrayed her inquisitive innocence. She possessed incredibly powerful haunches that enabled her to easily jump up and look me square in the eye, but her furry paws made it difficult for her to start and stop on a dime when the chase with Inky was afoot.

Although different in many ways, the one thing they had in common was an intolerance of beef, and too much cheese always put them off their normally healthy constitutions, as did milk, ice cream, or any other kind of dairy product. *Why did advertising often depict cats drinking saucers of milk when so many felines are lactose intolerant?* Cheetos were okay though. Go figure.

While Inky and Dinky hooved their breakfast, I enjoyed a long hot shower until my skin turned pinkish. After drying my hair, I put on a trace of eye liner and lipstick before I stepped onto the scale. My goal was to reach my pre-marriage weight and I had another eleven pounds to lose. When the digital numbers glared back at me, I groaned to see last night's pizza and wine splurge had set my diet back over two pounds. I knew eating five small meals a day and limiting my intake of sweets and carbohydrates was the key to losing the unwanted weight, but somehow living life always managed to get in the way. I accepted my temporary setback with grace. *Stumbling upon a murder victim has to account for some allowance*, I rationalized.

Returning to the kitchen, I made a cup of coffee. To my bowl of oatmeal, I added a dash of protein powder, a teaspoon of cranberry jelly, and a generous dollop of peanut butter, mixing the ingredients together into a nice mushy consistency. I sat down with my iPad and read about the murder while I ate.

With a big sigh of relief, I thankfully discovered my name had been omitted in connection with the discovery of Ken's body. The reporter quoted Police Chief Anderson as saying the police were conducting a thorough investigation of everyone present at the time of the murder. Several promising leads were being pursued and Anderson believed the department's investigation would lead to a quick resolution. The reporter expressed doubts in regards to Anderson's claim given the large number of suspects—

over sixty people were at the auction at the time of Ken's murder.

Hickory Grove was a sleepy burg. Nothing as sensational as a murder had happened here in a long time—over ten years ago according to the columnist. Crime had been kept to a minimum during Anderson's term in office for the last six years. Now, for the first time, he was on the hot seat. The reporter hinted at the possibility that the police force had grown lax under his leadership. The obvious conclusion reached after reading the article was that Anderson had better solve the murder quickly or he was likely to be out of a job come election time.

As my second cup of coffee was brewing, I saw the new percolator, a fifties piece made of bright blue aluminum I had won at an auction a couple of weeks ago. I hadn't had time to unpack it, but I was eager to try it out. Willing to sacrifice speed for the pleasing aroma percolators were known to emanate, I hoped the taste of percolated coffee lived up to my expectations and exceeded today's brewing systems.

Sitting down at my small kitchen table, I created a new note file on my iPad. I sipped my coffee and entered everything I could recall about Ken, Barry, Woody, Carole, Cyndi, Miss North, and Crazy Mary. I had almost forgotten about Mary. For some unknown reason, I had completely passed over her during last night's question and answer session with Jake. She was inside the storage shed at the same time I was there, only a few scant minutes before I stumbled onto Ken's body. It took me nearly forty minutes to enter all my notes.

Yesterday, I had lost my cookies, but today the mental picture of Ken lying on the cement floor with the dagger sticking out of his throat no longer repulsed me. Instead, it represented a puzzle—a puzzle I now yearned to solve. The woman-in-black was the first person on my list, followed by Carole. Besides being an artist and lifelong Hickory

Grove resident, I knew Carole had a boyfriend, Kurt. Denise had told me he and Carole were an on-again off-again couple. I also knew he had been arrested a couple of times as I recalled his being listed in the newspaper's police report section at least twice. I tried hard to dredge up why he had been arrested and I vaguely remembered one of the charges was for DUI.

Returning to Carole, I remembered Denise also saying Carole was having difficulty making ends meet and supposedly she had taken out a second mortgage on her home. According to Denise, Carole had stopped in Annie's on more than one occasion to see if she could sell some vintage items she had inherited in an effort to raise money. *Could she have had Ken appraise her heirlooms, only to be displeased later when the items didn't sell close to their appraised value? That's something the police would never figure out. Take that, Lieutenant Corso!* I placed a double asterisk next to my summation for future reference.

Ken's and Barry's names were next on my list. They had been companions for years, long before I married Richard and relocated from Chicago to Hickory Grove. Ken owned The Antique Shoppe that Barry managed. Annie had mentioned Ken also owned a storage unit rental business— a smart move since he had considerable storage space needs for all the items he purchased. Someone told Annie that Ken sold a lot of items on eBay, especially during the winter. He also appraised items for anyone who would hire his services in the northwestern suburban locality.

Barry was the doer; he restored furniture and ran errands. While Ken was the brains, Barry provided the brawn, although he wasn't exactly a poster boy for fitness. *What else do I know about Barry?* Very little. Strangely, I couldn't remember Denise ever talking about him. This fact stood out as doubly peculiar when I considered how often Barry visited the store. Denise always talked about everyone who patronized Annie's.

Ken and Barry had never struck me as a loving couple to judge from their interaction in public. Notwithstanding that fact, their lives and livelihoods were so intertwined I couldn't see how a split of a murderous nature would benefit either of them, although there was a financial angle to be considered. Most likely Ken had left everything to Barry in his will.

Did Barry kill Ken in a fit of rage, fed up with his bullying? Barry was so mild, almost meek in demeanor; I couldn't see him killing anyone. If I was to bet on either of them being a murderer, Ken would have been my choice. Everyone knew him for a bully—a bully who met his match as a corpus delicti. I entered my rationale into my notes, eased back into my chair and finished my coffee.

Scanning what I had entered thus far, I came to the conclusion I was long on guesses and suppositions, and short on facts. The woman-in-black still topped my list, but I knew very little about the mysterious Miss North. Maybe a call to Denise was a good idea after all. Pulling up my address book, I was about to select her number when my phone rang. Serendipitously it was Denise.

"Nikki, I read about Ken's murder in today's paper. Are you alright?" Not waiting for a reply she continued excitedly. "The article didn't mention your name, but I heard through the grapevine you discovered his body. Is it true?"

"I was one of the people there when he was found," I answered noncommittally.

"Who do you think did it?"

"Who knows? That's what the police are working on."

"How was he killed?"

"Somebody stabbed him in the neck with a knife, but only the coroner knows for sure what killed him."

"How dreadful," she exclaimed with false consideration. "He was an awful person, but can you imagine someone actually stabbing him at a public auction?"

"All too well," I responded sardonically.

Denise pumped me for more information, but I remained resolute in my reluctance to tell her anything more than what was in the newspaper. When her continuous stream of questions yielded little result, she changed tactics and switched to a more personal approach.

"Nikki, I just realized yesterday I never gave you a housewarming gift. You know how I love to cook, so I made you a rice and chicken casserole dish. Would it be okay if I swing by after work today and drop it off?"

"Sorry, Denise, but I'm on a strict high-protein, low-carb diet," I replied feeling a bit guilty in remembering my splurge last night.

"That's what I get for not asking first," she said with feigned disappointment. Without missing a beat, she said, "I know! I'll bring you a bouquet of fresh-cut flowers from my garden."

Denise often brought flowers to Annie's Attic. She loved to receive compliments about her gardening acumen. Given I wanted to speak to her about the woman-in-black, I gave in to her.

"That would be nice."

"I'll go home right after work and cut the flowers. I'd love to talk more, but I have to get ready for work now," she said and abruptly hung up.

I knew allowing Denise to visit me at home was like letting the wolf into the hen house. With a sigh, I began to pick up my detritus as a precursor to dusting and vacuuming. Denise had a steel-trap mind. She was sure to make a mental note of anything she could learn about my place and me—my furniture, my living arrangements—to relay through the grapevine

It was all relevant, I decided. After all, I had bigger things to worry about—like keeping my name cleared from Lieutenant Corso's list of murder suspects and watching out for my backside after receiving two nasty threats.

I busied cleaning up Inky and Dinky's loose fur left behind in their favorite areas and changed their litter box. The refrigerator was last on my list, not wanting to leave anything to chance. Besides being an unrepentant gossip, Denise was also a snoop. Without hesitation, I knew she would look in my refrigerator. I wrapped most of the leftover pizza into small packages and tossed them in the freezer. That left a pretty bare refrigerator, but better that than the alternative. Folding the empty pizza boxes, I put them in the garbage and took the bag out to the garage. Satisfied all was in order, I sat down and called Annie.

When she didn't answer her phone, I debated leaving her a voicemail message and decided against it. My finding someone murdered wasn't exactly the type of thing to expound upon in a message.

After my cleaning flurry, I eased back on my sofa, picked up my iPad, and reread my notes. An impulse struck me to go to the Fire Sign for lunch. Hopefully, Cyndi would be waitressing today. I was dying of curiosity to see how she would react to me after the strange experience at the auction when she had so curtly brushed me off.

My car was stifling when I climbed behind the wheel. Turning the air conditioning and the fan on high, I proceeded down the street. As I passed Carole's house, I remembered I had promised to get together with her after the auction to see if any of her artwork would fit in my show rooms at Annie's. I made a mental note to call her later and set up a time to meet. Pulling up to the old fire station that housed the Fire Sign, I parked and followed the winding pathway to the entranceway.

The Fire Sign was the most popular restaurant in the shopping district. The owners boasted an expansive patio where patrons could eat al fresco, enjoy a respite from shopping, and take in a bit of nature by watching the pair of swans that called the adjacent pond home.

Hickory Grove attracted a steady stream of affluent shoppers from Chicago and the surrounding suburbs. Long known for its quaint shops, unique goods, antiques, and ambience, the town had served as a getaway attraction for decades. Stores were spread out in a pleasant cobbled street walking district interspersed with small park-like areas.

The locale served my new livelihood well. I scoured estate sales, thrift shops, flea markets, even garage sales to create kitchen, bedroom, living room, and outdoor settings—anything I could piece together to create room ensembles in the space I leased at Annie's store. In exchange for leasing the space for a reduced fee, I arranged to work four days a week at the store for a small stipend. I usually had Friday, Saturday, and Sundays off to do my shopping and auctioneering.

I sought to appeal to customers who desired one-stop shopping, especially those individuals who lacked the decorating sense, or time, to complete their living spaces. I attempted to stage perfect settings wherein the customer couldn't imagine splitting up an ensemble—thusly increasing their inclination to buy the entire arranged set rather than dicker over piece parts.

For my living ensembles, I usually sought wood furniture pieces with unique characteristics like tiger oak, quilted maple, or a combination of woods. Most customers still found wood pieces warm and inviting as compared to the industrial look preferred by the younger urban crowd. To display three ensembles in my dealer space was a tight fit, and a special challenge to maintain a light and airy look while providing a cozy ambience. As a backdrop, I hung my framed artwork on the walls.

Although my idea was not a new concept, no one else in the area was doing anything similar, and the ensemble angle worked well within Annie's business. The other spaces in her shop were leased by various people and stocked with consignment goods sold by the piece.

One of the Fire Sign hostesses, a young woman I knew by sight, but not by name, greeted me inside the front door. I asked her if Cyndi was working and when she told me she was, I asked to be seated in her section. After leading me to one of the wooden booths next to the bar area, the hostess took my drink order and left.

Cyndi arrived and set my drink in front of me. "Hi Nikki," she said as if nothing untoward had occurred at the auction.

"Hi, Cyndi. How'd you make out at the auction?"

"Not so hot," she said ruefully. "The bidding was ridiculous. That's why I left early and I'm so glad I did after what happened. Were you there when they discovered Ken?"

Cyndi acted as if she didn't know I had found the body. Either she was a great actress or she was being sincere. I opted for the latter knowing what I did of her. Her ignorance over the affair revealed she wasn't in on Denise's Hickory Grove grapevine, and that fact notched her up in my estimation. "Yeah, don't tell anybody, but I was the one who discovered his body."

"Oh my God! How awful."

She isn't feigning ignorance that well, or is she? Scrutinizing her facial features for tell-tale signs, I saw no evidence she wasn't telling the truth. Then again, everybody was an actor or actress these days. Look at all the people on television who have disavowed knowledge of, or involvement in, something with utmost earnestness only to later admit their culpability. I was both intrigued and repulsed by their ability to turn their emotions on or off so easily.

"Yeah, it was awful," I agreed. "I don't think I'll ever forget it. It was an experience I could do without."

"Do the police have any suspects?" she asked nervously.

I'm not sure why I decided to tell her what I did. Perhaps an unconscious desire surfaced to see how she would respond, but I heard myself reply, "They think it was a woman," and I saw Cyndi noticeably pale under my steady gaze.

"A w-w-woman," she stuttered. "Why do they think that?"

"I'm not sure. Maybe it has to do with the way Ken was killed."

Cyndi, visibly shaken by my pronouncement, hurriedly took my order and rushed off without further conversation. While I sipped my protein shake, I considered her curious behavior. I'm not very good at subterfuge, so when she returned with my order, I said, "You seemed upset about something when you left the auction yesterday."

"Me?" she asked innocently. "I wasn't upset."

I decided to press her. "You were awfully abrupt when I offered to help you carry your items to your car."

"Oh that," she said breezily. "I'm sorry if I was, Nikki. Didn't mean to be. I was just pressed for time. I was late for an appointment."

"I understand," I conceded doubtfully.

She left to wait on another table and I weighed her explanation. I was so self-absorbed in my analysis of Cyndi and her answers that I didn't see Barry until he was standing over my table.

Pensively he asked, "Nicole, how are you?"

"Barry! I'm fine. How are *you*?"

"I'm as good as can be expected," he replied mournfully.

"Must be a terrible loss for you," I said clumsily, fumbling for words.

"Ken was a special person. He taught me everything I know about the business. I'm not sure if I can go forward without him—it's way too painful," he declared, tears welling and cheeks reddening.

"Give it time, Barry. Time has a way of working its magic. Just don't rush into anything and make hasty decisions you might regret later." My attempt at giving him sage advice left me feeling stupid and inadequate.

He shook his head sadly. "I suppose you're right, but my heart's not in it. Say, Nicole, do you know Carole Winker very well?"

His sudden change of subject caught me off guard. "N-n-no," I stammered. "I wouldn't say I know her well. We're both artists so our paths cross on occasion, but that's about all. Why do you ask?"

"I know she needs money and I thought she might help me with the business until I can sort everything out."

"What a great idea—definitely ask her. It's awfully tough to make a living as an artist these days."

"Yeah, it's tough all around. Well, it was nice seeing you, Nicole. Take care."

"Yeah, you, too, Barry," I mumbled as he walked away.

How odd. Isn't he a strange bird? It wasn't like Barry to be so outgoing, but like Cyndi had said earlier at the auction, he had always been kept on a short leash by Ken. In fact, I couldn't recall a time I had ever seen Barry unaccompanied by his deceased partner, except for the few occasions when he had stopped by Annie's Attic. During those times, he was all business, on a mission to do Ken's bidding. *Is Barry finally finding his way out from under Ken's auspices?*

Leaving a generous tip for Cyndi, I glanced at my watch. *Time for me to go; Denise is soon to come a-calling.* As I climbed into my car and began the short drive home, a funny sensation came over me. Looking in the rearview mirror, I spotted a silver sedan, but it was too far behind for me to make out the model or make. Unsure as to why I thought the car was following me, I turned right at the next corner and slowed down.

The car turned after me and pulled over to the curb. I was about to chalk up the happenstance of my pursuer to mere coincidence, but after I took a left at the next corner, followed by another left, my tail reappeared. I stomped on the gas pedal, made a right at the next corner, and beat a hasty retreat home.

My follower had unnerved me. *What should I do? Call Lieutenant Corso again and tell him about the incident?* No, I concluded, I'd feel foolish calling him—like a school girl running home to momma every time something went wrong. My decision was reinforced by the fact I had nothing to report to him except the color of the vehicle. And then, too, the vehicle may have been an unmarked police car. *That's probably it. Jake said they'd be keeping an eye out for me,* I told myself with a total lack of conviction.

Inky and Dinky were their usual buoyant selves at my return. I fed them and grabbed a diet soda. They soon joined me in the living room where I took a few minutes respite. Both clamored over me seeking affection, and we were playing together with a string attached to a book marker, when suddenly the doorbell rang. My shriek scared the kitties and sent them scampering into hiding. I was jumpy as a bullfrog. *Settle down,* I told myself, and peeked through the blinds to see who was at the door. I observed with redoubtable trepidation that it was Denise.

Straighten up. Don't let her see your anxiety. Brushing my hair back behind my ears, I composed myself, smiled, and opened the door. "Hi Denise, come on in."

"I picked you a special bouquet of flowers," she said, handing me an impressive display of calla lilies, zinnias, daisies, lavender, and dahlias before giving me an overly generous hug and kiss on the cheek.

"Wow, they're beautiful," I remarked with truthful admiration and sniffed their deliciously fragrant aroma.

Denise beamed at my exclamation. "Here, this was on your front stoop," she said holding out a basket of tomatoes and cucumbers.

"Oh, Mr. Campezi must have left them. He's a neighbor who promised me some goodies out of his garden. Would you like some?" I graciously offered, trying not to dwell on how seeing the silver sedan had upset me so much that I missed spotting Mr. Campezi's basket at the front door. *Not good, Nikki. What else have you missed?*

"Maybe a couple of each. I've thought about growing vegetables in my garden, but somehow I never have managed to include them."

"Everybody grows vegetables, but nobody grows flowers like you," I said effusively. *Geez, don't overdo it, girl.*

From the look on her face, Denise was eating up my every word of praise like a starving woman in front of a smorgasbord. "Let me put these in a vase, and I'll grab a bag for the vegetables. Make yourself at home," I added and immediately regretted my poor choice of words.

When I selected some tomatoes and cucumbers for Denise, I noticed a small note card had been slipped into the bottom of the basket. I left the card in place to read later, as I didn't want to leave Denise alone any longer than was absolutely necessary. When I rejoined her, I observed her scrutinizing my abode with tightly screwed up eyeballs.

"Here you go," I said handing her the bag. "Can I get you something to drink—a glass of wine perhaps?"

"That would be nice," she replied. "Thank you."

"Is cabernet alright?"

"One of my favorites."

"Why don't we stay and chat in the kitchen?" I suggested, motioning her over to a chair at the kitchen table. As I poured our wine, the idea of getting Denise a little lubricated to limit her impending interrogation occurred to me.

She took a sip of wine and looked around. "You don't have much furniture, do you, Nikki?"

"No, I let Richard keep our furniture with the house. I took the equivalent in cash," I declared without thinking.

Cripes. She's got you on the ropes already. Defend yourself and don't let her get the best of you. "I wanted the cash so I could buy exactly what I need to fit in with this style of house. Besides, the basement's cluttered with my stuff. I have much more I haven't brought up yet. I even have some goods down there I don't have space for at Annie's." What I didn't tell her was how I dreaded going through all my personal belongings and dredging up old memories.

"It's a good thing you left most things behind," she commented. "You'd never have room for it all here. What did you go from—a 4000 square foot house to, what is it, about 1100 square feet?"

"Yeah," I agreed, marveling at how she knew the details of my past and present living arrangements. "One thing I love about this place is the small-sized rooms with the unusually high vaulted ceilings, and all the woodwork—the beams, built in shelves, solid doors, wood floors. And I like the Art Deco touches in the bathroom, and kitchen," I added with a wave of my hand. "They don't make 'em with character like this anymore."

Denise can find fault with anything and my preemptive speech left her with a temporary loss for words. *Now who's on the ropes?* Taking advantage of the moment, I said, "The best part is the screened-in porch. I love the sound of the bugs, especially the crickets, at night. Inky and Dinky like it, too."

As I placed the flowers in a vase, I thought about asking Denise if she'd be interested in providing fresh flowers for my staging area. She has a small hothouse in the back of her house that provides her the ability to grow flowers all year long. *Don't get hasty and do something rash. Let's see how this visit goes today.*

Working with her at Annie's Attic was already a bit overbearing from being constantly under her scrutiny. Denise in small doses is okay, but doing business with her wouldn't be the wisest thing to do. If something went wrong, and knowing human nature it probably would, I'd be upset, and more importantly Annie would be displeased with having a personnel problem on hand at her workplace.

Denise wasted no time in switching subjects. "Wasn't it awful about Ken? I know what you said on the phone, but I heard you were the one who found him, Nikki."

Here it comes, the inevitable information gathering. While she worked herself up, I refilled her glass. "Me and a couple of the workers," I replied off-handedly.

"How was he killed?"

She was covering the same ground today as she had addressed yesterday, making sure no stone remained unturned.

"The coroner is the one to ask, not me."

"But you were there," she protested. "Wasn't he stabbed in the neck?"

"Yeah, but I'm not sure that's what killed him."

"You mean there was something else?" she asked excitedly, barely able to control her enthusiasm as she squirmed in her chair.

"I don't know."

My answer dampened her spirits. *Time for me to turn the tables.* "Denise, do you know a woman who dresses in all black? She was at the auction and won the dagger Ken was stabbed with."

She instantly perked up and asked raptly, "Do you think she was the one who killed him?"

"I have no idea." *Now throw her a morsel.* "But I did see her bawling Ken out about something at the auction earlier in the day."

That did it. Denise gulped a big swallow of wine, mindlessly wiping off a little rivulet of wine that dribbled down her chin with the back of her hand. "Describe this woman for me."

"Well," I said, while refilling her glass, "she looked to be in her early to middle thirties. She has straight black hair, a little longer than shoulder length that she ties back in a ponytail. Slim but muscular, she's about five-seven. Oh yeah, I think she drives a silver BMW," I added and suddenly recalled the silver car that had tailed me today. *Was she my tail? Was she the woman who had called and threatened me? Her harsh mannerisms at the auction fit the bill.*

"Nikki? Nikki!" Denise's voice eventually reached me, piercing my veil of inner-contemplation. "Where were you? You looked like you were a thousand miles away."

"Uh, no, sorry. I was only trying to see if there was anything else I could remember about her," I half-fibbed.

"From your description, it might be Julie Brandt."

"No, I know Julie. I think someone mentioned the woman's last name was North."

"North, hmm... No, I don't think I know anyone who fits her description by that name," Denise said with her face scrunched up in thought. "What was she wearing?"

"Black jeans, with a black silky blouse. A wide black patent-leather belt and black shoes or boots, I can't remember which now. She wore a similar, but different outfit the day before, too."

"Hmm . . . someone who wears all black," she said again as she continued to search her memory banks. "I don't think I know her. She's probably from out of town," she resolved.

Inky and Dinky picked that moment to make their appearance, Inky boldly treading over to Denise. "Hold out your hand and let her smell you," I encouraged.

In doing so, Inky instantly backed away and hissed at Denise's outstretched hand. She immediately withdrew her hand with a shocked look. She tried again, this time, saying, "Here kitty, kitty," only to have Inky turn tail and run. Denise's face flushed as a result of Inky's rejection. Normally, Inky and Dinky were friendly to everyone with some coaxing—the mailwoman, Mr. Campezi, even door-to-door solicitors, and when Annie and Burton are here, they'll readily jump onto their laps and demand their affections.

"It's not you, Denise. They're still getting acclimated to their new surroundings," I said to mollify her.

Denise harrumphed and took another sip of wine. Without losing a beat, she asked, "So how are you doing since the divorce?"

Damn, I should have seen it coming. Even on her way to getting half-crocked she's pushing for gossip.

"Not so good, huh?" Denise prodded hopefully.

No matter what I said, I knew Denise would distort and spread my words around town, and eventually they would return to Richard. "No, everything's fine. It's taken a bit of adjustment, but honestly I've been so busy working I haven't had time to think about it. How are things going with you?" I asked, redirecting the conversation and topping off her glass again.

"Same old, same old," she answered evasively. "Would it be okay if I use your washroom, Nikki?" she asked a bit sluggishly, setting her glass down a bit too hard and spilling a little wine.

"Sure, it's down the hall to your right."

Denise was only in the washroom a scant minute or two before a huge crash reverberated off the walls followed by a shriek, "Oh no!"

"Are you okay?" I shouted down the hall.

She opened the bathroom door, her face a bright red. "I was looking for an aspirin and the medicine cabinet fell off the wall."

I put my hand over my mouth to hide my smile. The cabinet had been a recent auction purchase and I hadn't the opportunity to properly secure it to the bathroom wall.

"Don't worry. The important thing is that you aren't hurt." I bit my tongue from not saying how I had taken an aspirin this morning and the yellow container was sitting in plain view on the sink.

Denise used the incident as a well-timed excuse to make her exit. After the front door closed behind her, I breathed a big sigh of relief and momentarily enjoyed the silence. "At least she didn't make it to the refrigerator," I said aloud to Inky and Dinky who stared at me from under the living room couch where they had sought safety after the calamity. I couldn't coax them to come out from under until they heard me open cans of cat food, and then they came galloping into the kitchen. They screeched to a halt at the kitchen table, hastily sniffed the area where I had entertained Denise, assured themselves she was really gone, and dived into their food. I released another sigh of relief when I heard their tongues roughly licking their plates clean.

Summarily rehashing my conversation with Denise, I realized neither of us had much to show for our efforts. I had managed to effectively thwart Denise's efforts to gain new information about my involvement in Ken's murder. And most importantly, I hadn't taken the bait, and had told her very little about my divorce. The worst she could do would be to talk about my small abode and furnishings. On the other hand, she didn't know the mysterious Miss North, and if she didn't know the woman-in-black, she didn't live in these parts.

After everything was restored to order in the bathroom, I jotted a note to go to the lumber yard and have a piece of mounting board cut to properly mount the bathroom cabinet. Then I recalled Brett had told me he was a retired carpenter. His card was on my bedroom dresser where I had emptied my pockets after the auction. I fetched the card and put it on the kitchen counter where I couldn't miss it in the morning. I'd call him then and arrange a time to get a quote on refurbishing the credenza and a number of other projects I wanted performed around the house.

I ate a small salad for supper and went over my notes again at the kitchen table. Something nagged at me, but I couldn't put my finger on it. In reviewing my notes, one thing stood out loud and clear: everyone I knew had acted out of character during the auction from how I knew them. Cyndi had acted strange, but yesterday she was her old self, still a bit nervous perhaps, but nothing like at the auction. When I considered the explanation she had given me to justify her abruptly rude behavior, something didn't quite ring true, although I couldn't point to anything specifically wrong per se.

Then there was Carole. I kept coming back to the fact she had lied to me about attending the Krieger auction. The more I dwelled on her deceit, the more it bothered me. I had to resolve that issue even if it meant having to confront her. It was impossible for me to do business with her knowing she had been untruthful. There had to be a reasonable explanation behind her mendacity. If she wasn't forthcoming with a good excuse for her deceit, it was too bad for her—I wasn't going to incorporate her artwork into my room ensembles.

Chapter Seven

With newfound intent, I locked up and walked briskly to Carole's house located a few blocks over from my place. My unannounced visit shouldn't be a surprise to her since we had already discussed getting together. Scattered clouds diffused the intense sunlight on the western horizon, but the humidity remained stifling. Nevertheless, I needed exercise, and walking—something I loved to do and needed to do more of—would do me good.

Carole's house, a modern two-story, was the very antithesis of my 1920s bungalow. White with black trim, it sat in the middle of the block surrounded by houses of similar appearance. She lived within a newer housing development begun in the 1980s, adjacent to the old, established neighborhoods. To me, all the homes looked alike with nothing much to distinguish one from the other.

Thankfully the same couldn't be said about my neighborhood where each house had been built according to each owner's individual taste. Mr. Campezi originally owned the tract of land by my house. His parents had been farmers and when they died, they left their only son their entire estate. He took over and worked the farm until he turned sixty. He had refused many developers' offers for the prime real estate. Instead, he sold off a parcel at a time to interested individuals who were to his liking. This accounted for the diversity in the homes surrounding mine and in the people who lived in them.

Carole's house was nicely appointed with bushes and trees. Her car sat in the driveway. Until then, I hadn't seriously considered what vehicles my private list of suspects owned, but seeing Carole's silver Chevrolet compact put my mental machinery to work. Walking around to the front of her car, I studied it carefully. It might have been the car that had followed me earlier in the day. Unfortunately, I wasn't very good in identifying one car from another unless some unusual feature caught my eye, like Mercedes' circled triangle logo or Ferrari's prancing horse emblem.

I had previously visited Carole in her house only one other time—during last year's Hickory Grove Art Crawl. All of the local artists banded together once a year aided by grant money and a grass roots marketing campaign complete with posters, brochures, and local media exposure, opening their work studios to the public. In this way, art patrons in surrounding communities became aware of and were exposed to various local artists' creations and work environments. The win-win being people would be induced to purchase local artwork and thereby infuse monies into our small community. Naturally, all the artists took time out to visit their co-creators and their environs.

The first year the event was held had been so successful that the art crawl became an annual event. Richard hadn't wanted strangers in our house when we were married, so I didn't participate as an artist and instead, I toured a number of the local artist's studios. Last year, I had visited Carole's studio. When I had told Annie earlier this year that I still wasn't going to be able to participate in the annual event because my bungalow was too small, she insisted I use her storefront to display my artwork for the duration of the art crawl. It turned out to be a good move on both our parts. People who came to her shop to see my artwork also ambled around to look over her vintage goods, and the increased traffic added to her sales.

As I approached Carole's front door, I was thinking about a specific piece of her artwork I had admired during the last art crawl that would look good in one of my room ensembles if she hadn't sold it to someone already. The work was a cleverly constructed three-dimensional paper house with windows that opened to reveal hidden meanings. It was a fun inspirational novelty item that would make a good conversation piece. I pressed her doorbell in eagerness to speak with her, but she didn't answer. I wasn't certain the bell was working since I hadn't heard a chime sound from inside, so I knocked on the screen door. As a last resort, I opened the screen door, and started to bang on the front door when it opened a crack under my exertion. Slowly pushing the door open further, I called out, "Yoo-hoo. Hello? Carole—its Nikki. Hello?"

Receiving no answer, I shouted my greeting louder—still no response. I knew from my previous visit that Carole's studio was in the back corner of her house. I called out again as I made my way toward her work area where I could hear country music emanating loudly from behind the closed door. Rapping my knuckles on the doorframe, I called her name again.

She didn't answer, so I cracked open the door for one last confirmation she wasn't present. Heavy drapes covered the windows shrouding the room in darkness when I snuck my head in for a peek. My hand found the light switch, and I flicked it on. A pair of woman's legs stuck out from behind a kiln near a row of pottery pieces stacked along the opposite wall.

"Oh no, not again," I cried feebly. Moving around a work desk, I looked down at Carole, her body curled in a fetal position. Blood stained her dress and the carpet where she lay. One look at her still body and ashen face was enough to tell me she was beyond resuscitation.

A loud, long keening moan escaped from my lips. Reaching out an arm, I braced myself against a work table and began to take quick, deep breaths to steady my nerves. *This can't be happening. Not two times. This is crazy, absolutely insane, first Ken and now Carole. What the hell is going on? Is there a serial killer on the loose?* I immediately dismissed the thought as the coincidences were too numerous for the murders to be unrelated. *But how are they connected?* That was the key question.

Backing slowly out of the room, I stumbled into the living room and sat down. After a moment, my curious nature, like that of typical cat owners, kicked in again and stirred me from the horror confronting me. I needed a moment to collect my thoughts. I wanted to run home, but knew I should call the police. For some inexplicable reason I was reluctant to do so. *How could I not be a suspect after finding both bodies? What are the chances?* It didn't take a Sherlock Holmes to figure out the murders were related and that somehow I was involved, if by no other means than by the unfortunate circumstance in knowing the two victims.

At that moment, I recalled something Richard had told me about his older brother. He said *things* always happened when his brother was around as a way of explaining the rash of incidents that occurred during his brother's one and only visit to our home. During his stay, a house burned down across the street, and a theft was committed down the block. The thief actually dropped his gun in our driveway as he tried to make his escape. Both outrageous events transpired during the first two days of his brother's visit. Another time and place, Richard had related how his brother had found a dead body in a friend's apartment. And there was the time someone tried to break into his brother's apartment while he was home. The intruder had actually attempted to force his way inside while his brother pushed to keep him out. *Am I becoming like Richard's brother—a human magnet for trouble?*

I needed to talk to Annie, and fast. She'd know what to do. I picked up my phone and selected Annie's number.

"Annie, I'm at Carole's and she's dead," I blurted out without thinking when she answered.

"Nikki, is that you?"

"Yeah, Carole's been murdered—just like Ken."

"Are you joking?"

"I wish I was," I replied shakily.

"Holy shit! What do the police say?"

"I haven't called them yet. They're going to suspect I did it. Especially since I found Ken, too," I added for emphasis. "What do I do?"

"Holy shit," she echoed. "Nikki, listen to me. You can't hide this from the police. Your fingerprints are probably all over her house. Call the police now. The longer you wait the more suspicious it will look. We'll be there as soon as possible—Burton and I just got home. Hold tight and wait for us, but call the cops now, sweetie."

"Okay, I will, but hurry."

"We will, sweetie, don't worry," she assured me before disconnecting.

Looking up Jake's number in my phone's recently called list, I shakily hit the numbers. He picked up on the third ring, "Corso here."

"Lieutenant, this is Nicole Carson. I'm at Carole Winker's house. She's dead. Somebody killed her."

"What?"

"It looks like somebody stabbed her."

"And you found her?" he asked in a voice resonating with suspicion. *See! He already suspects me!*

"Uh-huh. I only stopped by because we were supposed to meet. You see—"

"Stay there. Don't touch a thing. We'll be there in a few minutes," he ordered cutting me off mid-sentence.

A thousand thoughts raced through my brain as I waited. Time moved at a snail's pace. *What is taking them so long?* I paced Carole's living room like an expectant father, yet there was no bundle of joy to hold at the end of my waiting period. With each step I took, my curiosity increased until I couldn't stand it anymore. Resigning myself to an overwhelming desire to take one more look at Carole, I drew in a big breath and retraced my way to her studio.

This time I looked on the murder scene more dispassionately with a sense of detachment. There were no signs of a struggle. Either Carole's killer was known to her or had caught her by surprise. Looking around the studio, I concluded Carole must have known her murderer since there wasn't a hiding place anywhere in the room to provide adequate concealment. *Or did her murderer sneak up on her while the loud music masked his or her entry?*

Her studio had a closet with folding doors. With considerable trepidation, I opened the doors, and saw the closet was packed with her artwork and supplies. There was no space for the killer to have hidden inside. Besides, even if the killer had hidden away, a struggle would have ensued and the artwork that littered the studio—pottery, paintings, stained glass windows—would have been damaged or strewn about. That wasn't the case. The room was neatly arranged from a working artist's perspective. No, I was sure Carole knew her attacker. *But who could it be? Is her slayer her on-again off-again boyfriend, Kurt?*

The shock of first discovering her body had so overwhelmed me, I had failed to see that her right hand was tightly closed in a fist. Bending over her prone body, I pried open her stiff fingers until a piece of jewelry fell to the floor. Nudging it with my finger, I recognized the piece from the auction, one of the more valuable brooches made from a cluster of pearls and blue sapphires that had been kept in one of the glass cases at the auction on Friday.

"Hmm, that's strange," I said under my breath. I didn't remember Carole bidding on any of the jewelry. And being valuable, it wasn't the kind of costume jewelry she'd typically purchase for reuse in her artwork. *Was she reselling pieces on the side?* She'd kept mum about it if she had been doing so. If the rumors were true about how she was economically strapped, her buying the expensive brooch was doubly puzzling.

I stood up and surveyed the room again. My eyes spotted her iPad sitting atop a small desk positioned in the far corner. Picking it up, I turned it on. The logon screen asked for a passcode. Don't ask me why, but I returned to the living room and stuck her iPad into my purse moments before I heard police sirens.

Seconds later, two police cars abruptly pulled into Carole's driveway with a screeching halt, their lights flashing. The commotion stirred the neighborhood from its late Sunday afternoon lassitude. Doors opened and neighbors gathered outside on their front lawns to find out what the hubbub was about. A few brazen snoopy souls slowly made their way down the street towards the house.

Lieutenant Corso stepped out of the second police car and ordered one of the policemen to stay outside and fend off the curious onlookers. Sergeant Reilly accompanied him again. They walked through the front door as Annie and Burton's car pulled up to the curb in front. Burton exchanged a few words with the cop posted outside before they were let inside.

"We've got to stop meeting like this," I joked weakly to Jake.

Burton and Annie bustled in before Jake could respond. Annie hugged me and whispered, "Everything is going to be all right, honey, Burton's here." Burton, who knew Jake in passing, shook his hand and introduced Annie to him. Jake didn't waste time on additional formalities. Instead, he waved us all into the living room. He gave me one of his dark-eyed noncommittal looks and without artifice asked, "Where's the body?"

"In the back studio," I answered and motioned with a small wave of my arm.

He trod determinedly down the hall with his partner and Burton. I followed obediently, not knowing what else to do, ignoring Annie's protest. Bending over the body, Jake felt Carole's wrist. "She's been dead a few hours," he said to his partner. He squeezed around the kiln to get a better look at her back. Studying the body, I watched as he moved his arms about, emulating how the attack must have been carried out for her body to fall as it did.

He stayed on his knees until he was satisfied he had everything mentally catalogued, taking particular care in studying Carole's hand and the brooch. He looked at me and I quivered. *He's good, he's real good. He knows I messed with the evidence.*

He began an inspection of Carole's studio. About then, the medical examiner and a number of other personnel burst upon the scene. One fellow began to take pictures, while another placed various objects, including the jewelry piece, into evidence bags.

Jake turned and saw me standing there, took me by the elbow, and escorted me into the hallway. He told Burton to take me back to the living room where Annie gave me a big hug.

"Nikki, you poor dear. Are you alright? You look terrible."

"I'm okay, Annie. It's the stress. Seems like finding murder victims is becoming a habit with me." She scrutinized my face for reassurance. "Really, I'm okay," I persisted. Satisfied my emotions were under control, she took me by the hand and sat next to me on the couch. She cradled my head to her shoulder and gave me a motherly pat. Burton stood by stoically watching us, like a gargoyle guarding a castle. He was one in a million. Jake came into the living room, looked me over, and motioned to Burton to go with him into the kitchen.

"First Ken and now Carole. What the hell's happening, sweetie?"

"I wish I knew, Annie. I keep stumbling into the middle of murders and I'm beginning to feel like the walls are closing in on me. I've been threatened twice—"

"Threatened! Who threatened you?" she asked indignantly.

"I don't know who. After Ken's murder, a woman called and warned me to keep my mouth shut. Last night a man pushed his way into my home and threatened me, telling me to keep quiet or else. Luckily, a pizza delivery boy scared him off. I was going to tell you everything tonight when I called you."

"When the police are finished with you, sweetie, you're going to come home with us where you'll be safe and sound," she said giving me another big hug.

"Really, Annie, I can't impose on you and Burton like that."

"Nonsense! I insist. It's for your own good. Listen, Burton used to be mayor of this burg, and he's been the town lawyer for years. He carries a lot of influence. I'm sure he'll get a policeman assigned to watch your house."

A man's voice—impishly traced with affection—cut in, "You're sure about that, are you?"

"You better believe it, Burton! Imagine someone bursting into our house and threatening me."

"As usual you're right, my dear," he said with a grin. "I already cleared it with Lieutenant Corso. He's familiar with such requests—he's from Chicago. He's going to personally see that no harm comes to our wayward waif."

"Thanks, Burton. What would I do without you two? How can I ever repay you?"

"Now, none of that," Annie chided. Returning her attention to Burton, she said, "She's going to stay with us until the police catch whoever is responsible."

"It'll be nice to have a *young* woman around the house," Burton declared roguishly.

"Don't mind Burton, dear, he's getting a bit touched," Annie retorted, making a circular motion with her finger by the side of her head.

They were a loving, playful couple so I took their interplay as intended, with a light-hearted laugh. Burton was in his early seventies, but he retained the drive and energy of someone half his age.

Jake broke up our little fun as he strode over. "I need a few minutes alone with Ms. Carson."

"Don't worry dear, we're not going anywhere. We'll wait around until the police are finished with you," Annie assured me with a pat on my hand.

Jake led me to Carole's dining room. He pulled two chairs out from her large dining table and waved me into one of them. Turning his chair around, he sat, put his arms on the back, and without preamble ordered briskly, "Tell me from the beginning how you came to be here until the time you called me."

Wringing my hands in my lap, I stared into his big dark orbs. The feeling of becoming lost within them returned. His eyes welcomed everything inside and had a mesmerizing effect on me, like being under hypnosis.

Mechanically, I reiterated my earlier conversation with Carole at the auction—how we had agreed at the auction to get together to discuss the use of her artwork in my room ensembles at Annie's.

"When she didn't answer and the front door opened under my knock, I walked in and called her name. Loud music was coming from her studio area so I figured she was working and hadn't heard me. That's why I went into her studio and how I found her there laying on the floor."

"You didn't touch anything, did you?"

"Only the doorknobs," I said, and hesitated. "Hmm, I think I reached out to her work table and steadied myself when I found her body," I added. "It's a bit blurry." Then my curious nature took over again. "Say, Lieutenant, did you find any fingerprints on the knife Ken was stabbed with?"

He snapped his head up from his note-taking and scrutinized me with a steely-eyed look that gave me the heebie-jeebies. Deep inside, I was sure he was a no-nonsense guy. A guy who could be hard as nails when he wanted. He glanced around to see if anyone was within hearing distance before he answered, "I shouldn't say anything; this is not for anyone's ears other than yours, but the knife was clean."

"Someone must have used gloves or wiped the dagger clean afterwards," I whispered without thinking.

"Maybe you should take over the investigation," he suggested wryly.

"I'm sorry. I was thinking how the woman-in-black's prints had to be on the knives since she purchased them."

"Her name's Traci North, for your edification."

Learning the mysterious woman's full name was anticlimactic. "Somehow, her name doesn't fit her."

"Why do you say that?" Jake inquired leaning forward, his black eyes burning in intensity.

"I don't know. It's just an impression I have of her. She's a tough customer. I told you how she reacted when I bumped into her at the auction, and how she stood up and voiced a complaint in front of everybody about what Ken did. You know—over the cocktail glasses at the auction. And earlier, she called Ken to task about something missing from one of the display cases, too."

"What was missing?"

"I don't know. I didn't hear that part."

Jake inched closer and asked, "Was that when Ken called her a bitch?"

"When?"

"Right, when?"

"I think we're talking past each other. Do you mean did Ken call her a bitch when she accused him of taking something from the display case?"

He gave me an incredulous look and asked, "How do I know when he called her a bitch? I'm asking you when he said it."

"Oh, well, you didn't make that clear. So, you want to know when he said it?"

"That's what I just said," he replied in exasperation. "Tell me about that again."

"You mean the conversation with Ken or the complaint?" I asked getting more confused by the minute.

"Let's make this easy for both of us. Tell me about the conversation *and* the complaint," he clarified.

"You should have said that in the first place."

He rubbed his forehead with his hand, shut his eyes, and with strained patience said, "Start with the complaint, all right?"

"Sure. She complained about how the auction was being conducted. You see the auction helpers brought items out from the shed and set them atop the trailer bed. Other workers would then carry items from there to where Ken was sitting—next to a staging table in front of the trailer bed. On his end of the table, Ken would first arrange the various items into lots, and then he would move them to the other end of the table where they would be auctioned off by Woody. Once all the items were sold on the table by Woody, Ken would then stage other items to take their place. In other words, when bidding for choice would end for the current items in front of Woody, they'd be removed from the table, and other staged items at Ken's end would be moved to take their place, and so on," I explained.

Jake held up his hand. "'For choice'—explain that."

"I'm sorry. I should have realized you weren't familiar with auctions. When a number of similar or disparate items are put up 'for choice,' it means the winning bidder can choose one or more of the items they want from the lot. They pay the same amount for each item they take. After the winning bidder has claimed the items they want, the auctioneer usually offers the remaining items for the same winning bid amount to anyone else interested—any other takers. If no one accepts the same-bid offer, the auctioneer begins the bidding process again from scratch 'for choice,' and so on until everything is eventually sold. This process expedites things when there are a large number of items to sell."

"So what did Miss North specifically complain about?"

"Well, Ken bid and won one of the for-choice auctions. Instead of selecting items from amongst those staged for bidding at the end of the table in front of Woody, he selected items that weren't yet part of the bidding lot."

"In other words, he made his selection from items everyone understood to be amongst those staged for the next bid lot, not from the lot of goods currently being auctioned," Jake said in understanding.

His perspicacity impressed me. "Exactly," I affirmed. "That's when the woman-in—I mean, Traci North, complained. Woody, the auctioneer, didn't appear to be aware of what had occurred, but a number of us saw Ken's ploy. He slyly moved the items he wanted towards those being bid on, and when the auction ended he claimed the items were originally in the current bid lot. After Traci called Ken on his little ruse, Woody asked Ken what the ruckus was about. Ken said something in return I didn't hear."

"But that's when you heard him call her a bitch in front of everybody?" Jake asked with intense curiosity.

"Uh-huh. He didn't shout it at her, and I'm not sure if she even heard him. She was standing off to the side, near the rear of the bidders, but I heard him say it and so did a few others present."

Jake mulled over my information for a few seconds. "All right, tell me about the conversation you say she had with Ken earlier."

"What do you mean, 'I say she had'? You don't believe me?"

"Touchy aren't you, Ms. Carson?"

"So would you be if you were the one who discovered two murder victims," I reprimanded him.

"Okay, yeah, you have a point there," he conceded. "I didn't mean anything by it. My apologies," he said with a grin.

As I thought, he was one of those people who could turn the charm on or off with a drop of a hat. Beneath his calm demeanor there lie something dangerous about him—possibly a character trait acquired during his tenure as a big-city cop. I suspected he was a strong man of character, ethical to a fault, and anyone who crossed his line of decency had better beware. He didn't strike me as someone who would cut anyone slack from his tightly guarded principles, or anyone who crossed the legal boundaries.

"Are you religious?" I asked impetuously to check my deduction.

My question set him on his heels, a surprised look flashed across his face before his lips tightened. "I'm not a regular church-goer if that's what you mean. I'm not into organized religion. Guess I've seen too much in my time, but I try to live by a simple rule—the Golden Rule. If everybody abided by it, we'd all live in a better place."

"Isn't that the truth," I said. "Not that it's apropos of anything to do with why we're sitting here."

"Why'd you ask then?"

"Oh, no reason, really. Idle curiosity, I guess. You seem like a man of strong principles." Without allowing him the opportunity to comment, I continued, "Getting back to the conversation between Ken and Traci, I didn't catch it all," I hurriedly interjected. "She was threatening him, telling him that she had seen some object or objects that she claimed were missing. It sounded to me like she was accusing Ken of stealing because she told him he'd better make sure the items reached the bidding table. And in so many words she also told him it wasn't the first time she suspected him of mishandling objects. She said she was going to raise hell if the items didn't reappear and come up for bidding. Afterward, I saw Ken rush over to Barry and tell him something."

"Did you actually hear her accuse him of stealing?" Jake pressed me.

"Well, no, not when you put it that way," I said repentantly. "But she told Ken that he, not someone else, was responsible for seeing that the items made it to the auction block," I said with self-satisfaction.

"Did the items come up for bid?"

"I don't know because she didn't mention what they were by name."

"So she might have been talking about the daggers?"

"Maybe, but Traci made the fuss shortly after I saw the daggers in one of the cases and that was before the auction started. They could have been removed from the case after I had seen them. I do remember thinking at the time that she was referring to something she had seen in one of the display cases and only expensive items were in the cases. I don't remember exactly why I thought that, though. She must have said something or looked over there."

"So if she was accusing Ken of stealing, wouldn't the auctioneer know about it?"

"Now that's an interesting point. Ken was the appraiser and he probably catalogued all the items, too. If Woody, or one of his workers, didn't double-check the items during the cataloguing process, Ken could easily have walked off with some goods during his appraisal process or even during the auction set-up."

"Why do you include the auction set-up?"

"Because that's when it would be easiest for Ken to actually take something. Let's say he catalogued the items under the watchful eye of one of the auction workers at

Woody's auction house. Watchful eyes tire of the process after the first hundred transactions. So Ken goes through the motions, but makes no catalog entries for certain items, and makes no appraisal notes for those certain items either, conveniently omitting items he knows have considerable value based on his appraisal research. Then, during auction set-up, he directs Barry to remove the items from the estate. With the multitude of items in the estate sale, it's easy to see how Ken and Barry could work it.

"And after auctioning so many estates, it's likely a blur to the auctioneer just what items in what estate sale were sold, so no one would be the wiser. Who could say with one-hundred percent assurance what was what? That is, until someone like Traci North comes along. She puts two and two together and calls the kettle black, wherein someone else, like me, would give the auction house the benefit of the doubt when something turns up missing from one day to the next or one minute to the next. I'd just think someone moved it, or it was sold and we missed it, or some such thing. Understand?"

Jake didn't answer, but sat quietly and digested this latest tidbit.

"Do you mind if I ask another question?"

With a wry smile, Jake answered, "Sure, go ahead."

"What do you know about Traci North?"

"I can't tell you anything concerning the investigation," he replied noncommittally.

"I don't mean that. Where does she live? What does she do for a living? If you won't tell me, I can find out on my own."

"Maybe you should take the detective's test," he suggested sardonically.

"Maybe I should," I countered.

"You've got some grit, I'll give you that," he acknowledged.

"You think so? You really think I have grit?" I implored earnestly. For some reason, his opinion of me mattered greatly.

"Without a doubt," he said with a nod of his head. "Most people want a sedative after they discover a murder victim, but not you—you want a dossier on each of the suspects."

"That's the nicest thing anyone's said to me in a long time."

"W-w-what? Are you serious?" he asked looking up at me from his notes with wide, questioning eyes.

"Yeah, I am serious. My self-esteem's taken quite a bruising lately. You see, I just became divorced," I clarified and immediately felt regret about my personal disclosure. *Why do I care that he knows I'm divorced*? Silently answering my own question my cheeks flushed. I felt attracted to him, something I hadn't thought possible so soon after my failed relationship with Richard.

"Should I offer my condolences or my congratulations?" Jake asked somberly as his dark eyes drilled into mine.

"The latter," I said with a relieved grin. Evidently he didn't hold my divorce against me.

"That makes sense."

"What makes you say that?"

"It fits your character."

"Oh, really? You think you know me that well, do you Lieutenant?" I asked, unsure if I should be offended or flattered by his assessment of me.

"Hey, I didn't mean anything by it. Don't be so sensitive. You just strike me as an individual who knows what she wants in life—someone willing to do whatever it takes to succeed—someone who wouldn't stay in an abusive relationship without doing something about it."

"You're quite the detective aren't you? Were you good at your job in Chicago?"

"Too good," he said with a dour look.

"What does that mean?"

"I'll tell you someday when I know you better."

"Oh, so you don't really know me that well after all," I chided him with a smile.

He returned my smile and steered our conversation back to the present, asking what I knew about Carole. Disappointed in how he called a halt to our teasing interplay, I shrugged and related the little I knew about Carole—even less when he asked about her boyfriend, Kurt Manners. After I finished telling him what I knew about the pair, I asked, "Did you trace the telephone number for the woman who threatened me?"

"Yeah, like I thought, it was a public phone."

"Were you able to obtain any fingerprints from the phone?" I persisted.

"Uh-huh, the lab's checking them."

From his shortness, I knew further inquiries on my part were useless, so I shut up and let him ask his questions. Jake called to Burton when he finished and told him to make sure I got home safely. He shook my hand, somewhat tenderly, I thought, and reminded me to report to headquarters in the morning.

Annie gave me another motherly hug before they hustled me to their car for the drive to my house. She accompanied me inside and waited while I packed some clothes and toiletries. Lastly, I fed Inky and Dinky extra helpings of food and waited until their appetites were sated and then heaped more onto their plates to last them through the night. I had never left them alone overnight and I felt guilty in doing so, but they had each other and would be fine I assured myself.

"Be good tonight, girls. I'll see you tomorrow."

Burton took my overnight bag and stowed it in the back of their sedan before he drove us to their house. Upon arriving, Annie escorted me to a guest room, cleared a few antique accessories from a side table, and told me to make myself at home. The room was cheery, painted a perfect shade of yellow, and my spirits lifted immediately as I unpacked my belongings. Finished, I sat down on the bed with a loud squeak.

"Sorry, about that," Annie apologized. "I've been meaning to change out the furniture, but Burton insists we watch our pennies until we find our Florida home."

"It doesn't bother me in the least. You should hear the symphony my bed springs make."

"Supper will be ready in a jiffy," she announced after she showed me my bath.

Burton had reheated a large pan of homemade spinach manicotti and served us generous portions, along with hot Italian bread. *Here goes my diet again!*

I laughed when he poured the red wine, a label of a young Marilyn Monroe displaying her charms in old pin-up style adorned the bottle.

"Don't laugh," Burton exclaimed, "the Marilyn Merlots are quite collectible. I've seen this one go for well over a hundred dollars."

"I'm flattered," I replied.

"It's a special occasion. It's not every day one find's a murder victim, or two," he said tongue-in-cheek.

"Burton!" Annie admonished. "That's not something to joke about. The poor dear has suffered a terrible shock."

"I'm fine, Annie. Honest. In fact, I'm surprised at how good I feel."

"What did you and Lieutenant Corso talk about while you were in Carole's kitchen?" I asked Burton, my heart racing anxiously anticipating his answer.

"Mostly about you—he wanted to know about you. He was very concerned for your welfare."

"Yeah, I bet. He probably wanted to know if he should consider me their prime suspect," I rejoined.

"Certainly not. Don't take his attitude to disavow anything someone tells him to heart, my dear. You don't know cops like I do. They always suspect everybody. It comes with the territory."

"Seriously, do you think I should get an attorney?"

Burton gave Annie an inquisitive look, as if he valued her opinion even though he was the attorney in the family. She shook her head to him before he replied, "No need for that. I'm sure you're not a suspect." I supposed Burton probably had professional doubts about his advice, but followed Annie's instinctual lead. I let it go, knowing they'd let me know in a heartbeat if I needed representation.

"That's a relief. I don't know who I'd retain if I needed one. My divorce lawyer, Gene LaForte, is hardly qualified and I'd die before I'd ask Richard for a referral. He wasn't reliable as a husband and there's no way I'd trust anybody he'd recommend." My face flushed after I blurted out my feelings. Annie and Burton were like family, but I believed some things were best left unspoken. "I'm sorry, I didn't mean to vent—must be all the stress."

"See, I told you the poor dear is shaken up," Annie scolded Burton. "Don't worry, sweetie, everyone but you knew about Richard and his shortcomings. Forget him and move on."

Everyone? Was I that blind to the obvious? If so, could I be blind to who killed Ken and Carole, too?

The rest of the evening was spent in more light-hearted conversation. I retired early and stayed up reading a mystery I downloaded onto my iPad. Eventually I relaxed and grew sleepy. Setting the iPad aside, I curled up in bed and thought about Carole. *Earlier, I had Carole tabbed as a suspect for Ken's killer, but if she did kill Ken, who killed her and why?* I wrestled with the puzzle, until exhaustion conveyed me through a fitful night's sleep.

Chapter Eight

Monday

Even though the clock hands showed ten after midnight, I decided to go for a walk to clear my head. As I reached the street corner, a sliver of moon played hide-and-seek behind the clouds, and enveloped me in darkness. I turned at the sound of a twig snapping behind me, and saw a shrouded figure, wielding a long curved knife, walking steadily towards me. I began running as fast as I could, but the dark figure took up the chase and steadily closed the distance between us. I stumbled and screamed, my feet tangling in a neighbor's unwound garden hose. Twenty feet, fifteen feet, ten feet away—my attacker raised the dagger in readiness. The moon emerged from its cloudy veil and light beams glinted brightly along the knife's cutting edge. I screamed in terror—

"Nikki! Nikki!" A voice called to me from the dark. A firm hand on my shoulder stirred me and I awoke with a shiver until I recognized the familiar yellow walls of Annie's guest bedroom.

"You were having a bad dream, sweetie. You were moaning loudly and screaming."

"Oh, I'm so sorry, Annie, I didn't mean to wake you."

"You didn't wake me. It's almost seven. I've been up nearly two hours."

"Seven! Did you say seven? I'm supposed to be at the police station by eight," I said with a groan and scrambled out of bed.

"Wash up and join us for breakfast. Burton will drive you to the station house in plenty of time."

Burton greeted everybody with familiarity at the police station when we arrived, a few minutes to spare. Everyone liked Burton. He had an easy way about him and was an

108

exceptional communicator. He had served two terms as Mayor of Hickory Grove during the 80s and would have served a third term, but decided he had had enough. The town's people knew he was largely responsible for revitalizing the town into the tourist attraction destination it had become.

Dwayne Anderson, the Police Chief, invited Burton into his office and Burton introduced me. Sergeant Reilly then escorted me to a small room towards the rear of the station house.

Two hours later, I finished giving my statement to Lieutenant Corso and Sergeant Reilly, and then we aimlessly sat around another ten minutes before the officer who had typed my statement into a notebook PC had printed off a copy and handed it to Jake. Jake asked me to read it for errors and clarifications, and after a couple of minor corrections, I signed and dated the paper.

"You're free to go, Ms. Carson," Jake told me in a professional tone of voice, "but please don't leave town. We will need your testimony and we'll probably have more questions for you."

He acted a little embarrassed by his formal salutation and qualification. I knew the paperwork was standard procedure, but telling me not to leave town was not. I was on a suspect list. *Who did he think he was fooling?*

"More . . . questions, uh-huh," I replied. I gave him a hard look of my own to convey to him what I thought about his statement.

He returned my look, sighed, and rolled his eyes.

I found Burton idly chatting with the town clerk and pulled him aside, telling him I was free to leave. Once underway, I asked him to stop off at my house so I could feed Inky and Dinky before I reported for work at Annie's.

"I better go in with you," he said as he pulled up to the curb, "to make sure the coast is clear."

"All right, if it'll make you feel better," I acquiesced. Then I remembered how I had concluded earlier that Carole must have known her attacker and with that recollection, Burton's offer took on a more substantive meaning.

Inky and Dinky greeted us loudly when I keyed open the lock. They cried and ran around us heedlessly. Their antics were nothing compared to the agitation that ensued after they realized they were going to be fed. They pranced on their hind legs and practically jumped up onto the plates as I lowered them to their dining mats on the floor. I gathered their old dishes, put them in the sink, and topped off their bowls of dry food and water before I went to freshen up.

When I rejoined Burton, he was finishing wiping dry the dishes he had washed and rinsed. "You didn't have to do that," I exclaimed somewhat embarrassed. "I was going to do them tonight."

"You know me. I can't sit still. You'd be amazed at how much I get done waiting for Annie while she's getting ready to go someplace," he exclaimed with a grin.

"My ex used to take longer getting ready than I did," I retorted with a grin, recalling the time I had counted up his toiletries. He had twice as many as I did—a tribute to an enormous vanity that went hand-in-hand with his unbounded narcissism.

"It'll be a lucky man who snags you the second time around," Burton said with a hint of impishness. "If I wasn't married to Annie and forty years younger, I'd make a try for you meself," he added in his best Irish brogue.

"I bet you were a terror when you were younger," I jovially accused him.

"Ah, that I was," he acknowledged with a big reminiscent grin.

He courteously dropped me off at Annie's Attic before departing, explaining he had some errands to run. Annie met me at the door and asked me how things went at the police station.

"Lieutenant Corso instructed me not to leave town."

"What? That's ridiculous!" she exclaimed indignantly.

"Yeah, that's what I thought, too. But Lieutenant Corso qualified his order by explaining they may need to talk to me again."

"That may be true, but telling you not to leave town is stretching their power a bit."

"You know, Annie, something tells me the police department's investigation will cause quite a stir in this town before the killer is found."

"One thing's for sure; the chief is on the hot seat," Annie agreed. "These murders are the biggest thing to hit Hickory Grove in many years. Anderson's up for reelection this November. The voters won't stand for a long drawn out investigation. They want the murderer found quickly so they can shove the whole affair under a rug and go back to being just another sleepy suburb with only the usual crimes committed by a few errant teenagers. The local paper is already after Anderson's scalp. If he doesn't put the murderer behind bars soon, he'll be out of a job. Mark my words."

"Annie, do you know Brett Nielsen?"

"Yeah, but Burton knows him better. Why, sweetie?"

"Remember how I mentioned to you that he was at the auction Friday and helped me move the furniture pieces to your shop—how he was really nice and stepped forward to help without my asking?"

"Yeah."

"Well, I'm considering asking him to do a few odd jobs at my house and to restore the credenza."

"Sounds like a good plan. You want me to ask Burton what he knows about Brett?"

"Um, not right now—only if Brett shows an interest in being my handy man. You know, Annie, I can't thank you and Burton enough for all you do for me."

"No thanks necessary, sweetie."

"I know, but you two are awesome and I really appreciate your kindness. You do way too much—like having me stay at your place. I'm okay now, so I'm going to stay at home tonight."

"We really don't mind having you at the house, Nikki. In fact, we love it. Are you sure you don't want to stay longer?"

"Oh, Annie. I don't mean to sound ungracious, but I'm sure. Inky and Dinky need me around. They've never been on their own before. Besides, Jake said the police are patrolling my house regularly. Everything's fine."

"Have it your way," Annie replied with a shrug. "Oh, before I forget, there's a check here for you. Denise said a woman stopped in and bought your music cabinet."

"Great, I hoped she'd want it," I said happily as I punched Brett's number into my phone. When he answered, I said, "Hi, this is Nikki Carson, from the auction. Remember me? You helped me move the white monster."

He paused a moment and then answered, "How are you, Nikki?"

"Good and yourself?"

"I'm fine. What can I do for you?"

"I was wondering if you would like to stop by the shop and look at the credenza. I'm thinking about having the finish stripped off to reveal the wood. Also, I have a few odd carpentry jobs I've been putting off at my house. If you're interested in doing some remodeling for me, I can run you over to the house afterwards and you can take a look."

"Sounds interesting, but right now I'm in the middle of fixing the legs on an old Victrola. I can stop by this afternoon, oh, say about three. How does that sound?"

"That's good. See you then," I replied.

Annie and I were discussing the murders again, and exchanging viewpoints about possible motives and murderers when Denise walked through the shop door. "What are you doing here on your day off?" I asked innocently, even though I knew she came to gossip.

"Did you hear about Kurt?" she asked disregarding my question.

"Kurt? Kurt Manners? He's Carole's boyfriend, isn't he?"

My statement displeased her to judge by the sour expression on her face. "Yes. The police are looking for him," Denise replied sharply.

"You mean the police think Kurt may have killed Ken and Carole?"

"I don't know. That's why I stopped in. I thought you may have heard something," she said acutely, "since you've been talking to the police."

Leave it to Denise to know my every move. "I'd heard he was arrested for DUI once, but murder? That seems a reach, don't you think?"

"He's also been arrested twice for burglary and once for assault, but he's never been convicted," she quickly added. "He lives with two other guys at the Ridgeway apartments, but he didn't go home yesterday. Nobody knows where he is," she exclaimed while shifting from foot to foot, so wound up she couldn't stand still.

"I have a sneaking suspicion the police must be looking for him about something else."

"Oh, come on Nikki. What else can it be other than about the murders, especially since Carole did date him for a while?"

"That doesn't make him a murderer," I said surprising myself. I never thought I'd come to Kurt's defense, but falsely accusing anyone of murder wasn't right in my book. "I heard Kurt and Carole were tight, more than just dating."

"That's not true!" she shouted with a stamp of her foot. "She was a shrew hanging onto him tooth and nail."

"Wow, that's a pretty strong accusation against someone who can't defend herself."

"Your trouble is, you're too nice, Nikki," she snapped.

"Guilty as charged," I answered holding my hands up.

"Oh, you know what I mean. You're so nice—you think everyone else is like you."

Growing increasingly tired of our discussion and Denise's assessment of me, I told her, "You'll have to excuse me. I have someone coming in to check out my credenza."

But Denise had her own agenda; she wasn't through with me yet. "I found out who your woman-in-black is," she said smugly.

"You mean Traci North?"

From the look on her face, it was obvious I had stolen her thunder. *Score one for me.* Her mouth hung open, and she stared at me as though I was a telepath. She recovered quickly and countered, "Did you know she runs an antique store in Glenview?"

"Quite a way off her beaten path at Peterson's auction then, wasn't she?" I replied with more than a hint of conceit. *That's giving her some of her own medicine.*

"Yes," she reluctantly agreed. "She's very well-to-do. She only deals in high-priced items."

"Makes sense if her store is in Glenview." Denise didn't like me upstaging one of her gossipy moments. But then her mention of 'high-priced items' was not exactly a subtle comparison to the wares in Annie's store and her thinly disguised slight rubbed me the wrong way. "I have to go and prepare," I told her and walked away. As I made my way to my room, I heard Denise talking to Annie about Carole's murder. Denise was like a hungry lioness—you never wanted to turn your back on her.

Three o'clock rolled around and Brett arrived a few minutes after the hour. He wore a freshly ironed blue jean shirt and jeans with creases. The light blues looked good on him and went far in accentuating his rugged countenance. I found myself wondering if he ironed his own clothes or if he ran them to the dry cleaners. I was taken aback a bit when I sensed myself assessing him. *Nikki, for goodness sake, like Denise said, he's old enough to be your father.* While I led him to my leased space, I thought I smelled Old Spice and did a slight swoon. My dad used to wear the manly fragrance. *Miss you, dad.*

"This is quite a shop, Nikki. I know it's been around for a while, but aside from helping you the other day move some pieces in here, I've never been inside before. You said this was Annie Edward's shop, right?"

"Yeah. She's the owner and has run it for about twenty years or so."

"So just how do you fit in?"

"I work here a few days a week and lease space from her. I put together room ensembles to sell." I pointed to the credenza. "The white beast you helped me move is going to be part of an Art Deco living room I'm putting together. What I'd like to know, Brett, is do you think stripping the credenza is a good idea?"

"Let's take a look at what's underneath and see," he replied.

We moved the piece out from the wall and he tilted it toward me. I struggled to hold the unwieldy furniture piece in place to prevent it from tipping over while he inspected the bottom. Dusting off his knees, he stood up and announced, "The wood's good, no water damage. It's maple underneath, but we won't know if the rest is the same until we strip it."

"If it's all maple, how do you think it'll look redone?" I asked expectantly. "There's an impression on the back that reads, 'Made in France.'"

"I think it'll make one hell of a showpiece. If it's European maple, a few coats of polyurethane should really spruce it up once we strip the paint off. You should easily be able to get a couple grand for it. The piece looks fairly old, but looking at the joints on the bottom, it's very well made. The wood the craftsmen of that time period would have used to make furniture like this should prove to be top-notch. These other two pieces will complement the credenza nicely if the cabinet turns out how I'm thinking. I could add a few coats of polyurethane to them, too, to pull them together as a set."

"How much will it cost?"

He surveyed all the cabinets for a few minutes. "What's going to take most of the time is getting all the old finish out of the seams and detailed areas. Staining and finishing doesn't take much time at all. Seeing as you're a first time customer, I'd say seven hundred, plus materials, should do it."

"That's quite an investment. I don't mean to be insulting, but I'd like to see some of your work before I commit to that big of a cash outlay."

"I understand," he replied calmly. "You mentioned some other work?"

"Yeah, at my bungalow. I know I told you I'd drive when I called, but I spaced and forgot I didn't drive in today. Do you mind if we go in your truck? It's only a couple of miles from here." I didn't feel comfortable explaining to him about my break-in, discovering Carole's body, and subsequent lodging at Annie's—the real reason I didn't have my car.

"Not at all. My truck's out front," he said with an easy grin. I hurried along to keep up with his long-legged strides.

He suggested we stop at his house first so I could see some of his work and I agreed. He crossed town going east until he pulled up to the curb in front of a cozy craftsmen-style house. It was painted in earth tones, a fern green, with burnt sienna, and cream colored appointments. It stood out like a ray of sunshine on a cloudy day from the other homes lining the street.

"Did you build this?" I asked awestruck, especially enamored by the flagstone pillars.

"Yep. You like her?" There was that easy style again.

"It's gorgeous. I can't wait to see the inside," I gushed.

We walked toward the rear of the house and he led me to his workshop that abutted the house's screened-in porch. "I'll show you the inside first since you're interested, and then we'll go to my workshop."

"Wow! I love the wood archways," I said upon entering.

"African mahogany," he told me proudly.

I was overwhelmed with the quality and detail of the wood and stonework and told him so. He beamed like a school boy to my superlative appraisals, explaining what kind of wood he had used for each separate feature. It was obviously a man's house, but his exquisite taste made it something much more—something special.

"C'mon, let's go to my workshop," he invited.

"I'm sold already after seeing the job you did on your house."

He unlocked his workshop and ushered me inside. When I stepped over the threshold, the smell of sawdust pleasantly assailed my nostrils. The first thing I noticed was the old Victrola he had mentioned and a pair of elegant side-tables that sat upside down on a large sturdy table in the center of the room. He saw me looking at the side-tables. "I'm working on those for a client. So far I've stripped them and repaired a couple of the legs. They were knocked up a bit. Next, they get stained and shellacked."

"They're quite unusual, aren't they?"

"Yeah, they're from France also—from the 1800s. At least that's what the owner told me. Look here," he said turning one of the pieces over and showing me the front.

"What kind of wood is that? It looks three-dimensional."

"It's what's referred to as quilted maple. It's fairly rare, especially when it's this good. The wood has to be quarter-sawn just right to gain this much effect. Kind of looks like rolling clouds, doesn't it?"

"Uh-huh. I've never seen wood like it before," I exclaimed in admiration. "I love how the pieces are matched so perfectly."

"Who knows? Maybe your piece is made of quilted maple."

"I should be that lucky," I laughed.

"So what do you think, Nikki? If you're still unsure about my workmanship, I can give you some references if you want them."

"No, I'm sold. When can you start?"

"Next week."

"Perfect! I'm afraid my house is going to be a letdown to you after seeing your home, though," I said humbly.

"Let's go see what you have."

With a last look, I surveyed his work area. Everything was neat and orderly which didn't surprise me. The inside of his house had been the same way. As I walked to the door, something caught my eye along the side wall, set back amongst the shadows. If I didn't know any better, I'd swear it looked like one of the glass cases from Peterson's auction. *It couldn't be!* Surreptitiously, I meandered over toward the piece to take a better look while Brett busied with rearranging the end tables he had shown me. *It is one of the cases!* I was doubly shocked to see there were items inside. *How the hell did Brett get this case? He wasn't even at the auction the second day. Or was he?*

In the case were a few pieces of jewelry, small oriental figures carved from jade, two meerschaum pipes, and closest to me lay two curved middle-eastern daggers. I didn't recall any of the items in the case making it to the auction block. I was dumbstruck. A chill raced up my spine and I stumbled toward the door.

"I'm sorry. I should have warned you to be careful," Brett said, rushing to my side and grasping my arm for support. "I salvaged this building from the original estate. It used to be a servant's quarters. The floor's a bit uneven. One of these days I'll fix it. You know how it is with craftsmen. They always put off doing their own work till last."

"Uh-huh," I replied numbly, shaken by my discovery and not knowing what to think.

During the drive to my house, all I could think about was how I could be inviting the murderer to my bungalow. *Brett didn't seem like a bad man, but neither did a lot of serial killers to their victims.* And Brett fit the size and shape of my intruder. In fact, upon further recollection, his voice was almost identical to that of my home invader. *Oh my gosh, what have I done? I could be with a killer!*

Taking long, deep breaths, to steady my nerves I glanced at Brett. He didn't appear to sense my anxiousness. *What should I do? If I don't go through with showing him my house, he might get suspicious. And if I do go through with it, he might murder me. Stop being silly! You're being paranoid. Why would he murder me? I haven't done anything wrong. Sure, the intruder warned me to keep my mouth shut, but after Carole's murder, he had to know the police would question me. But what about the display case and auction items? How did Brett acquire them if he wasn't at the auction on the second day? Remember what I learned about situational awareness, stay alert and don't turn your back on him.*

We arrived at my bungalow and after I opened the front door, I waved Brett inside ahead of me as a precaution. Oddly, neither Inky nor Dinky made an appearance.

"This is a great house," Brett said appraising my living room. "It's got great character, a lot of potential. Do you mind if I look around?"

"N-no, not at all," I said, remaining at the front door I kept half-open. He walked from room to room, looking at the ceilings, the walls and floors, and he even pulled out a couple of the built in drawers for a closer inspection. "They don't make 'em like this anymore. Has to be from the twenties," he enthused.

"Nineteen twenty-three," I affirmed.

He nodded his head and said, "Do you mind if I look at the foundation?"

"The basement door is off the kitchen." I kept my position of safety and waited, listening to him bound down the stairs.

He returned in a couple of minutes. "There's been some settling, but nothing to worry over. No signs of dampness or mildew either. Did you have an inspection done on your house when you purchased it?"

"Yep. There were a few things found, but nothing structural."

"Good. So what projects did you have in mind?"

"You're the craftsman. Maybe the best thing to do is have you jot down your ideas," I suggested, explaining, "I don't want to taint your creativity with preconceived notions."

"I can do that. I have to warn you, though, these old houses can be hell to work on to modernize them and bring them up to code, but it's usually well worth the investment."

"Sounds good, but I better get back to work," I said holding my wrist out and feigning a look at my watch. All I wanted to do was leave as soon as possible.

"I'm going to need some time to look at her in detail before I figure out what I think you should do and what's possible," he said with a last look.

"Let's plan to do that after you finish the credenza. That way I can hopefully turn it around and have enough cash to help budget some of the work on the house," I said to hurry us along.

My explanation satisfied him from the look and nod he gave me. I locked up and we walked to his truck. Breathing a big sigh of relief, I climbed in. He dropped me off at the shop's back door.

"Do you want me to take the credenza now?"

"No, it can wait until you're finished with your current projects. It'll take up a lot of space in your work area," I added as an afterthought to help explain my reluctance to move forward in using his services until my suspicions of him were confirmed or proven false.

"I'll give you a call then," he said with that same easy smile and drove away.

I entered the shop before I realized with sudden fright—Brett had driven directly to my home without asking me for directions on how to get there.

Chapter Nine

That night, Annie insisted I stay for supper before she would allow Burton to drive me home. I readily agreed as I didn't feel like cooking, even if it was only to heat leftovers. Knowing I was on a diet, she made a light salad with chicken much to my liking. While I set the table, I debated about mentioning my suspicions regarding Brett to her. Undecided, I instead told Annie what Denise had said about Kurt and Carole.

"Denise is a good worker, but I've never met as natural a gossip in all my life. Talking about people is normal, I suppose, but she shouldn't cast ill-founded aspersions on anyone without having facts to back them up," Annie declared.

I nodded my head vigorously in agreement. "She does go overboard. Speaking of facts," I said with a look at Burton, "can you look up Kurt Manners' police record?"

He gave me a wry grin. "One of the suspects? Are you playing detective now?"

"No, but if there's something I can do to help solve the murders, I'm going to do it," I averred. "The police must consider me a suspect. Even though they haven't come right out and said it, they did tell me not to leave town. I'd feel a whole lot better being able to go out in public without having everyone, like Denise, giving me strange looks and talking behind my back."

Annie chimed in, "The sooner the police catch the killer, the better. Business was slower than usual today. Some of the other store owners are saying the same. I've heard tell that some people are even afraid to go out of their homes."

"Human nature, my dear," Burton replied.

"You mean human stupidity, don't you," Annie said stridently. "The murders weren't random—the work of a serial killer. Ken and Carole were killed for a reason."

"Yeah," I agreed. "I've given this whole thing a lot of thought. The common denominator appears to be auction going, or more specifically, the Peterson auction. What else would link Ken and Carole? They don't do business together as far as I know. Carole went to auctions to buy materials for her artwork. Ken attended auctions for bargains he could resell in his shop and online. Carole used Ken to appraise some of her items that she later sold to raise needed money. Instead of appraising the items too low, like he did with you," I said to Annie, "he valued them too high to increase his fee. It would explain why she was upset with him at the auction."

"Makes sense," Burton relented. "But I don't see why somebody would kill them just because they attended an auction or because they did some business together."

"Yeah," I reluctantly agreed, "there must be a deeper tie-in somewhere. I have a nagging feeling I'm missing something obvious. The thing that's crazy about my hypothesis is Carole's behavior at the Peterson auction. She told me she thought Ken had appraised the items too high and that would result in Woody starting bids higher than normal. Why would she care? People are only going to pay what they want to regardless of what they've been valued by others."

After we finished eating, Annie served up coffee and we continued to bounce ideas off each other for another hour. Time was getting late.

"I need to get home to my kitties," I announced. "Thanks again for everything, you two. You're the best," I told them before I gathered my belongings.

Burton drove me home. Reaching in my pocketbook for my keys, I suddenly remembered that the tablet I pushed aside was Carole's iPad, not my own. Guiltily, I reached under it and retrieved my keys.

Burton waited at the curb for me to unlock the front door and give him a thumbs-up signal that no masked murderers were waiting inside. I carefully opened the door to avoid Inky and Dinky from getting outside, but I needn't have bothered. Oddly, they didn't greet me. I did a quick check of the house, returned to the front door and waved goodbye to Burton. He waved back and drove away.

"Inky? Dinky?" I shouted as I walked from room to room. "That's funny," I said aloud when they still didn't respond. Then I remembered they hadn't been around earlier when Brett was here either. I started to get worried, and more than a little scared. This wasn't like them. I flicked the light switch on in the bedroom and looked under the bed, but they weren't in their usual hiding spots. Continuing to call their names, I carefully made my way towards the kitchen. Stopping to turn on all the lights within reach, I saw the door leading to the basement was ajar.

The basement had never been finished and still bore the stone walls and hard-packed floor from when it was built. I didn't allow the kitties downstairs because the old exterior cellar doors didn't close all the way. Possibly Brett had left the basement door in the kitchen open earlier during his inspection and hadn't closed it firmly. Most of the doors in the house were warped with age, one of the many things I hoped Brett would fix. The old wooden stairs creaked as I made my way down to the dank basement. Inky let out a "meow" when I pulled the light cord at the bottom of the steps. She jumped down from a stack of boxes to greet me. "Here you are. Now what are you two up to?"

Dinky didn't make an appearance, and a moment of panic struck me when I looked at the gaping space between the cellar doors—easily large enough for the kitties to squeeze through to mischief outside. Walking over to the boxes where Inky had been a moment before, I happily spotted a whitish-gray tail sticking out from one of the boxes. Relieved, I pried back the box flaps. Dinky stuck her head up and gave me a quizzical look and a pitiful silent "meow."

"You poor little baby. Got yourself in, but couldn't get back out, huh?" I cooed and reached to pluck her out of the box just as the front doorbell rang.

I hastily stuck several boxes in front of the cellar doors to block the gap, scooped Inky and Dinky in my arms and dashed up the stairs. Closing the basement door with my foot, I set Inky and Dinky down and hurried to the front door. A brief glance through the side curtain revealed Lieutenant Corso standing patiently on the stoop. I unlocked the inside door and screen door and said, "Come in, Lieutenant. You're working late."

"Jake, please," he said in answer to my invitation.

"Can I get you something to drink?" I asked after I ushered him into the living room.

"No thanks," he said with a stern countenance. He had a look about him, as if he was in a fight against time—a fight to the death.

"Uh-oh. Am I in trouble?" I asked in response to his look.

"No," he answered with deadly seriousness. "I just need to ask you a few more questions."

"Whew, that's a relief. You look like you mean business." He gave me a brief, mirthless smile in return. "I'd hate to be a criminal under interrogation from you, Lieutenant. One look and I'd confess every guilty thought I ever had," I teased.

This time, my utterance evoked a genuine grin. "I find that hard to believe, Ms. Carson, and please call me Jake."

"I think that was a compliment, although I'm not sure," I laughed lightly. "And if I'm to call you Jake, the least you can do is reciprocate and call me Nikki."

"Deal," he agreed. "Nikki, I'd like you to tell me everything you can remember about Carole at the auction—anything you might have forgotten."

I motioned for him to take a seat in the living room. After we were settled, I said, "I'm afraid there's nothing new. No, that's not really true," I amended deciding to tell him about how Carole lied to me at the auction. "I don't know if it's important, but I asked Carole about a previous auction held the week before in Walnut Grove. She denied being there when I know I saw her there."

"This was the Saturday before?"

"Uh-huh."

"You're absolutely sure about this?"

"Yes, she was there."

He leaned back with a self-satisfied look.

"What does it mean? I've been wracking my brain trying to figure out why Carole lied to me."

Before answering, he gave me a pained look. "Nikki, I can't say."

"I'll bet it has to do with Kurt Manners."

Jake raised his eyebrows. That meant a 'yes' in my book. *So it did have something to do with Kurt,* a*nd Jake isn't telling*. I fought hard to hide a self-righteous smile, knowing I had ascertained the truth.

He shook his head at my expression. "Do you remember anything else about Carole—when you said she was talking to Ken?"

"No, nothing new. Sorry."

Jake took my disappointing news in stride. He was staring off into space, thinking to himself. I followed his gaze and goose flesh crawled up my arms and the hair tingled on the back of my neck. His eyes were fixed on Carole's iPad that I had carelessly placed on the living room table when I had come home. I put it there so I'd remember to do something about it. *Did he know it was Carole's? Why else would he be staring at it?*

Be calm. Act natural. How could he know it wasn't mine? And where did I leave mine? I thought with a surge of panic. I tried to casually survey the room to see if mine was lying within eyesight. I didn't see it, but I was so nervous I couldn't think of where I had last set it down.

Forcing myself to return my concentration to the subject at hand, I steadied my nerves through a tremendous effort. "Carole must have lied to me about the auction, and it must have something to do with Kurt." Then it came to me. "Of course! Carole lied to protect him from something."

"Go on," Jake encouraged.

"Kurt was a burglary suspect, right? I read in the paper there was a burglary committed on Saturday, but I can't recall where. Kurt's a suspect and Carole's his alibi. It makes sense, doesn't it?" I proclaimed proudly.

"Possibly," Jake acknowledged with a satisfied look.

"If Carole denied she was at the auction, and someone could prove she was in fact there, she'd be guilty of perjury—if she made such a claim to cover up for Kurt. But she was there and she did buy something," I said all excited. "I remember her buying a box of empty picture frames. Why else would she lie than to provide him an alibi? And Denise Barrington had told me he had a record of burgling. She doesn't always get things right, though. Does he have such a record?"

"His past burglar offense is public record. Don't jump to conclusions, though. His past record isn't proof he pulled the job on Saturday."

"All right, but let's say Kurt was the burglar. Then he could have been my home invader. He told me to keep my mouth shut about Carole—meaning not to tell anyone she was at the auction. If that's the case, Carole must have told Kurt what I said to her at the auction. And she had to be the one who called me—telling me to mind my own business. She disguised her voice because she knew I'd recognize her as the caller," I enthused as everything fell into place.

"Could be," Jake said while studying me.

Somehow his scrutiny scared me and excited me at the same time. Looking askance, I continued, "Sure, that all fits. But why would Kurt murder Carole? She was his alibi for the burglary—unless he thought she was going to retract her alibi. But would he kill her for something like that? It seems pretty farfetched if you ask me. And even if he did, why would he murder Ken? Jake, who was burgled? You can tell me that can't you? It must be common knowledge by now. The newspaper must have printed the location in their police report coverage."

"A storage facility was broken into on the other side of town."

"The office or a unit?"

"You sure as hell are persistent," he commented. A slight grin creased his lips. "I'll cut to the chase. It was Ken Lawton's facility and one of his own units was burgled."

"Oh my gosh. That's the common denominator between Kurt, Ken, and Carole—" then the full impact of what I was saying hit me. "Wait a minute," I cried, "that's why Carole was arguing with Ken at the auction. Their argument had nothing to do with Ken doing an appraisal for her. She was defending Kurt, and if I know Ken, he was all over her about her boyfriend. Which means only Kurt is left," I said as my voice drifted off, my thoughts racing ahead of my words.

"Kurt's the killer and he was the one who broke into my home. He might have killed me, too," I said shakily, "and now he knows I know and he'll try to kill me for sure!"

"Get ahold of yourself, Nikki," Jake said soothingly. "First off, Kurt knows by now we're looking for him. With Carole killed, there's no reason for Kurt to come after you because of what you know. I imagine he's too busy worrying about his own hide to worry about yours. Plus, we've set up a schedule to regularly cruise this neighborhood and we've issued an alert for Kurt."

"So you agree Kurt's the one who broke in and threatened me?"

"I didn't say that," he said holding his hands up defensively.

"But you didn't deny it either. Not only that, you haven't denied Kurt is under suspicion for murder. Was Kurt ever arrested for assault against Carole?"

"Yeah," Jake said reluctantly. "It's public information."

His answer left little room for doubt. I mulled over his reluctance to name Kurt the killer. "It looks bad for Kurt," I said summarily.

"Yeah," he said again without conviction. "Do you know Kurt?"

"Only to recognize him. I've never spoken to him."

"How about any of the women he dated?"

"Women? Carole's the only woman I know he's dated."

An awkward silence ensued. Finally, Jake said, "Well, I better leave. Thanks for your time, Nikki."

"Anytime, Jake," I said with a smile. He gave me a small nod and started to say something, but stopped and strode to the front door. He looked pensive, his head hung deep in thought as he walked out.

After he left, I sat and thought about his visit. No matter how much I tried to concentrate on Carole, Ken, and Kurt, I found my thoughts returning to Jake. He fascinated me in an inexplicable way. I had to admit, I was a bit frightened by his intensity. At the same time I felt a deep seated attraction to him, like a moth to a flame, yet I felt safe in his presence.

My phone rang and I went into the kitchen to retrieve it from my purse. "Nicole, are you okay? I've read about the murders. It must be awful for you."

"As if you care, Richard," I said spitefully, surprised at my sudden vehemence.

"But I *do* care, Nicole. Even though we're not married anymore, it doesn't mean I don't have feelings for you."

"Uh-huh. What do you want?"

"I wanted to see how you're doing."

"I suppose you expect me to believe you."

"Maybe I'll call another time when you're in a better mood," he said in his hurt little boy tone of voice.

"There's nothing wrong with my mood. I'm just busy," I avowed.

Suddenly he switched gears and asked, "Nicole, remember that harvest table we had in the living room?"

"Yeah," I replied hesitantly. *Here it comes.*

"Well, I've decided to redo the house and it doesn't fit in with what I have in mind, so I thought I'd give you first option on it."

The table had always been one of my favorite pieces of furniture. Even though the table was too big for my small bungalow, I could easily turn it around for a quick sale. I tried hard to keep the enthusiasm out of my voice at the chance to acquire it. "I'll gladly take it off your hands."

"Great. I think twelve hundred is a fair price. Don't you?"

Damn, damn, damn. I let him sucker me again. Why did I leave myself open to his advances? Determined not to make a bigger fool of myself than I already had in thinking he was going to give me the table for nothing, I replied, "I'll consider four hundred."

"Nikki, you know how much we paid for it. It's a steal at twelve hundred, but I'll tell you what. You can have it for eight hundred."

"Nope, four hundred's my limit," I replied stonily.

"I can't let it go for that," he whined.

"Then you know what you can do with it, Richard. If you change your mind, let me know. I have to run now," I said and disconnected.

"What a bastard," I shouted and began to pace back and forth between the living room and kitchen. "First, I was his personal maid and cook, and now he's trying to use me as a cash cow. Asshole!" I ranted. "Nothing that putting a block-caller for his number on my phone won't fix," I said in disgust and tossed my phone onto the kitchen counter.

Inky and Dinky hadn't come into the kitchen for food. *Why?* Then I saw the basement door ajar again. In my haste, I hadn't closed it properly. The door was becoming a real nuisance. *What's so interesting in the basement anyway? There must be a mouse or something to keep them so preoccupied.* I quietly returned downstairs to see what they were up to. Inky was lying on top of an adjacent box, watching her sister paw away at the folded carton flaps—working feverishly to gain entry into the same box I had retrieved her from earlier. I reached over and picked up Dinky and set her on the floor. "No, no, li'l one."

Curious as to what she found so stimulating, I lifted the box and carried it under the light to get a better look at its contents. With a start, I dropped the box and shrieked. The box hit the floor with a loud crash and tipped over, the items spilling onto the floor. I recognized a couple of the items as being from the Peterson auction. I didn't know who had won them; I only knew they weren't mine. But that wasn't what made me shiver. It was the small jeweled dagger that had rolled out of the box and settled next to my foot—one of the three daggers won by the woman-in-black at the auction. Dried blood clearly showed on its blade. Something inherent within me told me it was the dagger used to kill Carole.

Chapter Ten

How did it get here? I asked myself incredulously, knowing the answer but not wanting to believe it. *Someone must have come in through the cellar doors and put the box in the basement. Why?* The obvious answer was to set me up for Carole's murder. *What did someone have against me?* That was the main question. *And just who was trying to set me up?* Again, the answer was clear: the killer must have figured I was a prime candidate to frame for the two murders since I had discovered both bodies.

After overcoming my initial shock at discovering the knife, I retrieved some paper towels from the roll dispenser by the washing machine. Careful not to touch anything, I placed the items, one by one, back into the box while I fended off Inky and Dinky. Lastly, I picked up the knife with one of the paper towels and laid it on top of the other items in the box before I folded the flaps closed.

If the killer was setting me up, it meant they would anonymously tip off the police to my being in possession of the murder weapon or plant clues that would lead them to me. Either way, I had to dispose of the knife pronto. How, and where, to get rid of it was the problem now confronting me. I couldn't just throw the knife in the garbage. A dumpster. No, that's no good. The knife might have the killer's fingerprints on it and then I would be destroying valuable evidence as well as committing a felony by obstructing justice. I didn't know a great deal of law, but I did know that much. *But I can't just leave it here. I need to rid myself of it post haste, but where?*

I carried the box upstairs, calling the kitties up behind me, shut the basement door as tightly as I could, and pondered the problem confronting me. A glance outside revealed a cloudy, moonless night. The darkness made it unlikely anyone would see me carrying the box to my detached garage. I peeked out the back door and saw that no lights shone in my back yard from the neighbors' homes. I quietly opened the back door and shuffled quickly to the garage. I opened my car door and placed the box on the passenger seat. I stole another quick peek out the garage door to see if anyone was about.

Out of breath from my stealthy excursion, I stood inside the garage doorway and took deep breaths to steady my nerves. *The police might show up at any second. I hved to move the box and move it quick, but where? Should I leave it at Carole's? No, the police might have her house under surveillance.*

I grabbed my purse, fished for my keys, climbed behind the wheel and began to drive, eager to get as far away from the house as possible, without any particular destination in mind. Driving away from my house set me more at ease, but I couldn't just drive around all night. Hopefully, some inspiration would come to me soon.

I drove for what seemed like hours in a daze trying to come up with an answer to the dilemma facing me. I must have been driving a lot less than I thought, though, because when I suddenly took notice of my surroundings, I discovered I had unconsciously driven only fifteen miles or so into neighboring Walnut Grove. A few blocks more brought me to a busy thoroughfare. Turning right, I pulled over to the curb and sat for a minute to collect my thoughts. The only place I was familiar with in this burb was Ken and Barry's antique shop. Maybe it was providence, but without having a better idea, I took out my phone and asked for directions to The Antique Shoppe—Ken and Barry's business.

The building was dark as I drove past. I went down to the end of the block and turned right. I turned right again, into an alleyway leading behind their store and flicked off my car lights. Pulling over to the side, I left the car running and climbed out. I walked down the alley looking for the rear entrance to their store. I approached an old dilapidated garage that sat directly behind their shop which was a relic of times past when the store had once served as a Victorian-style mansion for a wealthy family. A combination lock was looped through a metal catch on the wing-doors. Upon closer inspection, the wood doors appeared weathered, showing signs of water damage along the bottom edges. When I put pressure on them, the screws that held the metal catch moved slightly.

There were no signs of life around as I took another quick look up and down the alleyway. This time I tugged on both door handles. The screws pulled out a fraction of an inch. By varying my efforts, pushing and pulling, I managed to loosen the screws enough on one side of the catch to pull the hasp all the way off the door.

Dashing back to my car, I grabbed the box from the front seat and hustled toward the garage. With one last quick look, I cracked open the garage door and squeezed through, my feet hitting something as I stepped inside. Holding the box under one arm, I reached out into the darkness with my free hand and turned on my small LED keychain light. I had stumbled into a stack of boxes. I was in luck. Ken and Barry used the garage for storage. I set my box down by my feet and grabbed the top box off the stack. I then set my box on the stack and returned the box I had removed onto the top of the pile.

Shuffling my feet to hopefully blur any telltale traces of my footprints should there be any imprints in the dust and dirt covering the floor, I made my way back outside. It was easy to push the screws that held the hasp back into the door. I firmly pressed both sides back into place. Satisfied with my efforts, I returned to my waiting car, my adrenalin pumping big time from my escapade.

Now what do I do? Should I leave an anonymous message for the police telling them where to find the murder weapon? I didn't want to unfairly cast suspicion on Barry. After all, there was no reason why he would have killed Ken, let alone Carole. Besides, Barry hardly seemed the killer type. No, it wouldn't be right to call. I'd let the weapon simply be discovered in time. *But what if the killer struck again and I could have prevented it by disclosing the evidence to the police?* With a pang of guilt I considered the possibility. I'm not sure why, but I felt Carole and Ken were killed for a reason that started and ended between the two of them. *No, I'll leave things alone and wait for further developments.*

With one dilemma temporarily solved, my thoughts drifted to Richard and his telephone call. It still irked me. Maybe I should have moved away after the divorce to another town, or better still, a different state. *Look what's happened since our divorce became final—I find two dead bodies and become a murder suspect. And if that weren't reason enough to relocate, my husband—correction, my ex-husband—calls whenever he's lonely or decides to hit me up for money by selling our former possessions back to me.*

With those pleasant thoughts circling in my head, I returned home and pulled into my garage, parked, and slammed the door shut. Richard could keep the table for his next wife for my money. Rumors were already circulating he had someone special in his life.

Not more than five minutes after I walked in the back door, my doorbell rang. It was Lieutenant Corso. *He must have been tipped off to the knife being here.* Sudden panic raced through me again. In my haste to dispose of the errant box of items, I hadn't performed a search to see if anything else had been planted about the house to throw more suspicion my way.

Opening the door, my elevated blood pressure pounding in my ears with a steady drumming, I asked casually, "Jake, did you forget something?"

"No, but I need to ask if you've seen or heard from Cyndi Comings lately?"

"Cyndi? I saw her yesterday at the Fire Sign. She waited on me."

"You haven't heard from her since?"

"No. Why? Don't tell me she's dead or missing now," I asked in alarm.

He gave me one of his steely-eyed looks for a moment before he gave a slight nod. "Yeah—missing. She didn't report for work today and her landlord said she never returned home from work yesterday."

My head reeled under the weight of his statement. *Cyndi! Was she involved in this mess?* It certainly appeared that way from Jake's interest in her disappearance.

"By the way, where were you? I stopped by earlier and you didn't answer your door."

Involuntarily, I gulped and stammered, "I-I w-went for a drive for some fresh air. I was hot and feeling a bit cooped up sitting around staring at the four walls."

He studied my face closely and casually commented, "Nice night for it."

"Do you think Cyndi's the murderer?" I asked to his retreating back.

He shrugged his shoulders, and without a word, continued to walk to his car.

Deep inside, I knew Jake knew I had lied. I felt bad about it. *But what was I supposed to do—tell him I had to take a ride to dispose of one of the murder weapons?*

Chapter Eleven

Tuesday

I spent another restless night tossing and turning and mulling over the murders and everything that had occurred since the first day of the Peterson auction. My head felt like a bee hive as ideas and fleeting notions swirled in my head, while I vainly attempted to discover an answer amongst the seemingly disparate events.

Feeling the worse for wear, and thankful Annie had instructed me to come and go as I pleased this week at the shop, I climbed out of bed, put on my robe and shuffled to the kitchen. After feeding an unrelentingly expectant pair of kitties, I made a cup of coffee and returned to bed. I saw my iPad was where I had left it last—on my nightstand. I picked it up and once again reviewed my notes—what I had begun to think of as my suspect list.

Cyndi's disappearance added a new twist to things. Cyndi knew Carole, probably better than I did, and she knew Ken, too. Beyond that, I couldn't come up with anything to tie the three together except for the fact they all had a penchant for attending auctions. Cyndi could be considered a rival to Ken, but in a small way, because, like him, she bought auction items to turn around and flip for a profit—for her son's future college tuition.

As if two murders weren't enough, Cyndi had now joined Kurt in the missing person's category. If either of them were the murderer, they had to be responsible for planting the auction goods in my basement. It didn't seem possible Cyndi could be the killer. On the other hand, her behavior towards me at the auction, so abrupt and curt, wasn't what I thought her capable of until I observed it first-hand. *How much does one really ever know about people, and what they're really capable of doing?*

I picked Inky up off my lap and set her aside as I crawled out of bed and returned to the kitchen for a refill. As I reached for the coffee pot, my gaze fell on the vegetable basket Mr. Campezi had left on my stoop on Sunday. His note remained in the basket unopened. Picking up the small envelope, I lifted the flap and extracted a folded sheet of paper. Unfolding the paper, I slowly deciphered Mr. Campezi's scrawl: *Hope nobody steals this. I saw a stranger hanging around your house.* He signed the note, *Walt.*

I carried my coffee and phone back to the bedroom and called him. "Hi Walt, this is Nikki," I announced when he answered.

"Did ya get the veggies I left for ya?"

"Yes, they're great. Thanks for thinking of me."

"You're welcome, you gorgeous hunk of female pulchritude," he teased.

Walt was like that—a sweet old man who everyone in the neighborhood cherished. He could be a little coarse at times, but he was harmless. He was a bit of a throw-back. The characterization brought Jake and Brett to mind. They fit a similar mold—the kind Denise had referred to when she said, 'they don't make them like that anymore.'

"You're a flirt, you know that don't you?"

"If I was only thirty years younger, I'd give you a run for your affections."

"I wish," I said forlornly. "I called to thank you for the vegetables, Walt, and to talk to you about your note. You said you saw a stranger around my house?"

"Yep, young fella. Average height, slight build, dark hair, wearin' black."

"'His description immediately made me think of Traci North—the woman-in-black. Are you sure it was a man, could it have been a woman?"

"'Suppose it coulda. Hard to tell nowadays. Didn't get a good look at 'im. Took off when I reached the corner. I

138

walked 'round the block, but didn't see hide nor hair of 'im."

"Do you remember what time that was?"

"Must have been about seven or so Saturday evening."

"From your description, it might have been the fellow who tried to break into my house late Saturday night. Lucky for me, the pizza delivery boy interrupted him."

"Did he get anything? He might come back again you know."

"No, he was scared off. Don't worry. I reported the break-in to the police and they're patrolling my house regularly."

"Don't you go takin' any chances, young lady. Keep your doors and windows locked. I'd hate to see any harm come to such a fine specimen of nature."

"No harm done, I guess," I replied, smiling to myself. Richard had always made me feel like chopped liver, but with Mr. Campezi, I felt like someone special. "Thanks again, Walt, for the veggies and warning. I'll return the basket in a few days, okay?"

"No hurry," he said.

Walt's description of the snoop was so vague I saw no reason to tell Jake about it. *What good would it do?* I finished my coffee, returned to the kitchen and made myself a piece of toast with peanut butter and blueberry jam.

While I ate at the kitchen table, I picked up Carole's iPad and turned it on. The opening screen appeared, asking me to enter a security code. If Carole was like me, she only used a four digit code, never bothering to add a more elaborate and safer passkey. From experience, I knew I had only ten tries to get it right. After that, the tablet would lock up and I'd never have the opportunity to see what information she had input while at the auction or otherwise.

Fetching a telephone book from the shelf, I looked up Carole's address. It was 1107 N. Campezi Lane. I entered the street number in the iPad and it was rejected. One down, nine tries to go. Next I entered the last four digits of her phone number. Again, failure—only eight more attempts to get it right. Grabbing my phone I called Annie's Attic. Denise was working and when she answered I asked her if she knew when Carole's birthday was. "Hold on and I'll look in my contacts file," she replied. *Her contact list probably contains half the residents in Hickory Grove.* After a minute or so, Denise said, "October twenty-third," proudly. "Why do you need her birthday?" she inquired.

"I'm trying to figure out why she bought certain items at the auction," I feigned.

"With a birthdate? Don't you think the police can solve the cases?" she asked acerbically.

Obviously she didn't believe my lame explanation. "They haven't so far," I countered. "If you ask me they can use all the help they can get."

"I'm sure they can do without your help," she fired back at me tartly. Something was certainly eating her to judge by her snappish behavior.

"Thanks for the info, Denise. Gotta run now," I said, taking what my dad used to say was the 'high road' in letting things go that people either said or did that were irritating but trivial in the big scheme of things.

I set Carole's iPad aside and picked up my own. I hadn't had a chance to read Monday's news yet. The front page featured Carole's murder with a big bold title, *2ⁿᵈ Unsolved Murder in Two Days*. To my surprise, the reporter said the police were looking for Kurt Manning to question as a possible murder suspect. According to the reporter, Kurt had been living with Carole until recently. How odd, Denise had said Kurt lived with two friends. *But then, Denise has a flagrant disregard for facts*, I reminded myself. It wouldn't be the first time she had been completely wrong. Kurt's previous arrests were listed and the article strongly suggested Kurt had killed his girlfriend after killing Ken for what was, as yet, an unknown reason. *What about the accused being innocent until proven guilty?* I finished reading the article and set the paper aside.

Carole had been thirty-three years of age according to the reporter. I picked up her iPad again, turned it on and entered her birth year for the security code. Entering one-nine-eight-three into the code field, my attempt was rejected once more. Four down, six more tries to go. Next I tried one-zero-two-three, her month and day of birth. Again, the entry was rejected. That left me five more attempts before I'd be frozen out. I reversed the month and day and tried again. No luck. I'd eliminated the most common possibilities; anything else I tried at this point would be like throwing a dart in the dark.

I eased back in my chair and mulled over other possibilities she may have used as a security code. *Wait a minute! What an idiot I've been.* The reporter probably didn't know Carole's exact day of birth. Carole would have turned thirty-three this year, but it was only August now and her birthday wasn't until October. Since she was born in October, it meant she was born in 1982 not 1983. I picked up the iPad and expectantly entered her correct birth year. Bingo! I was in. With unbridled ebullience, I let loose a cry of success and quickly scanned the icons displayed on her home screen.

I searched for and found Carole's notes app. Opening up the app, a number of files appeared, one was labeled *Auctions*. I opened it and began to read her notes arranged by date. The first date listed was from May of this year. A generic list of items appeared, and after each one she had entered a dollar amount. Scanning down, my eye stopped at a June nineteenth entry. This time specific items were listed with details and corresponding dollar amounts. All the ensuing entries were similarly included. Her attention to detail had increased over time, leaving me the impression she was learning about items and their corresponding worth.

Why would she care about documenting such details unless she was interested in each item's investment potential? Maybe I've been all wrong about Carole and she was buying and selling goods to flip in order to earn badly needed money. That would explain the piece of jewelry I found clutched in her hand.

I continued down the list to the latest dated entries. Again, Carole had entered items with what I assumed were their corresponding dollar amounts. I recognized enough of the items listed to know they were from the Peterson auction. One thing I found puzzling was while Carole had won some of the items she had listed; she hadn't won all of them, nor was the list complete of all items sold. Ken had won one or two of the items, and the rest I wasn't sure about. It was odd she had listed only certain items.

Why enter items she didn't win? Or more importantly, why had she listed items Ken had purchased as well as her own? Carole needed money according to a number of sources. Could she have been checking prices to educate herself in preparation for buying and selling auction items? If so, she was going about it in a terribly haphazard manner to judge from her lists unless she was concentrating on only specific categories of items. With that thought in mind, I reexamined the list. I could discern no rhyme or reason to the items, no categorization according to price, type, or age. Yet, Carole struck me as being a methodical person. The few occasions when we had discussed art, she had presented an exacting method behind each of her creations. No, I was convinced Carole had only listed certain items for a very specific reason. *But if the reason was according to what items had come to market at the auctions, the knowledge would be of limited utility and why would she post them?* There had to be a better reason behind her notations, but what that reason was escaped me at the present.

I examined the other apps Carole had on her iPad. They were the usual—games, video-streaming, music, and a few productivity apps. I found nothing of interest until I opened up her e-mail and scanned the sent file. It felt strange reading Carole's e-mails—like I was eavesdropping. Denise would have had a field day reading someone else's mail, but it made me feel guilty.

The first e-mail was from Carole to Jenny and concerned their mother. Jenny must be a sister, I guessed, from the language and tone of the message. Two more e-mails were exchanges between them. The last e-mail was from Kurt. The body of his e-mail had two terse sentences: *I checked. You were right.* That was all. A quick scroll downwards revealed his e-mail had not been a reply to an e-mail Carole had sent, but was a standalone. Other personal e-mails of seeming insignificance were found in the deleted and trash folders.

Turning off Carole's iPad, I lifted up the top on my stove and placed the iPad underneath and popped the top back in place. It wasn't the best hiding place, but it would have to do for now.

After washing up, I threw on a pair of jeans and a loose fitting top. It was crazy, but I was determined to confront Brett about the auction items I had spotted in his workshop. I just couldn't bring myself to hire a man I didn't trust.

I needed to check out my basement first, though, to see if my intruder had left anything besides the box of auction items and murder weapon. I performed a quick, but thorough search and discovered nothing untoward. Satisfied, I went upstairs, closed the door, grabbed my purse, and as an afterthought, I retrieved Carole's iPad from the stove and put it in my purse. I spotted Inky and Dinky laying together in the sun on the couch. "Be good girls," I told them and I petted their sleepy heads as I walked by.

Brett didn't answer when I used the old fashioned knocker affixed to his front door, so I walked around to the back figuring he was at work in his shop. The shop door was closed, but the high-pitched whine of a machine increased in volume as I approached. He didn't respond when I knocked, so I tried the doorknob. It was unlocked. Opening the door, I spotted him leaning over the work table in the middle of the room with his back to me. He was cutting an intricate design into a large piece of wood. I didn't want to startle him and cause an error in his work so I stepped back to the door and knocked as loudly as I could on the frame while I shouted his name. He turned, held up a finger for me to wait, and continued his work for a few more seconds before turning off the machine.

"Hey, what brings you to this neck of the woods again?" he asked, removing what looked to be a painter's mask from his face.

"I need some help. It's kind of an emergency," I replied, and casually walked by the glass cabinet as I closed the distance between us. Noticeably glancing at the pieces held within, I said, "Hey, these are from the auction, aren't they?"

"Yeah," he answered laconically, giving me a strange look.

"I don't remember you bidding on anything. Were you at the auction the second day? I don't remember seeing you there." I tried not to stare at the contents behind the glass enclosed case, but one particular item, the old pipe, caught my eye again. I looked at the other items more closely and a breath stuck in my throat. From what my quick perusal revealed, all of the items had been listed in Carole's iPad. *What were they doing here? Had she won them?* No, I knew she hadn't. Carole didn't win the case or items because they never made it to the auction block before the discovery of Ken's murder halted the proceedings.

"I didn't attend the second day. A client dropped the case off," Brett replied coolly.

Why would Carole give Brett the case with stuff in it to work on? Maybe she didn't give it to him. I came up with only one viable answer: Brett must have killed Carole to get the case, but that didn't make sense. There wasn't anything extremely valuable sitting in the case to kill someone over, and why would he be fixing the case and have it sitting out in the open where anyone who came into his workshop could see it? None of it was making sense. It was highly unlikely Carole would have had time to give the case to him before she was killed, even if she did acquire it somehow. That meant he took it or was covering for someone else.

So who is his client? The most likely answer is Woody because the case would have remained in his custodial care. The case may have been damaged during the ensuing mayhem after finding Ken's body. By having the cabinet repaired, Woody could be exercising proper care, but that doesn't explain the items inside. Nor does it explain why Carole had entered them into her iPad.

I tried to subtly hint for answers, but to no avail. It was obvious Brett felt uneasy talking about the case when I tried to extract more information from him. He deflected a pointed question regarding the identity of the owner, instead asking me what my emergency entailed.

"It's my cellar doors. They're badly warped. They don't close all the way and don't lock. I'm afraid my cats will get out one of these times when I forget to close the inside door in the kitchen leading to the basement. The cellar doors are so rotted I don't think screws will hold to install a catch and lock," I explained half-heartedly.

"Why don't we go take a look now? I could use a break. I've been working on this piece since seven this morning.

It's a neighbor's emergency, too. You know how business is; it's always feast or famine."

We took his truck. Even though he had evaded answering my earlier questions, I ineffably wanted to trust him. And I desperately wanted to know who really gave him the display case to fix. I tried to think of some way to find out without directly asking him as we walked around to the rear of my bungalow. Unfortunately, there wasn't a way to get the answer from him without making an unmitigated snoop of myself. *Maybe a better time will arise later.*

When we reached the cellar entrance, I pointed at the doors and said, "See what I mean?"

Brett pulled the doors open and the sunlight blinded Inky who stood blinking rapidly at us in return. "You little rascal—how'd did you get down here again?" I picked her up and walked down the small creaky cellar steps into the basement. Dinky was back on top of the box where the other box with the knife had been stacked earlier.

Oh no, don't tell me my visitor left something else. And to think I've invited Brett here, just like I invited him the first time. I let his nature put me at ease, leaving me vulnerable. When will I learn?

"Curious creatures, aren't they?" Brett asked directly from in back of me.

"Aaaaa," I shouted, startled by his sudden closeness. "You scared me."

"Sorry, 'bout that."

I have to be more careful until the murders are solved, I admonished myself.

"What do you think?" I asked motioning toward the doors with a shaky finger. "The door that leads to the basement doesn't stay shut either, so it's imperative I do something to fix that problem, too—it's how the kitties keep getting down here."

He ignored my nervous gesture. "The cellar doors are pretty bad alright—must be the originals. They need to be replaced. Can't get to them or the basement door for a while, though," he added, petting Inky's backside as she curled her body around his legs.

"Can you do anything to keep the cellar doors closed in the meantime?" I asked pleadingly, picking up Inky and Dinky who thought the doors had been opened just so they could amble outdoors.

He walked back outside and examined the tops and bottoms of each door. "Do you need to get into the cellar from the outside until I can put new doors on?"

"No."

"In that case, I can put a couple of longer pieces of wood across the top and bottom. Screws should hold sufficiently near the perimeter where the wood is a little sturdier."

"Sounds good to me."

"Yeah, that ought to keep the little ones in. I'll see what I have in my truck."

While he was getting what he needed from his truck, I put Inky and Dinky upstairs in the kitchen, closed the basement door tightly, and went back downstairs. I saw Inky extend a furry paw under the door and heard Dinky give out a cry.

"I'll let you two check things out later," I said with a smile, and went to join Brett outside.

He returned in a couple of minutes carrying three boards and an electric screwdriver. "If you don't care what it looks like, I can screw these in place."

"Go for it."

He began to work, and I interrupted him by asking, "Brett, how did you know where I lived yesterday? I didn't give you directions to my house."

He gave me a funny look before he replied, "You laid your auction receipt on the music stand after the auction and I caught a glimpse of it. Guess I was curious to see if you were a local."

"Oh, that explains it," I said doubtfully.

"You're awfully suspicious, aren't you?"

"I guess maybe I am. You would be too if you discovered two murder victims."

"Yeah, I might at that," he agreed. Surprisingly he made no further mention of the murders or my involvement in them. He was done in less than five minutes, having put boards across the gap to block the kitties escape. *Sometimes it really is nice to have a man around.*

"That ought to do it," he said testing his workmanship by lifting up on the handles. The doors stayed firmly in place. "Just remember, you won't be able to get in or out through the cellar until I take these boards off."

"Not a worry, and thanks, Brett. I'll rest a lot easier knowing Inky and Dinky can't get out."

He chuckled. "You might want to put a chair under the basement door as a brace to keep it closed until I can fix that door, too."

"Of course, I should have thought of that myself as a temporary fix."

"Since we're talking about fixes, I've been working through a few ideas for your house. What do you think about rounding off the doorways—making the entranceways and doors into oval shapes, frames and all. Since the doors, as they stand now, don't close well, it would be a good time to make an overall modification rather than just fix what you have."

"Wow, that sounds incredible! Reminds me of a Hobbit house," I replied enthusiastically.

"Yeah, kind of wished I'd thought of it when I was doin' my place."

We talked about what woods to use and their relevant costs during the ride back to his house. He walked me out to my car, chivalrously opened my door, and told me he'd check back with me in a few days. I asked him how much I owed him and he waved me off saying, "Forget about it. It was just a few scrap pieces of wood."

I thanked him profusely and climbed in my car. *Brett doesn't seem a dangerous type, but isn't that what the neighbors always say upon learning they had lived next door to a murderer?*

My next destination was to see Burton. Annie was undoubtedly at work, but I hoped to catch Burton at home. He had said he was going to check into Kurt's arrest record and I was dying to hear the inside scoop on the police investigation of Ken's burgled storage unit.

"There she is. Fresh as a daisy and twice as pretty," Burton exclaimed when he opened the front door.

"Flattery will get you everywhere," I said and gave him a kiss on the cheek. "I stopped by to see what's new with your friends down at city hall."

"Might as well make yourself comfortable," he said waving me into the living room. "You know the police are looking for Carole's boyfriend, don't you?"

"Yeah. Is Kurt their primary suspect?"

"He's one of them, that's for sure. Anderson is mighty charged up over this. He knows his butt's in the fire and somebody's head is gonna roll if the police don't turn up something quick."

"What about Cyndi Comings? I heard she's missing, too?"

"Cyndi? That pretty little waitress at the Fire Sign?"

"Yep."

"Missing? When did you hear this?"

"Lieutenant Corso stopped by yesterday to ask if I had heard from her. He gave me the impression the police think her disappearance is somehow connected to the murders."

"First I've heard of it. Nobody said anything about it to me when I was at the station house this morning."

"What about Traci North?"

"Ah, now there's one interesting gal. The police are trying to find out more about her and her business. They've drawn a blank so far."

"What do you mean?"

"They know she owns and operates an antique store in Glenview. She bought the store a couple of years ago. The previous owners weren't doing very well with the business and sold out to her. She's made quite a go of it since she took over—turned it into a gold mine according to what I was told. The police are trying to figure out how she's been able to turn a profit so quickly. They didn't come right out and say it, but I think they suspect her of dealing in stolen goods. Oh, I forgot to tell you, the police had the dagger that killed Ken analyzed—"

"I know. They didn't find any prints," I interrupted him.

Unperturbed by my rude interlude, Burton, continued, "Yeah, but did you know they discovered the dagger was worth a lot of money—something in the neighborhood of twenty thousand dollars. Guess it must have been the real McCoy."

"Twenty thousand! Are you kidding? There were three of them," I wailed, realizing I had let sixty thousand dollars slip through my fingers at the auction. I moaned again when I remembered the dagger that had been planted in my basement was one of the three. Possession would have been nine-tenths of the law. But then again, tampering with evidence, obstruction of justice, and a multitude of other crimes I had undoubtedly committed when I took it upon myself to hide the murder weapon in Ken and Barry's garage was the law, too. With a shrug, I accepted the loss graciously and mentally moved forward. After all, the loss of twenty thousand seemed small potatoes compared to twenty years behind bars.

"Burton, do you know anything about Brett Nielsen?"

He returned my question with a peculiar look. "Yeah, a little bit. Why?"

"I'm thinking of using his services for my business. You know, fix and refurbish furniture—do some work on my bungalow as well."

"That's your business, of course, but just be careful."

"Careful? Why do you say that?" It was uncharacteristic of Burton to be so reserved with me. He had definitely put his cautious attorney's hat on.

"Well," he said, hesitating for a few seconds while carefully choosing his words, "I seem to recall a bit of trouble he was in a few years back. A long time ago, mind you, right after I was elected mayor for the first time—something about another man's wife. I know he was arrested for assault with a deadly weapon, but I don't remember whatever came of it. I think the charges were dropped and it was hushed up for some reason. He went away for a while afterward. I don't mean jail," he clarified. "He just left town and came back a number of years later."

I was shell-shocked. The Brett I knew, albeit briefly, was so mild-mannered, so laid back that I couldn't imagine him ever getting angry enough to commit felonious assault against anyone. Yet, I did have him on my murder suspect list. "You wouldn't happen to remember what kind of weapon it was, do you? Was it a gun?"

Burton scratched his head, concentrated for a few moments and declared, "No, I seem to recall it was a knife."

Chapter Twelve

Burton's story upset me so much that I mindlessly began to drive toward Richard's, our old house, before I realized what I was doing. *Pay attention and concentrate on your driving. This is how accidents happen.* Making a U-turn, I drove back to town, to Annie's Attic. I parked in the alleyway and entered through the back door. I counted my blessings as I spotted Annie helping some customers who were examining the contents of one of the locked cases of pricey paraphernalia sold on consignment. I waited for her to finish with the customers and return to her usual station behind the square counter set in the middle of the store.

"Annie, do you know Woody, the auctioneer, very well?"

"What are you doing here? I thought you were going to rest up some?"

"Yeah, I was, but I started to think about the murders and I may have come up with something. What about Woody?"

"We know each other. We're friendly, but not close friends. Why, sweetie?"

"There are a few questions I'd like to ask him about the Peterson auction. What sold for what and to whom—those kinds of things. Do you think he'd tell me if I asked?"

"I don't know," she said, pondering my question. "It might be considered private information. Besides the police probably have his ledgers. Let me give him a call." She picked up an old tattered phone book to look up his number. Annie never bothered to adopt new technology; she only carried a cell phone for emergencies when she travelled. She claimed she was too old to change, but she recognized the advantage technology afforded those who used it in our business.

"Hi, this is Annie Edwards. Is Woody around?" she asked when her call was answered. After a few seconds wait, she asked in a cheerful voice, "Hello Woody, how's business? Anything good on the horizon?" After a lengthy pause, she added, "That sounds interesting. I'm sure one of the gals here in the shop will be interested in learning that's coming down the pipeline. Her name's Nicole Carson."

I could hear Woody's voice, but couldn't make out his words. After a moment's interruption, "Yeah, that's her, Woody. She's good-looking with dark brown hair, blue eyes. Listen, would it be okay if she stopped by to ask your bookkeeper a few questions? She was so upset by what happened at the Peterson auction she can't find her receipts and you know how the IRS is in this business if you get audited. Good," she said and gave me a wink. "Two o'clock?" she asked giving me an inquisitive look. I nodded an affirmation. "That works. She'll be there at two. Make sure and tell her about that upcoming auction. Thanks, dearie. Don't make yourself such a stranger, Woodrow. Who knows? If Nikki doesn't take over the shop one day, I may need you to sell everything for me," she told him greasing the skids for me.

"You're good," I told her when she disconnected.

With a broad smile, she said, "You have to be in this business, sweetie." She jotted on a piece of paper, tore it from the notepad and handed it to me. "Here's his address. It's a big red pole barn. He holds consignment auctions there. He didn't mention anything about his records being confiscated, so they must be available. He also said a big estate auction is coming up in a couple of weeks—another collector who has stashed stuff away for fifty years. Make sure and ask him about it."

"Thanks, Annie. And you don't have to say it. I'll be careful."

Inky and Dinky came bounding to the back door when I arrived home. Nearly one o'clock, I fed the girls and grabbed a protein shake for a quick lunch. Sipping my shake, I thought about what Burton had told me regarding Brett.

Here I am behind the eight-ball with Brett, again. He exhibited a fair amount of reticence to my inquiry regarding the auction items in his workshop. And Burton says Brett had once been charged of assault with a deadly weapon—a knife no less—the same instrument used to kill Carole and Ken. Maybe Brett should become tops on my suspect list.

Picking up my phone, I dialed Jake. "Jake, this is Nikki." I thought I heard an audible groan at the other end.

"What's up?"

"Can you see if a gentleman by the name of Brett Nielsen was ever arrested and convicted for assault with a deadly weapon? It would have happened over ten years ago."

"And why do I want to do this?" he asked sharply.

"I can think of at least three good reasons," I replied curtly.

With resignation in his voice, he said, "All right, I'll bite. What are they?"

"Well, first, there's the fact that he was at the auction on Friday. Second—"

"Wait a minute," Jake interrupted. "What about Saturday? Was he at the auction then?"

"N-no, not that I'm aware of, but he told me he went to auctions a lot," I replied ardently. No mistaking it this time, Jake definitely groaned. "He was once arrested for attacking someone with a knife. And," I continued quickly, "the third reason is that he has a knife and some other items from Saturday's auction in his workshop. I asked him about them and he told me they were from a display case a client hired him to fix. The display cases definitely weren't sold during the auction."

"Are you certain the case was part of the estate?"

"Well, no. I guess the case could have been the auctioneer's, or even Ken's for that matter. But the items inside were definitely up for sale at the auction."

Jake was silent for a few seconds. "You saw these items in his workshop?"

"Uh-huh, they were there this morning."

"I'll look into it."

"You'll let me know what you find out, won't you?" I asked beseechingly.

"Oh sure, I wouldn't think of keeping Hickory Grove's private eye out of the loop."

"Hey, I'm only trying to help," I protested.

In a more subdued voice, he responded, "I know, I know. It's just that the chief is climbing the four walls and my ass is on the line. Let me check into it. That was an ADW, right?"

"Huh?"

"Assault with a deadly weapon," he patiently spelled out.

"Oh, yeah, a knife."

After talking to Jake, I finished my shake and played an exhaustive game of hide-and-seek with Inky and Dinky until it was time to depart for my appointment at Woody's.

Woody's Red Shed Auction Enterprises was housed in a large pole-barn variety building set back from the road to allow for parking in the front. A counter was set off to the left side when I entered, but no one was present. "Hello," I shouted and was soon greeted by Red who had graced the trailer at the Peterson auction. She was wearing an overabundance of dark eye shadow and eyeliner, jeans, and a black *AC/DC* t-shirt.

"What can I do for you, honey?" she asked between pops of her gum.

"I'm Nikki, from Annie's Attic. Annie talked to Woody earlier and set up a meeting for me."

"Woody mentioned something about someone looking at the Peterson records," she acknowledged. "I remember you from the Peterson auction. You're the new divorcee."

"How do you know I'm newly divorced?"

"I remember how confused you were over your address at the auction. Plus your tan line shows where your rings were. My guess is it's been less than three weeks."

"Wow, you're good."

"Naw, I've been there, though. Just hang in there and you'll do okay. I was in the same place you are now a couple of years ago and today I'm doing great. A bit of air conditioning in the trailer would help, though," she conceded with a sardonic smile and blew another bubble that burst with a loud pop.

"Thanks," I mumbled numbly, feeling slightly off-base by her encouragement, realizing she meant well.

But how could sitting behind a trailer window issuing auction numbers be a boon? Then again, it's not so easy to identify the haves from the have-nots these days. Either that or her definition of doing well was strikingly different from mine. Surely, working at an auction house has to merely provide for the bare essentials in today's economy.

I thought back to what my attorney, Gene LaForte, had advised—that I would need well over a million dollars in assets in order to retire comfortably. Red hardly seemed qualified as set for life, but unlike her physical characteristics, perhaps she hid her financial assets well.

Looks can be deceiving.

"Follow me, ma'am," she instructed and walked around a partition to her left where a small office was situated. She pulled a chair up for me to sit in and left me for a few moments while she went to retrieve the records.

When did I go from being a 'miss' to a 'ma'am'?

It seemed just like yesterday when I was being carded whenever I made a liquor purchase. Why, it was only last week when the clerk asked to see my driver's license when

I went to buy champagne to celebrate Annie's sixtieth birthday. I was floating on air until he ruined my momentary elation and qualified his ID request by saying, "Sorry, lady, but it's a new policy. We have to card everyone now. I know it doesn't make sense, but I don't make the rules." Annie had a good laugh over that one when I shared my cold-slap-of-reality moment with her. She said she couldn't wait to patronize the store and be carded. With her gray hair and walking stick, she said she was going to have some fun!

Oh, well. I had chalked the experience up to one of life's rich pageantries, just like the weight I had gained while being married. I had slowly climbed from a size seven to a size twelve before I realized I had lost my girlish figure. Well, I couldn't control being carded by the establishment, but I vowed to Annie I could and would control my weight. She seconded the motion without a blink of the eye, "You shed Richard, honey—you can shed the pounds, too."

There was much to admire about Annie. She had carved out a nice living for herself after her first husband had been killed in a car accident nearly thirty-seven years ago. Shortly after his death, she left Hickory Grove, her birthplace, to live in Chicago. Barely able to make ends meet in the city, she returned to her roots and worked to become a big fish in a small pond. She beat the odds and succeeded.

When she was in her early fifties, she married Burton Edwards. Their marriage was the icing on her cake. I counted Annie, now a young-at-heart sexagenarian, as my best friend. While waiting for my divorce to become final, I had ventured into her shop one day to see if I could place my artwork in her eclectic store. She liked my work and we immediately hit it off. I'm not certain what she saw in me, but during the ensuing weeks, our friendship blossomed, and I was soon 'Nikki' to her, the name I adopted after my divorce. Richard had never liked the shortened version of my name, always insisting I use 'Nicole' around his friends and acquaintances. *Who knew why?* This peculiarity was only one of many instances when he exhibited his control-freak nature.

Annie normally took in works from artists on a consignment basis, but after a couple of weeks, she took me under her wing and let me lease space in her store. She taught me the antique and collectibles business, and now her shop was proving to be a great place to sell vintage goods I picked up, along with my artwork. I was currently putting together room ensembles, hoping to sell an entire room, rather than items piecemeal to those who preferred one-stop-shopping. Like I said, Annie's motives for taking me in weren't purely altruistic—she hoped I'd buy her shop one day. That was fine by me—but a bit scary.

I was stirred from my thoughts by a loud thump as Red placed a thick ledger on the desk and began to flip through the pages.

"Do you want Friday's or Saturday's transactions?"

"I bought items on both days. Do you suppose I could look at the ledger? It would save us time since I have to look up the item descriptions on my tablet first."

"Naw, just let me find your auction number for each of the days and I can read you our description and you can compare it with yours. How's that, hon?"

I couldn't very well tell her 'no.' "Okay," I agreed reluctantly, thinking this was going to be a waste of my time. When she found my bidder's number for Friday, she scanned the rows of items until she found the first item I had won and told me the description and price. I feigned checking my notes on Carole's iPad, all the time trying to think of a way to find out from Red who had purchased the items Carole had listed in her notes app.

My opportunity came when Woody stuck his head into the office, and said, "Scarlet, can you help me a minute. I'm having trouble cataloging some items." His hair was messy as though he had been running his hands through it and his face bore a look of utter frustration.

"Thanks for helping me out, Woody. I'm Nikki, Nicole Carson, the one who Annie Edward's called you about," I said by way of introducing myself, and rose from my chair to shake his hand.

"Sure, I remember you. You discovered Ken's body, didn't you?"

"Unfortunately."

"Terrible thing. His death has caused me a lot of work, I can tell you," he exclaimed running his hand through his hair.

It wasn't very good for Ken, either. "Did Ken do all your appraisals?" I asked innocently.

He shook his head. "He did most of the major ones for us. Now we're left high and dry."

"I don't mean to overstep my boundaries, but you might want to ask Annie to fill in. She knows as much about antiques as Ken did—probably more."

Woody's face brightened noticeably at my statement. "Do you think she'd do it?"

"I don't know, but it never hurts to ask," I encouraged.

"Does she have appraiser certification?"

"I don't know, I think so. Woody, did Ken also catalog all the items for the auctions he appraised?" I asked as an afterthought.

"Yeah, that's what I'm having trouble with now—trying to categorize everything properly for our next auction. Ken knew his stuff, but in a way I'm looking forward to having someone else appraise and catalog items for me. He was a pushy so-and-so. Thought he was boss—always giving me orders. I took the bad with the good, but more times than not he was a big nuisance."

"That explains it," I mumbled to myself thinking about the interactions between Woody and Ken I had witnessed at the auction.

"What's that?"

"Oh, nothing," I replied evasively. "I was thinking if Annie takes the appraiser job, I'd offer my help to catalog everything. I'm sure she'd want me to do that because she has plans for me to take over her business someday."

"That's awfully nice of you, Ms. Carson," Woody said appreciatively.

"Please, call me Nikki."

He held out his hand for me to shake and said, "Hope everything works out, Nikki. I'm going to call Annie right now and see what she says. If she agrees to do it, it's sure going to be a load off my mind."

Woody wasn't gone more than five minutes before he returned. "Annie told me she'd think about it and call me back. She's licensed, but said she wanted to talk to you first," he said with a beseeching look.

"If it's up to me, we'll do it."

Woody rubbed his hands together and beamed from ear to ear. "Let me know as soon as you know, will you?"

"Sure."

"Oh, I almost forgot, Nikki," Woody added. "Real quick—Annie said you'd be interested in a big auction coming up in October. Two doctors—they have several outbuildings full of three generations worth of collectibles. I told Annie we'll be posting the auction in the beginning of September. If you want, you can come by while we're sorting the stuff and get an early looksee. They're open to wheeling and dealing beforehand on some of the big items. Call us after Labor Day for exact dates. In the meantime, I need to borrow Scarlett for a few minutes. Make sure and have Annie call me," he reiterated to my nodding head, before he walked away with Scarlet, gum popping, in tow.

As soon as they had left the office, I flipped the ledger book around and hastily scanned the pages to locate the items Carole had listed in her iPad. Brief descriptions of the items were listed next to the winning bidder's number along with catalog information.

After identifying the first eight items, a pattern began to emerge. All the items had been purchased by one of three bidders. I flipped back to the beginning of the auction notes where the bidders' information was listed along with their respective auction numbers. The numbers belonged to Carole, Barry, and Traci North.

I checked for items on day two of the Peterson auction and the pattern held true again. Carole only listed items purchased by these same bidders. As I mulled over my discovery, Red returned and interrupted my thinking. "I hope you don't mind, but I finished while you were gone. Thanks for all your help."

She smiled and said, "Who knows? Maybe we'll be working together."

"I hope so," I responded brightly. "We've never been formally introduced. I'm Nicole Carson."

"I'm Scarlett Mix."

Her name fit her perfectly and I'd have no trouble remembering it. I thanked her again, and departed.

I drove straight to Annie's Attic to clear the air with Annie. Hopefully, she didn't think I had overstepped my bounds by offering her expertise to Woody. When I entered the store, I spotted Barry leaning on the counter, talking animatedly with Annie. He gave me a nod of acknowledgement as I opened the partition and entered the office area.

"Is Denise gone for the day, Annie?" I asked.

"Yeah, she said she wasn't feeling well. Everything go okay with Woody?"

"Great," I acknowledged. I was dying to know what she thought about filling in as appraiser for Woody, but it didn't seem right to talk about it in front of Barry. It might appear as if we were vultures trying to take over Ken's appraiser business at first opportunity which was the furthest thing from the truth.

A glance at Barry told me he wasn't happy when he heard I had been with Woody. Oh well, one can't go worrying too much about things one can't control.

"How are you doing, Barry?"

"I'm fine," he said with a piercing look. "I came by to see if anyone here is interested in buying some goods. I want to reduce my inventory. Ken bought so many things over the past few years—we have storage lockers filled."

At his announcement, my face flushed thinking about the box of goods I had added to the hoard in their garage. "I'd be interested, but I'm a little cash strapped right now."

"If you bring in what you have with you today, I'll take a look at it," Annie offered.

"Can you give me a hand?" Barry asked me.

"No problem."

We walked out to his truck parked in the alley. Boxes were stacked neatly in the bed. *Oh no*, I thought. *What if those boxes are from his garage?*

"Sorry to hear about Carole," he said. "She was a good friend of yours, wasn't she?"

"We were friends, but never really close." His question about my relationship with Carole once again was odd, but I let it pass.

"I guess I thought you two were closer since you're both artists," he said as he handed me a medium-sized box. "What did you see Woody about?" he asked off-handedly as he repositioned the boxes he lifted.

His question stopped me in my tracks. I certainly didn't want to tell him about the possibility of Annie taking over Ken's duties as appraiser. "I was just double-checking some of my records with him," I replied vaguely. From the look on his face, I knew he didn't believe me. I rushed ahead of him, tucked my box under one arm and held the door open for him.

In all, it took us six trips to carry all the boxes inside. Annie was going to have quite the job to examine everything Barry had brought. After we carried in the last load, I told Annie I was leaving for the day and apologized for not putting in my usual time. She waved me off and told me not to worry.

Inky and Dinky greeted me when I opened my abode's back door. Dinky jumped up on the kitchen counter and tried to climb onto my shoulder when I set my purse and keys down. Picking her up, I stroked her fur and she began to purr. Inky meowed in protest to the attention I paid her sister. I set Dinky down, gave Inky a quick hug and opened the refrigerator and retrieved their food. As soon as they heard the telltale sound of me snapping the plastic lids off the cans, they began to meow in unison. I spooned out equal portions of food onto their respective plates and set them on their mats. They voraciously ate their food, noisily gnawing away at the shredded meat. Dinky gulped her food and greedily eyed her sister's plate. She knew I was watching her and I could see she was thinking about making a play for her sister's food.

"No, no, none of that now," I said preemptively. Reaching in the fridge, I took out Dinky's food and spooned out another helping in an effort to buy time for Inky to finish eating.

I made a cup of tea, and sat down at the kitchen table with Carole's iPad. Scanning her auction lists, I tried to see if something more was to be had of her lists after what I had discovered at Woody's. I still had two burning questions. *Why did Carole track items she didn't purchase, and more importantly, why did she only track some items purchased by her, Ken, and Traci North?*

A niggling thought tickled at the fringes of my inspection. Something was important about Carole's notes, but I didn't have any idea how the information tied in with the two murders. Whenever I figured out a motive for

Ken's death, my reasoning fell apart in applying the same logic to the cause behind Carole's murder. The same held true when I reversed the situations. The more I thought about it, the more my brain hurt. There seemed to be too many confusing cross-purposes at work to tie the murders logically together. My number one suspect ranking changed so frequently, my head spun. Kurt, Cyndi, Brett, Traci, Carole, Barry—all of them were possibilities, and none of them were ruled out by me or the police if I interpreted the limited information Jake had provided me correctly.

I checked the note files and e-mails again. There was Kurt's one message. He had checked something to substantiate Carole's suspicions about something. Carole had listed items bought by Ken and Barry and Traci. Burton had told me in so many words that the police suspected Traci of selling stolen goods.

That must be it. Carole must have become suspicious of Ken stealing goods and fencing them through Traci's antique shop. She had Kurt check on it and he sent her the e-mail confirming her suspicions. That's the missing link between Ken and Carole's murder which makes Traci my number one suspect again.

Then I thought about Traci's confrontation with Ken at the auction. She had warned him, even threatened him, about missing items. *No. It doesn't fit. If Ken was using her to move stolen goods, why would she be accusing him of stealing auction items?* Another of my bright ideas shot to hell. Every time I thought I had things figured out, I returned to ground zero.

Absentmindedly, I opened up Carole's picture app and flicked through her folders. A lot of the pictures were of Kurt or selfies of the two of them. I studied his facial features—dark, intense eyes stared back at me, reminding me of Jake's. Except Jake's eyes revealed an honest frankness underlying a hard exterior. Kurt looked equally hard, but I had an impression of unruliness—traced with danger lurking behind his wild black orbs. There was no trust to be found in those shifty eyes. His unkempt, curly black hair framed a strong, handsome face. *His looks fit the perfect toxic bachelor profile*, I thought, based on what I knew of his past and his tempestuous relationship with Carole. I felt sorry for her as I reexamined the pictures. *He doesn't look like a one-woman-man, but looks can be deceiving,* I reminded myself once again.

The last folder I opened contained copies of pictures Carol must have scanned into her tablet. I judged them all to be old—most had creases, yellowing, and stains. Suddenly, I came to a picture that took my breath away. Denise stood, looking back at me from the photograph, and beside her stood Barry. She wore a white dress and white hat, and Barry was dressed in a dark suit, his arm around her waist. Both of them looked like they were eighteen years old. Their age didn't shock me; it was the fact Barry and Denise wore wedding rings and looked to be a happily just-married couple.

Chapter Thirteen

"Naw, it couldn't be," I muttered in disbelief. "No way,"

I picked up my phone and called Annie. Without returning her 'hello,' I spluttered, "Annie, you're not going to believe this, but I think Denise was married to Barry when they were teenagers."

"What?! Whatever gave you that crazy idea?"

"I came across an old wedding photo of them. She's wearing a white wedding dress and he's in a suit. He's holding her close, and they're wearing wedding rings."

"Holy shit," she said verbalizing my thoughts exactly.

"Did she ever talk about being married before?"

"Yeah, but that was to Bob Nelson. She married him about six years ago and it only lasted about a year."

"Well, I think she was married to Barry first. You know she talks about everybody who comes into the store, but I can't remember her ever mentioning Barry. How long has he been with Ken?"

"I don't know, sweetie. I only met them about ten years ago."

"I figure Barry must be about forty now, so he was with Ken at least since he was roughly thirty. Geez, you don't suppose he left Denise for Ken, do you?"

"Wouldn't that be a lark—Miss Busybody with a hidden skeleton in her own closet?"

"Who could we ask who would know for sure?"

"Umm, I can't think of anyone off hand."

"Not to change the subject, Annie, but how did things work out at the shop with Barry?"

"Nikki, you have to see some of the glassware Barry sold me," she gushed. "He discounted everything so much I couldn't resist buying almost everything. The prices he asked were extremely reasonable—a quarter or less of the retail value."

"Great, I can't wait to see everything you bought. If you don't mind, I'll probably be in and out again tomorrow."

"You do what you have to do, sweetie. If I need help, I'll ask Burton since Denise called in sick."

"Denise is sick? Again? Annie I can't leave you in a lurch. I'll report first thing in the morning."

"Nonsense. Some honest work will be good for Burton for a change. You take your time."

"Well, I better let you go, it's almost closing time. I had to tell you about Denise. I can't wait to hear what Burton has to say about them."

I no longer disconnected my call with Annie, when my phone rang. It was Jake.

"I'm reporting in," he announced snidely.

"You sound happy," I observed disparagingly.

"Tickled to death to be of service to you. I couldn't find anything on your boy, Brett."

"So my source was wrong," I said, surprised by the bum steer Burton had given me.

"I didn't say that," he clarified. "The old court house had a fire about ten years ago and all the records were destroyed."

"Oh, so if what I heard is true about him, the incident must have happened before then. Does the state keep records, or how about the jails and prisons?" I pursued.

"Yeah, they all do, but this is the end of the line for me—there's too much red tape to go through to check elsewhere."

"Did you ask Brett about the auction goods?"

"Not yet. It's not a priority. We're tracking down other leads for now."

I was glad he hadn't followed up on the information I had given him because Brett would have instantly known I had tipped the cops off about the display case and contents.

"Carole was keeping track of items Ken bought at the auctions," I told him impetuously to assuage some of my guilt over having taken her iPad.

"How do you know that?"

"She told me about it," I fibbed. "I just remembered it."

"All right, Miss Sherlock, why was she tracking items Ken purchased?"

"I think she thought there was something funny about the prices he paid for the items," I answered vaguely. I wanted to tell him she also followed Traci's purchases, but couldn't think of a way to do it without divulging my secret source of data.

"How the hell can there be something wrong with what he paid at an auction?"

"I don't know, but there had to be a reason she said what she told me."

"You've got a screw loose. You know that?"

"All right. Believe what you want to, Lieutenant Corso, but I know I'm onto something," I said and disconnected. It was obvious Jake was feeling the strain. Every time I talked with him, he seemed more irritable.

Hickory Grove had its share of crime, but nothing to match the big city. An unsolved murder in Chicago was de rigueur, but in this sleepy burg such news made front page news for days. Annie was absolutely right in her earlier assessment of events. If the murder victim wasn't arrested soon, there'd be a major shakeup in town from the Mayor on down and that possibly included Jake, too. Suddenly, I felt sorry for him. I picked up my phone again and hit the last received number.

"Jake, this is Nikki. I've been thinking—" There was that audible groan again. "I know working on these murders has consumed you. Why don't you come over for dinner tonight? I promise not to talk about the case."

He didn't respond to my offer. "Jake, are you there?"

"Yeah."

"Does that mean yes, you're there, or yes, you're accepting my invitation? Or does it mean yes, you're there, but you're thinking about accepting my invitation? Or—"

"Enough already, I'm accepting your invitation, but no talking about the murders," he snarled.

"You don't sound very thrilled about it."

"I'm pleased. I'm tickled. I'm happy as can be. All right?"

"Now you're being snotty. I think I'll retract my invitation."

"Look, I'm sorry, Nikki. I haven't had much sleep lately and when I don't get my eight hours, I get cranky. I'd very much like to have dinner at your place and forget about this case for a while. Does your offer still hold?" he asked with a strained tone of voice.

"I guess so," I said giving him some of his own medicine in return.

"That doesn't sound inviting," he remonstrated.

"Let's start over, shall we, at the point where we agree you're coming to dinner. What would you like to eat?"

"Anything—except sushi," he quickly qualified.

"What's wrong with sushi?"

"It's a long story and involves a murder case I was on in Chicago a few years back."

"I don't think I want to know," I said, as revolting possibilities raced through my mind. "What time do you get off tonight?"

"Five."

"Come by about six then, all right?"

"See you then, and thanks, Nikki," he added quietly.

"Hold the thanks until after dinner—what I don't know about cooking could fill a dozen cook books."

My pantry was depleted and I ruled out the leftover pizza sitting in the freezer from the other night. A glance at my kitchen clock told me I barely had time to shop and prepare dinner before Jake was due. Grabbing my purse and keys, I went to my car and drove to the nearest grocers. As I went up and down the grocery aisles, I considered what Jake most probably liked to eat. He definitely struck me as a meat eater, so I bought a filet for him and a package of chicken strips for me. I picked up a few produce items and a pastry in case Jake had a sweet tooth.

I headed for the check-out and spotted Cyndi with her son in tow. She was pushing a cartload of groceries out the door to the parking area. She didn't look missing to me—being out and about in public and doing normal chores.

I saw Cyndi too late for me to call to her, and other patrons had already queued up behind me in line. I could barely hold still while the cashier slowly scanned the woman's groceries in front of me. When the lady withdrew her checkbook from her purse, I groaned. *Now I'll never catch Cyndi in the parking lot.* The woman took forever to complete her transaction. *Hurry, hurry, hurry!*

My purchases were small, barely enough to fill one bag. I immediately paid using my phone after the cashier scanned my last item. Grabbing my groceries, I ran through the doors into the parking lot. Frantically searching left and right, up and down the parking lot aisles, I looked for Cyndi and her son. There was no sign of them. Crestfallen, I carried my groceries to my car and drove home.

Jake arrived right on the dot, six o'clock sharp. Somehow I knew he would be on time as he seemed the punctilious sort. He was still dressed in his work clothes, a suit, dark blue shirt and a red, silver and blue tie. His shirt and suit coat were wrinkled, and his countenance matched the wearisome look of his attire. His eyes were bloodshot, and it looked like he hadn't shaved for two days. I found his somewhat disheveled appearance sexy. He appeared more vulnerable compared to his usual reserved rigidity.

"Hungry?" I asked after he followed me into the kitchen where I checked on the fresh green beans I set to steaming on the stove top.

"Yeah, and tired. You'll have to excuse my appearance, Nikki, but I didn't have time to wash up. A late call came in and I came here straight from work."

"Take your coat and tie off and make yourself comfortable while I check on the grill. There's beer and wine in the refrigerator, help yourself. And the bathroom's down the hall."

Jake was sipping a bottle of Guinness when I returned to the kitchen. I was right to figure him a Guinness drinker. "Do you want a glass?"

"No, I'm good."

Inky and Dinky made their appearance and smelled every inch of Jake's pants legs. Dinky jumped up onto his lap and I quickly rushed over to set her down. "Sorry."

"It's okay. She probably smells my cat."

"You have a cat?" I asked in amazement. "Somehow I can't picture you having a pet."

"I like animals; especially cats. They're low maintenance and work out well with my schedule."

"I'll give them some food so they don't bother us when we eat. It'll only be a few more minutes." After Inky and Dinky set to their meal, I laid out place settings and put a bowl of fresh salad on the table topped with olives and Mr. Campezi's cucumbers and tomatoes.

"Can I help you?"

"Sure, there's a bottle of white wine in the refrigerator. The opener is in the drawer by the sink. You can pour me a glass," I said and stepped out the backdoor to check on the grill again.

I was pleased with how the meal turned out since I hadn't cooked much after my divorce. Jake devoured every morsel, so it wasn't necessary for me to ask how he liked it. While we ate, he pleasantly surprised me by telling me about the time he had lived in Ireland for a year after he graduated from college. We discovered we had a lot to talk about, as being part Irish I had always wanted to visit the home of my ancestors.

After dinner, I invited him to sit in the living room and poured out two small snifters of Benedictine. Inky and Dinky were showing off in front of Jake, running around, jumping on the furniture, and taking turns chasing each other when I walked into the living room with our drinks. They seemed inordinately happy with having him for company.

Jake eyed the glass I held out to him warily, and asked, "What is it?"

"Benedictine—a liqueur. Everyone thought the Benedictine monks invented it, but now it's attributed to a Frenchman from the 1800s who supposedly stumbled upon their old recipe. The ingredients are a closely guarded secret. Only three people besides me know it."

"You?" he asked doubtfully.

"Yeah, I could tell you what it is, but I'd have to kill you afterwards," I said with a grin.

"Ohh, did I fall for that one," he grimaced and examined his glass. He sniffed it and took a small taste. "Hey, that's not bad," he exclaimed and took a bigger sip.

"I have a passion for liqueurs and like to share them with others when I can. They're much more interesting than most alcoholic beverages. Liqueurs are culturally tied to the roots of the people who make and predominantly drink them—and their local ingredients. Except for the newer commercial ones; I stay away from those out of principal."

"Yeah, I can see how that would be," he said and swallowed the last of his drink.

"Unfortunately, good liqueurs tend to be pretty expensive, not something that goes down well with a starving artist. Would you like some more?"

"No, but I'll have another Guinness."

"Help yourself—there's also a pastry in the white bag in the fridge if you feel like something sweet—I can make coffee if you want a cup of java instead."

"No thanks, I'll stick with the Guinness and check out the sweet treat."

As Jake went to the refrigerator, the doorbell rang. I peeked through the side window and eyed Richard standing on the stoop. *He always did have perfect timing—perfectly bad.* I debated whether or not to greet him. Finally, I decided to just find out what he wanted and send him on his way as fast as possible.

"What are you doing here?" I asked, after opening the front door.

"Can I come in and talk to you for a minute?"

"No, now's not a good time. I have company."

"Something sure smells good."

"What do you want, Richard? I'm busy."

"I stopped by to tell you I've reconsidered your offer for the table. I'll take four hundred, even though it's highway robbery."

"I've reconsidered, too, and I've decided I'm not interested in it anymore."

The initial shock at my statement wore off his face quickly, and he objected, "We had a deal."

"No, I said I'd consider paying four hundred. I considered it and decided I don't want it," I corrected him.

"But I passed up a deal for four hundred already," he pouted.

"Too bad for you, but I don't want anything to remind me of our marriage."

His smile changed into a smirk. "You always were a shit, Nicole."

"Why, because I don't worship at the great Richard's altar?"

"Is there a problem?" Jake asked coolly from behind me, munching on the blueberry tart. In my preoccupation with

Richard, I had forgotten all about Jake and hadn't heard him walk up behind me.

I turned toward Jake, and in so doing, purposefully let Richard have a good look at him. "No problem. The Dick is just leaving."

Richard's mouth fell open in surprise. I didn't know if his reaction stemmed from my statement or Jake's presence. Speechless, for a couple of moments, he mumbled something too low for me to hear, turned, and walked back to his car.

"Sorry about the intrusion, Jake."

"For a minute there, I wasn't sure if you were talking about him or me," he said grinning.

I laughed and said, "You're a dick, but not a *dick* if you know what I mean. At least I don't think you are."

"Thanks . . . I think," he said returning my laugh. "I presume he was the ex?"

"Score one for the detective. It's over. He's gone. Let's relax," I said and resumed my position on the sofa. "Hey, it almost slipped my mind. I know I said we wouldn't talk about the murders, but this isn't about the murders. At least I don't think it is."

He received my comment with a knowing scowl. "Go ahead. I knew it was too good to be true."

"I saw Cyndi and her son today while I shopped for groceries."

Jake immediately sat up on the edge of the sofa. "Are you sure?"

"Why do you always ask me if I'm sure about what I tell you?"

"Sorry. Force of habit. Where and when did you see her?"

"At the grocery store. She was pushing a cart full of groceries out the door when I stepped in line to check out. I searched for her in the parking lot after I paid, but there was no sign of her."

"What time was this?"

"About four-thirty or so." I saw his mental gears kick into high. "Darn it, you're thinking about the case again aren't you?"

"Occupational hazard," he acknowledged ruefully. He took a small notebook from his hip pocket and questioned me thoroughly, asking me to describe what she was wearing, if I had seen the vehicle she was driving, and a dozen more questions. Unfortunately, there was little I had to add to my sighting of Cyndi.

Jake abruptly stood up and said, "I better go to headquarters and report this."

"I don't understand. Since she isn't missing, and she and her son are all right, what's there to report?"

He hesitated before he answered, "We think she's taken up with Kurt."

Stunned, I blurted, "Cyndi with Kurt? Cyndi Comings?"

"Yeah, seems she's his latest love conquest. We discovered he frequents a joint up in Fox Lake. It's his little love nest where he takes all his girlfriends. The bartender positively identified Cyndi when we showed him her picture and told us she'd been coming in with lover-boy over the past month."

"Unbelievable."

"That's not all," Jake continued in a weary voice. "I probably shouldn't tell you this, but your coworker has been up there with him, too."

"What?" I cried. "Not Denise Barrington?"

"Yeah."

"Unbelievable! Are you kidding? This is unreal! First, I find out she may have been married to Barry and now I discover she's involved with Carole's boyfriend."

"Did you say Denise was married to Barry? That wouldn't be Barry Dynel, Ken Lawton's partner?"

"Oops, I didn't mean to let that one out of the bag. I'm not positive they were married, it's just hearsay."

"Jaheeesus," he said in a long drawn-out manner. "Is everybody in this town related to each other?"

"That's small town living in a nutshell. You know what they say. Between Hickory Grove and Walnut Grove we're home to all the nuts."

"Ohh," Jake groaned in response to my witticism. "Are you sure Denise Barrington was married to Barry Dynel?"

"There you go again, questioning me."

"I'm sorry, dammit," he declared self-deprecatingly.

"No, I told you I wasn't sure. I just heard about it earlier today and I haven't had time to learn the truth. Hey, you can find out though, can't you?"

"I knew it," he cried in a plaintive voice. "Why me?" he asked looking upward in exasperation.

"That's what comes from being a dick," I replied smugly.

He fought hard, but finally gave in and laughed, shaking his head back and forth. "You're incorrigible, you know that?"

"Uh-huh," I confessed. "You've got to promise me you'll tell me what you find out. Denise is the biggest gossip in town. I'd love to have something on her to put her in her place."

"If she's the biggest, you must run a close second."

"Hey, I resent that. I'm nothing like her," I bellowed. "She's malicious and mean. All I'm trying to do is help you solve two murders."

"Don't be so sensitive. I didn't mean anything by it. Listen, I really gotta run," he said anxiously. He shocked me by stepping over to me, giving me a light kiss on the cheek. "Thanks for dinner. I had a real nice time, Nikki. The best in a long time."

"Me, too," I told him truthfully. He fetched his tie and coat from the back of the kitchen chair where he had left them, stooped to pet Inky and Dinky, and departed without another word. I felt where he kissed me and a warm glow suffused through my body. I liked Jake, but knew so little about him. And it was going to take a long time before I became seriously involved with another man. No way was I going to make the same mistake I had made with Richard.

Calling it a day, I cleaned up, slid into my pajamas, and lay down on my bed. The house was stuffy with leftover aromas from dinner. Opening the windows provided little relief from the warm summer night, not even the faintest breeze stirred the curtains. No two ways about it, I'd have to budget for an air conditioner before next summer.

I grabbed my iPad from my night table and set the alarm so I wouldn't oversleep. I needed to return some normalcy to my life, regardless of Annie's offer for me to take all the time off I needed. Reaching into the top drawer of my bedside table, I located the bag of crispy Cheetos I had purchased at the grocery store. While crinkling the plastic wrapping, I called out to Inky and Dinky. They galloped around the corner of the doorway and leapt onto the bed, meowing in anticipation.

"I should have named you Rocky after the flying squirrel," I said to Dinky as she climbed up on my chest and tried to stick her head into the open bag.

Dinky inhaled the bits of Cheetos I meted out while Inky primly savored each morsel. Three for Dinky, one for Inky, I counted. After a quarter of the bag had been devoured, I folded the top and returned it to my bedside drawer.

"That's all for tonight, girls," I announced, as I grabbed a mystery book by Nicolas D. Charles from my nightstand. He was a new author I hadn't known about until a friend turned me on to him. After reading the first short story in his book, I was hooked. Charles brought a fresh perspective to his detective fiction that could have been written during the pulp magazine era. In fact, the interwoven stories all took place back in the 1930s. The work was refreshingly entertaining, just what the doctor ordered.

Inky and Dinky were keyed-up after their treats. The pair raced around the bed, batting a small ball of yarn back and forth while I curled up on top of the duvet. "I wish I could just cocoon with you two and not interface with another soul—just read and read and read," I told my two playmates.

I read until eleven o'clock. Turning out the lights, Inky and Dinky jumped off the bed for their evening vigil. I lay thinking about Jake's earlier exclamation about everyone being related: Denise and Barry, Barry and Ken, Denise and Kurt, Kurt and Cyndi, and Kurt and Carole. What an entangled mess!

There were more facets to the people involved in this case than on the Hope Diamond. One thing seemed clear, though. I'd lay even money that Denise wasn't sick in the traditional sense. Knowing her grapevine, she probably had uncovered Kurt's dalliances with Cyndi.

It's my guess she's suffering from heartache after discovering Ken had taken it on the lam with his latest conquest.

Somehow the knowledge of Denise's past, cast her in a worse light than I had previously held her. If she had been married to Barry, she had kept it a secret from everyone who knew her—everyone except Carole since Carole had a copy of a photograph of the couple on her iPad.

"Oh my god," I exclaimed aloud. Denise ties everything together. She could have murdered Ken because he took Barry away from her years ago, and then killed Carole because she knew about her former marriage. Either that or Denise thought Carole was taking her man, Kurt, away from her. I could easily envisage Denise being very vindictive when it came to affairs of the heart—effortlessly committing murder in the throes of passion. But then I reined in my thinking and reminded myself she wasn't at the auction. I was letting my mind run off. Discovering the latest Hickory Grove entangled relationships had me imagining murderers behind every tree.

With what I knew about Denise's past, I had a mighty
sword to hold over her head to keep her from ever
spreading gossip about yours truly. With that comforting
thought, I drifted off to sleep to the soothing rhythmic
sounds of crickets chirping.

In my dream, I saw toy soldiers lining up to attack a
crystal palace that refracted bright sunlight into a myriad of
colors. Looking over the wall of the palace stood a figure
shrouded in black. The figure slowly turned towards me,
and I was paralyzed with fear to see Ken's face staring at
me—a silent scream on his lips. His face, contorted in pain,
was exactly how he had looked when I had stumbled upon
his body at the auction. I heard myself scream and awoke
with an anxious start—my body tense, and my hands
clutching the duvet as if I was holding on to it for dear life.

Inky leapt on the bed and sniffed my face. I told her
everything was all right in my most reassuring voice and
petted her until she bedded down by my side. Lying back, I
attempted to calm my mind and body according to what I
had learned in yoga class, concentrating on tensing and
releasing each body part starting with my feet, working my
way up, and ending with my facial muscles. My body
reluctantly released the tension built up from my dream as I
slowly began to relax.

I thought of other things besides the murder case, like the
work Brett was going to do on my bungalow. My mind
started to drift and cloud with thoughts of him. I felt sure he
was also tied to the mystery behind the murders in some
way. Tomorrow, I'd come right out and ask him about the
assault charge Burton had related to me. Glancing at the
clock on my bed stand, I saw it was half past midnight. I
had to get some sleep; I had to stop thinking about things.

I felt hot and sticky from the oppressive heat and needed
relief if I was to fall back asleep. Gathering up my bed
linens and pillows in my arms, I went to the screened-in
porch. Much cooler there, I spread the bedding out on the

floor to the delight of Inky and Dinky who thought I did so just for them. A sheet provided the only topping I required and I slowly began to drift off to sleep again.

No sooner had I fallen asleep, than I awoke to Inky hissing at the screen door. There was barely enough light for me to make out a form stealthily creeping up the walkway that led from the detached garage to the back of the house. The moon was to the figure's back, making identification impossible. And from my vantage point, I wasn't able to discern the person's size and shape accurately, nor to say if it was man or woman with any degree of certainty.

Reaching out an arm, I lifted Inky and Dinky into my arms and darted into the kitchen where I flipped on the lights. I frantically locked the inside porch door behind me after setting the girls down on the kitchen counter. I ran pell-mell through the house, clicking on every light I encountered, closing and locking all the windows I had carelessly left open after Jake's initial warning waned. When I peeked through the kitchen window curtain, my mysterious visitor was nowhere in sight.

I nervously waited in the kitchen and listened intently for the slightest sound of an intruder. *Where were the police when I needed them?* Twenty minutes passed in anxious anticipation before I felt confident I had scared off the prowler. Nevertheless, I kept the windows locked and went back into my bedroom to join Inky and Dinky who had curled up in my usual sleeping spot on the bed. *All must be well now, since they're in here sleeping.* My nerves still a bit on edge, I read for a couple hours before I finally turned out the lights again. As I lay staring at the ceiling, an idea began to form about the various players, particularly Cyndi.

Chapter Fourteen

Wednesday

When I awoke to the beeping alarm of my iPad, I was sticky, frazzled, and drained. I thought about making a hot cup of coffee, but dismissed the idea. The last thing I needed was caffeine and something hot held little appeal. As I bathed, I debated whether I should ask Annie if I could stay at her house again. After feeding the kitties, I made oatmeal with my usual dollop of peanut butter and sat at the kitchen table with my iPad reading the news.

All but two columns of front page news were devoted to the two murders. The police said they believed the two murders were linked on the basis of the coroner's report. The stab wounds were caused by similar sharp instruments according to the autopsy findings. What I found significant was what the police didn't say—that both victims were killed by the same individual.

The mayor was fending off reporters with a bunch of political-speak. Already a couple of the town's council members were calling for the Police Chief's resignation—both councilmen known to have political ambitions. Tensions were reaching a boiling point. Soon the councilmen would be openly calling for the mayor's head to be placed on the chopping block. How short-sighted, I mused. Ensuing grudges were going to run deep—long after the murders were cleared up one way or the other.

Reading the next article, the reporter's lead-in line was: *Will there be three deaths before this murder rampage is over?* The catchy title was followed by references to how Traci had reported she had placed three daggers in her car and all three had gone missing. The reporter interviewed a number of police personnel, and Lieutenant Corso was quoted as saying the investigation was progressing accordingly and the police were chasing down a promising new lead. *Is that the information I told Jake last night about Cyndi. If not, what was the new lead?*

The weather forecast foretold of another hot humid day, with the temperature returning to the upper-nineties. I slipped on a light, bright flowery summer dress and a pair of open-toed sandals. After I fixed up my face, and refreshed the kitties' water with some ice cubes, I locked up and walked to the garage. I looked, but I could see no evidence of last night's prowler. The neighborhood boy had cut my lawn recently, leaving the grass too short for anyone but a trained tracker to identify any footprints, especially since this latest heat wave had burnt most of my lawn to a crisp bristly tan carpet.

Cautiously, I opened the garage door and looked inside. After assuring myself the killer wasn't hiding behind my car or in the back seat, I climbed in and drove to Brett's. I wanted to clear the air with him once and for all before I reported for work. All the stress and strain I caused myself by worrying about whether he was involved in the murders was too much a weight for me to carry, on top of everything else I had experienced as of late.

Brett struck me as an early riser, so I figured to catch him early in the morning. I wasn't disappointed. Machine noises emanated from inside his workshop as my sandals rhythmically flip-flopped on the pathway leading to its open door. I knocked on the door frame, but he didn't hear me, so I stepped inside and walked up to him. He was drilling holes into a piece of dark walnut wood as I stepped around in front of him and shouted my greeting.

He looked up, turned the drill off and said, "This is becoming a regular occasion, Nikki. Maybe we should set up a meeting time. What's up?" he asked with a twinkle in his eye.

"Brett, I have a problem and I need to talk to you."

"Sounds serious," he said studying my face. "Let's go inside and I'll make us a cup of coffee."

I accepted his offer and followed as he led the way through the back entry of his house. I sat at his small kitchen table while he brewed us coffee. In a few seconds, he set a steaming mug of java in front of me and took a seat across from me. "What's on your mind?"

"It's personal, but I'd feel much better clearing the air if I'm going to enlist your services for my house and business," I said trying unsuccessfully to hide my anxiousness.

He listened intently to my preamble, his eyes riveted to mine. "Okay, shoot," he said tersely.

"Someone, who I trust implicitly, informed me that you had been arrested for assault with a deadly weapon—a knife—a number of years ago. And . . . well . . . with the recent murders, I can't help but think of the coincidence of it all. I mean, you were at the auction and you do have one of the cases from the auction in your shop. Plus, you were rather evasive when I asked you about the case, and—"

"That's enough," he shouted brusquely lifting his hands from the table top, palms toward me. He was clearly upset.

His violent reaction was out of character from the mild mannered man I thought I knew, and I was taken aback. Sitting rigidly, in readiness to leave, I changed my mind when he said, "Sorry, I didn't mean to be rude. You hit on the one thing I'm sensitive about." Silence ensued. His face went through a myriad of contortions as he appeared to wrestle with how to address my concerns. After a while, some of the tension left his face and he spoke quietly, "I know how hard it must have been for you to come here, Nikki. You took quite a risk, didn't you?"

"Did I? I'm glad you see my side. I'm sorry to dump this on you, but if we're going to do business going forward, I need to trust you implicitly. I already know you're a brilliant craftsman, but I don't really know who you are otherwise." I eased back in my chair, not realizing how tense I had been—perched on the chair's edge—my entire body poised to flee at the slightest provocation.

"I'd want to know what happened if I was in your position, too. I'll tell you, but it's for your ears only and I never want to hear about it again after this," he said sternly.

"Agreed."

"I was building a house for a well-to-do couple. I won't name names. Anyway, the wife was a drinker. One day, while I was working on their mantelpiece, she got drunk and came on to me. I was fending off her advances when her husband arrived at the building site. To hide the truth from her husband, she lied and made up a story that I had tried to attack her. He believed her and came at me with one of my wood carving knives. We fought. I managed to get the knife away from him, but not before he accidentally cut his arm. His wife called the police and had me arrested. I was held in jail for two days before her husband dropped the charges against me. I think he knew his wife had lied, but it took him a while to face the truth. They eventually divorced, but that's neither here nor there. After I was released, I moved away because it's a small town and you know how people talk in a small town," he said giving me a knowing look.

My face flushed under his intense scrutiny. "It wasn't like that, Brett. I didn't hear anything about you through the grapevine." I believed him and felt foolish for confronting him with the injustice from his past.

"Oh no? Then how did it surface? It's been over ten years. I should have known better than to think enough time had passed for people to forget."

"You can blame me. I asked a trusted friend for a character reference on you. Like I said, I don't know you as a person. The person I asked isn't a gossip. I'll pass the facts along and you have my word it will go no further."

Brett gave me a skeptical look. "I doubt that."

"One thing in your favor is that all the police records went up in flames years ago," I said consolingly.

"Yeah, but people's memories didn't."

"True, but with these murders headlining the news, I doubt anyone will be talking about your past. Like I said, it only came up because I sought out a reference."

"That's a rather backhanded way of looking at things."

"I suppose it is, but it's true. People latch onto the latest sensationalisms. And speaking of the murders, I might as well jump into the fire all the way. What's the story behind the showcase and the auction items in your workshop?"

"What makes you think there's a story?"

"It's written all over your face."

A small grin crossed his countenance. "All right, Ms. Gumshoe, or should I call you Ms. Nosy Parker? I didn't want to say anything, but you've forced my hand. Carole Winker dropped off the showcase and asked me to hold everything for her. She's been a good customer, so I did as she asked without further explanation, but it did seem a bit out of the ordinary to leave the case with everything inside. After the murders, I didn't want anyone to know I had her stuff until the police caught the murderer. I was afraid if the police found out, they'd trace things back to Carole and that auction, and then they'd go digging into my past. If they put two and two together with that old assault charge, what do you think they'd come up with?"

"But you said those charges were dropped."

"Do you really think that would matter to them?"

"N-no, I suppose I'd think the same thing if I were in your shoes."

He gave me a self-assured nod of his head. "Exactly. Are you satisfied now?"

"Yeah. Thanks, Brett, for being so understanding. This conversation never need come up again as far as I'm concerned either. Are we still friends?" I asked sheepishly.

"Sure. Do you still want me to work on your house?"

"Most-assuredly," I said and held out my hand. "Friends?"

"Friends," he replied shaking my hand with a smile. "You know, in a strange way I'm glad you brought that incident up. I've never talked to anyone about it in all these years. Feels like a weight has finally been lifted off me by telling my side of the story."

"No charge for an initial consultation," I said with a smile. "I think it's admirable of you to return to Hickory Grove. And I know the nature of small towns only too well. Can you imagine the backlash I'm going to be subjected to? For years, people will point to me and tell their friends how I was the one who found the murder victims—and that will be the good side. The downside will be a lot of them will probably think I had something to do with the murders just because I was there."

"Yeah, to tell the truth I had no intention of ever returning here, but the D.A. called me about a year after the incident and apologized. He found out the truth and told me he cleared the charge from the books."

"That was good of him."

"Maybe, but I don't think he was being altruistic. He had political aspirations and probably wanted to clean up his office. Like you said, it's a small town and he didn't want to get blindsided by his opponent digging into the past and bringing a mistake to light."

"Still, it took a lot of inner fortitude for you to come back."

"I suppose," he acquiesced. "I thought about it for a long time. I finally figured it would be too much like admitting defeat to not come back. Sometimes I wonder if I made the right decision."

"Understandable," I empathized. "You have a good way of looking at it. I'll have to remember that when my going gets tough. I have one suggestion for you, though. Don't you think you should hide Carole's stuff?"

"Absolutely not!" he replied stridently. "That would be all I'd need. If the police caught wind that I had some of Carole's stuff here, they'd think I was guilty for sure if they found it hidden. If they discovered I concealed anything that might be connected to the murders, my picture would be on their wanted posters before you could say 'post office'."

True. And then I remembered the police already knew about the glass case and enclosed items because I had told Jake about them. I could feel blood rush to my face in embarrassment over my indiscretion.

Boy, am I going to feel like a heel if Jake follows up on the information I had told him. If he does investigate it, I will have assuredly driven a figurative knife of my own into my brief friendship with Brett. I thanked Brett again for his indulgence and excused myself saying I was going to be late for work. *What kind of a mess have I gotten myself into?*

Chapter Fifteen

I entered Annie's Attic through the back door and flipped on the light switches. I reversed the open/closed sign in the front window and turned on the cash register. Annie arrived twenty minutes later in a chipper mood. She and Burton had enjoyed a barbecue at the home of friends the previous evening. Not wanting to rain on her parade, I fought down an impulse to tell her about my midnight visitor. *No, it's time I fended for myself. Stood on my own two feet—not lean on her or anyone else.*

She ushered me to a back room where she stored surplus items until display space in the front opened up for them. Bending over one of the boxes stacked on the floor, she extracted a couple of glasses and held them to the light for my inspection. They shone a brilliant crystalline green.

"Wow! Those are gorgeous."

"They're Murano," she said proudly.

"How much did Barry charge you for those?"

She puffed out her chest and replied, "A hundred for the entire set."

"You're kidding!"

"Nope. They're easily worth five times that."

"You weren't kidding when you said he's come down on his prices."

"Wait till you see what else I bought, sweetie," she said aglow with excitement. She showed me a box of Steuben glassware, and I recognized a couple pieces as those purchased by Ken through Barry at the Peterson auction. Another box contained vintage toys—sock monkeys and other Americana— many of which were highly collectible. A third box contained antique firearms. By the time Annie finished showing me all the items she had purchased, I was overwhelmed.

"What a goldmine. I love everything, Annie, especially those old sock monkeys. They always make me smile."

"Barry is going to come by again today with more items. He's really clearing house. You should get in on the action."

"I wish I could, but my funds are tight right now. I'm contracting Brett to do some major work on my house."

"Tell you what I'll do, sweetie. The monkeys are yours— a gift from me. It's good to see you smile again. And if I buy anything today, consider it yours, too. You can pay me back when you have the money."

"I'll take the monkeys, thanks," I said, giving her a big hug. "And I really appreciate your offer, but I won't let you float me. I want to make it on my own, Annie. Besides, what would Denise say if she ever found out you didn't give her the same offer?"

"It'll be our little secret," she said conspiratorially, "and I'll give her an opportunity to purchase anything left after you've looked everything over. What do you think now?"

"I'll do it under one condition—that you charge me the going rate of interest and call it a loan."

"It's a deal," she agreed without hesitation. "Let me do the buying, though. That way Barry won't try to pull a fast one. You know, I think I intimidate him," she said with a boisterous laugh.

We were interrupted by a customer who sought assistance with items in one of the locked cases. Lucky for me, one of my oil paintings depicting a young boy painting a Mona Lisa was also of interest. The patron had a great sense of humor to match the mood I was in when I had painted the spoofy piece. Anyone who wore a long cape and a hat adorned with a feather on a smoldering August day had to be a bit quirky—perfect for the piece. The sale made my week and would help me pay back Annie for any of Barry's treasures I purchased.

With the afternoon came the good old Midwestern storm we had needed for weeks. With each thunderclap, the building shook and the tinkle of glassware echoed throughout the cavernous building. Rain was always good from the store's perspective as it invariably drove customers into the shop.

This day was no exception. A couple in their mid-30s inquired about my Art Deco living room display. They were dressed for success—her in yoga pants, stylish heels, and a chic top with a wide belt. His sports coat and slacks were a dark grey, offset by a black shirt and lighter gray tie. They exuded money. When I explained my settings and intention to include the credenza and side pieces in the set after it was refinished, they were keenly interested. After showing them the *Made in France* stamp on the back of the credenza they went off to a corner and excitedly discussed things in hushed tones. I left them alone so as not to seem overbearing, even though I was almost beside myself in anxious anticipation of a whole room ensemble sale.

The couple approached me as I was writing up a receipt for an elderly woman who had purchased a sweet pixie figurine for her daughter's coming birthday. I rang up the woman's sale and turned my attention to the pair.

"I'm Russell Marks and this is my partner, Beverly Jones. Our firm is in the Merchandise Mart," he said handing me his card. "We're impressed by what you're doing here and want to know if you'd be interested in doing business with us."

The Merchandise Mart was in the heart of Chicago, a monument to the past. When it opened in 1903 it was touted as the largest building in the world. Today, it hosted a number of high-end furniture wholesalers and retailers, amongst a myriad of other businesses.

I asked them what they had in mind, and Beverly told me they would be interested in buying my room ensembles for resale downtown. "You have a very keen artistic sense," she said. "It's perfect for what we want to offer our clients. What kind of a deal can you give us on the Kountry Kollectible Kitchen and the Art Deco Living Room?"

I warily thanked her for the compliment. *Are they going out of their way to be nice to me, buttering me up for a lowball offer?* I contemplated bringing Annie into the picture to negotiate a price for me and then decided against doing so, reminding myself that I was determined to make a go of it on my own. Besides, she was busy doing her own thing, cataloging and tagging the items she had purchased yesterday from Barry.

To my surprise, I managed to strike a deal in no time for the two room arrangements. Russell and Beverly were confident they could double their investment, and my share of the deal exceeded what I had hoped to collect for the ensembles. The only stipulation they insisted upon was that I arrange for delivery at my cost. I hoped Brett would be amenable in helping me out in that area since we had cleared the air between us. If not, I was certain Burton would pull a few strings for me and shanghai a couple of his cronies to load the items into a truck and deliver them for me. And the best part came when Russell promised future business if the initial rooms sold well. He left me a non-refundable check as money down to hold the ensembles before they left.

I was on cloud nine. If my staging areas became a hit at the Mart, the possibility of my work taking a new direction could derail Annie's plans for me to take ownership of the store. On the other hand, a lucrative tie-in to the city might lead to an expansion of my business here, whereby I could hire a helper and take on both outlets. *Nicole Carson Enterprises. Look out world, here I come!*

Time went by quickly as the downpour continued, and customers flocked into the store in droves. Business was so good I had a crisis on my hands. After committing two of my three furniture settings to Beverly and Russell's business, all that remained was a single setting and a scattering of small odd pieces. I needed to quickly replenish my inventory.

Annie taught me how important inventory turnover was in this business. If I wanted to make money, I needed to build up a surplus of goods for when my stock became depleted, like now. I knew, going forward, I needed to better manage both my money and inventory in order to succeed. I had to hand it to Annie for all the years she had made her business profitable. I was learning how difficult this business could be—more so than I ever imagined.

I was fretting over my situation when Barry entered the shop carrying three boxes. I told him Annie was in back and hustled him to her storage room. She remained with Barry for nearly two hours going through a total of ten boxes. When she eventually escorted him out from the back room, she gave me a big smile and wink indicating success. *Yes!* And Barry seemed pleased with his dealings with Annie as well. He smiled broadly at me and said, "Your boss drives a hard bargain."

"Someday I hope I'm half as good as she," I replied. Deciding to jump in with both feet with what was on my mind since I had seen that photo of him and Denise, I lowered my voice and asked, "Barry, can I ask you a personal question?"

From the look on his face, I thought he took offense to my prelude and I was going to retract my statement, but he stoically replied, "That depends on the question."

"Fair enough, after all, it's none of my business." Since I didn't know how to ask without seeming to pry, and I wasn't one to pussyfoot, I decided to just blurt it out like I did with Brett, just put it on the table, "Were you and Denise ever married?"

A number of emotions crossed his face ranging from fear to chagrin to resignation before he tiredly responded, "Yes, a very long time ago."

"Before you met Ken," I offered in an attempt to stay the awkwardness surrounding what was probably the time-frame of when he accepted the fact he was gay.

He gave me a small contrite frown. "Uh-huh."

"Don't worry. I won't tell anybody—"

"Worry? I'm not worried. What would I be worried about?" he extoled loudly. "Who told you about Denise and me?"

His sudden outburst shocked me. "C-C-Carole," I volunteered and immediately regretted it.

Barry gave me a peculiar look. "That figures."

I didn't know what to say. I think he interpreted my silence as meaningful in some unintentional way because he abruptly turned and marched out the door.

"What's with him? What did you say to him, Nikki? I hope you didn't piss him off—he wants to bring in another load of goods tomorrow," Annie said coming over to the counter.

"I asked him about his marriage to Denise."

"You did what? You're kidding? What did he say?" she asked with eyes intently ablaze.

"He said they had been married a long time ago."

"I'll be damned," she said with a slap of her thigh. "Doesn't that beat all?"

"There's more, too. Denise was seeing Kurt who dumped her for Cyndi Comings."

"Holy shit," she blustered. A knowing look came into her eyes and she burst out, "So that's why she's been calling in sick. She's sick all right—love sick."

"Yeah, that's what I figure, too."

"When I asked if she could come in tomorrow, she told me she's been running a fever. What she didn't tell me was that the fever was in her pants. That gal sure gets around."

"And spreads it around."

Annie guffawed—one of her big boisterous laughs. "You can say that again, sweetie."

We shared a couple more laughs before she enthusiastically ushered me to the storage room to show me the purchases she had made on my behalf. My wishes were granted ten-fold as she withdrew piece after piece from the boxes—everything from jewelry to a case of wine. I wanted to buy all of it and tried not to feel guilty about Denise not getting any of it.

"The wine's for Burton, though," Annie explained. "Sorry, but burgundy is his favorite."

"I understand," I said, and hesitantly asked, "Was Barry selling as reasonably today?"

"Even more so. Let me go add everything up and I'll tell you exactly how much you owe. He said he's bringing twice as many items in tomorrow. What say we split what he sells tomorrow? With what he brings in tomorrow and what I bought already, I may not need to purchase goods until the New Year."

"It works for me," I automatically responded before a twinge of buyer's remorse hit me, followed by fear. *Would he bring in the box containing the dagger I had planted in his garage?* I shrugged off my discomfiture. Why worry about what I couldn't control.

"He's really opening up since Ken's death. It'll be interesting to see what he ends up doing with the store. It's funny, isn't it?" Annie proffered. "I can't attest to Ken and Barry's personal relationship, but from all outward appearances, Ken made all the business decisions. Of course, it takes two to tango, but now that Ken is gone, Barry seems like a whole new person. He told me how he's implementing some plans for the store he must have worked out prior to Ken's death. I suspect he's wanted to make changes to their business for a long time, but Ken always held him back. He mentioned several times about his dislike over the number of storage units Ken had filled."

"So it would seem, to judge from this inventory liquidation."

"Barry told me they have six storage bins, a basement, and a garage full of stuff."

I involuntarily flinched with the mention of the garage, but Annie didn't appear to notice. "He doesn't even know what's in them all."

I know of one thing!

"Apparently, Ken often purchased things unbeknownst to him, and he was very secretive and never let Barry look at the books. Barry thinks it's going to take him weeks to sort through everything."

"Isn't it odd how two people can be intimate in a relationship, yet not share their finances with each other? I always find it so strange when couples function that way." Even Richard and I had been able to reach an equitable understanding in dealing with money matters, though I recalled a few times when he dipped into my pocketbook without telling me.

Annie agreed, and we exchanged our knowledge of partners who kept separate finances before she continued to catalog and tag the items she had just procured. If tomorrow's items were anything like Barry's last two hauls, Annie and I stood to make a very healthy profit over the next couple of months. All the items were top drawer. Ken had a very discerning eye.

I waited for Annie to do her accounting, anxious to price and display some pieces for immediate sale. Closing time approached, so I locked up shop and counted the cash. It had been a really good day for the store—the best since the murders. When I figured in my anticipated sale to Beverly and Russell, it was by far my best day.

"I spent $2,735 of your money, honey," Annie announced, tapping the eraser end of her pencil on the sheet of paper in front of her.

I was elated. The total was far less than I thought it would be. "That's fantastic, Annie. How much do you think the items will fetch?"

"Easily four to five times what you paid for them," she boasted.

"Wow! Now I know why Burton calls you 'Eagle-eye Annie.' The timing couldn't be better. I met a couple today who want to buy two of my stagings. If all goes well, I'll be able to pay you back next month."

"That's fantastic, sweetie. I told you, you have a natural knack for the business."

"I'm starting to believe it myself," I said with bolstered spirits.

Annie stayed to finish her paperwork while I turned off the lights in the rooms and flipped the door sign to 'closed.'

The rain was coming down in a steady drizzle when I opened the back door and dashed to my SUV. I went on automatic pilot mode as I drove home—all excited about my business prospects. It wasn't until I was half way there I realized I was driving to my old homestead again.

Taking a left, I turned onto a rarely used gravel road that ran adjacent to a farmer's field in order to cross over to my neighborhood. As I approached the intersection, I waited for traffic to clear before turning onto Campezi Lane. After driving a couple blocks, I spotted a myriad of blue and red flashing lights ahead. Two police cars were parked in front of my house and I spied another squad car parked in the alleyway by my garage.

Chapter Sixteen

Jake hustled over to me as I climbed out of my car. "Sorry to have to do this, Nikki, but an anonymous tip came into the station house this afternoon saying the murder weapon is in your house. We have to follow up every lead. Do you want to see the search warrant?"

"Murder weapon in my house! Are you kidding me?" I shouted in an outraged voice. *Maybe I'm not a bad actress after all.* "Somebody's trying to set me up. Was it a man or a woman?"

"We don't know. The caller disguised their voice."

Waving my hand insouciantly, I replied, "Have at it." My nonchalance took Jake by surprise. Little did he know how right the tipster had been. *So, I am right about the murderer planting the weapon in my basement. But who is it?*

I unlocked the back door and waved Jake and two other officers inside after making sure Inky and Dinky didn't escape. "Do what you have to do. Just make sure you don't let my cats out," I ordered. "Is it all right if I go out for a bite to eat?"

"Better not, Ms. Carson," Jake replied business-like in the presence of the other officers.

'Ms. Carson,' indeed! Okay, if that's the way he wants it, fine by me. With a shrug, I put the kitties in the powder room where their cat box was and closed the door. I went to the kitchen while Jake supervised his co-workers in their methodical and thorough search of my humble premises. As I sat at the kitchen table and nibbled on a few of Mr. Campezi's vegetables, I started to think things over. The more I thought about everything—from the search warrant to the squad cars with their lights going full tilt—the more agitated I became. With each passing minute, my outrage increased.

I heard Jake scold one of the cops for handling my goods roughly. He ordered them to leave everything as they found it. His efforts did little to assuage my anger. In thirty minutes they finished searching my living quarters, and proceeded to the basement. I silently wished them luck in searching through the mess downstairs. Two hours later, they trod heavily upstairs with dirty clothes and exhausted countenances. Jake told the pair to search the garage next, and came into the kitchen.

"Sorry about the intrusion, Nikki."

"You're damned right you are," I lashed out. "What'll my neighbors think? What's the idea of the squads' flashing a light show?"

My vehemence set him on his heels. "The boys got a little overzealous. It's their first murder case," he explained apologetically.

"Yeah? Well that doesn't excuse you, does it?" I said, trembling with indignation as I stood up, and pointedly stabbing him in the chest with my finger.

"Okay, okay," he cried holding up his hands. "You win. I was wrong. Feel better?"

"I'll feel better when you and your stooges get the hell off my property," I yelled.

"What the hell's gotten into you?"

I began to give him a piece of my mind, but stopped short, instead saying, "Just get the hell out of here, will you?" I half-turned so he couldn't see the tears welling in my eyes.

Thankfully, his cell phone rang, giving me time to compose myself. After answering the call, he looked at me, and said, "Repeat that."

The party at the other end said something in return and his face flushed a deep red. He held the phone away from his ear and said, "Cyndi Comings is at the station house. She's asking for you."

"Me? What does she want me for?"

"How the hell do I know?" he fired back, giving me a dose of my own medicine.

Things sure come around quickly. "Somehow we always get off on the right foot, but never end that way," I remarked repentantly.

"Are you going to the station with me or not?"

"I'll follow you, *if* I can use my own car now, Lieutenant."

"All right then, let's go."

"Is that an order?"

"Take it however you want."

"Then I'll think about it."

"Hold on chief," he said red-faced into his phone. "Yeah, I'll tell her."

"The Police Chief requests your presence," he said loud enough for the chief to hear as he held his phone toward me. "Will you please honor us with your esteemed presence, Ms. Carson?"

"If you and your fellow Huns are through ransacking my home . . . or maybe you're not done and want to search me, too."

He put the phone back to his ear and said, "We'll be there in a few minutes, chief."

Whew, my bluff worked. I didn't know what I would have done if he had searched my purse and found Carole's iPad.

His fellow officers soon reported they had found nothing of interest after searching the garage. Jake told them to return to their duties, and wordlessly motioned for me to follow him.

At the station house, Jake led the familiar way to the office whose closed door had Chief of Police, Dwayne Andersen printed in gilt letters on frosted glass. He knocked, opened the door, and motioned me inside.

The chief looked up from some papers he was filling out and said, "Ah, Ms. Carson, please have a seat."

"I thought Cyndi Comings wanted to see me," I said suspiciously. "Was this a ruse to get me down here for further abuse?"

"No, I assure you we don't operate that way," Andersen said.

"Uh-huh," I replied dubiously and sat on the edge of a worn leather chair.

Jake stepped forward. "You'll have to excuse Ms. Carson. We arrived at her premises right before she did. It was quite a shock to her to find us there. We were following up on the anonymous caller's lead we received, and we just finished searching her property."

"Find anything?"

Jake shook his head and replied, "Clean as a whistle."

"Do you know why anybody would want to implicate you in these murders, Ms. Carson?"

"No. Do you?"

He didn't bother to answer my question. "Do you know why Ms. Comings has asked to see you?"

"Haven't the slightest."

"Officer Wilkins picked her up this afternoon for running a stop sign. When he asked her for identification, she became belligerent with him. Wilkins called the incident in, and after he tagged her he brought her in for questioning in connection with the murder case. She's refused to answer our questions. Instead, she's insisted we contact you. You have absolutely no idea why?"

"None," I answered laconically.

The fact he didn't like the situation was clearly written on his face. He drummed a pen on his desk, leaned his chair back, and stared at the ceiling in thought. Plopping his chair forward, he told Jake, "Take Ms. Carson and Ms. Comings into one of the back rooms," before he addressed me. "Need I tell you Ms. Carson that withholding evidence in a felony case is against the law?"

"What evidence?"

He ignored my question again. "Don't let her leave without reporting back to me," he ordered Jake. He was going to say more, but thought the better of it and summarily waved us out of his office.

Jake led me to a small meeting room at the rear of the building and told me to wait while he fetched Cyndi. A few seconds later he escorted Cyndi into the room. "When you're done, knock loudly on the door," he said to me and quietly left, locking the door with a loud click behind him.

"Thanks for coming, Nikki," Cyndi said dolefully.

Her blond hair was streaked from crying, her eyes red and swollen. Dark circles lined her face and her hands shook slightly as she grasped mine across the table.

"My goodness, Cyndi. What's going on?"

"I'm sorry I asked for you, but I had nobody else to turn to. The people I work with would have given me a hard time, and all my relatives live in California. You've always been so nice. You're the only person I feel I can talk to who won't judge me."

"Thanks for the vote of confidence."

"It's about Kurt," she unburdened. "I've been dating him for about a month now."

"Go on," I urged gently.

"I overheard him talking to someone on the phone about a week ago. He told the person to stick to their story or he was going to kill them."

"You heard him actually say the word, 'kill?'"

She nodded her head, "Uh-huh."

"So why tell me? Why not tell the cops."

"I can't, Nikki. I'm going to have his baby. That's the real reason I was short with you at the Peterson auction. The nurse had just called me with the lab results."

My jaw dropped in shock. When I looked up, desperation was written all over her face. "Oh, Cyndi," I declared in a long drawn out voice. I stood up, walked around the table and held her in a motherly embrace. I thought about the negligible difference in our ages, and the ludicrousness of the situation hit me.

"What am I going to do?" she wailed. "I love him, Nikki. I can't testify against a man I'm going to marry. I won't do it!"

"Let's hold on a minute and compose ourselves," I said compassionately. After a few minutes, Cyndi stopped sobbing and I returned to my seat. "First, you have a choice whether to have the baby or not."

With a horrified look, she asked, "You mean I should get an abortion?"

"I'd never give you advice on what to do with your baby, Cyndi. It's your decision and no one else's. I simply stated your options. Think of your child. If Kurt *is* a murderer, do you really want to have his baby?"

"Murderer? Kurt's not a murderer," she shouted.

"I'm sorry, I didn't say that well. What I meant to say is you need to think of what is best for you and your baby."

"You *are* saying I should get an abortion," she said accusingly.

Raising my voice, I rejoined, "No, I'm trying to help you sort out your life. You have choices. If you don't want my help, just say so and I'll leave."

"N-n-no. I know you mean well, but I can't get an abortion, no matter what."

"Has Kurt proposed to you?"

"Well, not exactly. But he's talked about getting married."

"Cyndi, before I came in here, the Police Chief reminded me that withholding evidence in a felony case is a very serious crime. Don't compound your problems by breaking the law. You have to tell the police what you know about Kurt, what you told me he said, and let things work out as they will." The implications of my advice hit home. "And so do I, otherwise I'll be committing a crime, too." I tried to hide the guilt I felt from giving her advice I hadn't followed myself, especially considering I had Carole's iPad with me, not to mention hiding one of the murder weapons in Barry's garage.

"But they'll arrest Kurt. He has a record and they'll dump everything on him even though he's innocent. He wouldn't hurt a fly."

"That's just an expression of speech, you really don't know what he did or what he's capable of—you've only known him for about a month. Only Kurt knows what he did or didn't do. If he hasn't done anything wrong, he has nothing to hide."

"Why do I have to tell them anything? They'll never know what Kurt told me if we don't say anything," she said belligerently, as if she had recently acquired some newfound brilliance.

"I just explained that," I said patiently. "You've confided something to me that may implicate Kurt in the murders. If I don't tell the police what you've told me, I could go to jail. I won't do that for anybody."

An ugly look suddenly transposed itself onto her face. She shouted venomously, "I thought you were my friend. I thought you'd understand."

"I understand a lot of things, including the law."

"I shouldn't have trusted you," she lashed out vehemently. "I confided in you and what do you do? You tell me to get an abortion and then rat us out to the cops."

"All right, we're done here," I said and stood up from the table.

Cyndi yelled a vindictive string of swear words at me that would have put a longshoreman to shame. I pounded on the door with all my might, and Jake opened it almost immediately. I stepped outside and he quickly shut the door behind me to Cyndi's shouts of enmity.

"You okay?"

"Yeah, I'm okay. Let's go talk to your boss."

Taking seats in the same chairs we had previously occupied, I cut to the quick. "I know you were listening in on the conversation, so let's spare any pretense. We know Carole must have been the individual Kurt was talking to and threatened to kill during the conversation Cyndi overheard. Carole probably found out about Kurt's tryst with Cyndi and out of vindication threatened to withdraw her alibi concerning his storage unit break-in."

Jake cocked an eyebrow at my foresight, but Chief Andersen looked surprised. "She reads mysteries," Jake told his boss as way of explanation.

"Cyndi's your problem now. I tried to help, and now she hates me. That's what I get for trying to play Good Samaritan. What's the old adage, 'no good deed shall go unpunished'?"

"Welcome to our world," Jake returned sourly. "Do you have any idea where Kurt might be hiding?"

"No, but from the cart of groceries I saw Cyndi rolling out to her car, I'd guess she was buying for her and Kurt. I remember seeing a case of beer in her cart and all I've ever known Cyndi to drink is wine."

Andersen gave me a discerning grin and said, "Thank you for your cooperation, Ms. Carson. Also, you have this department's formal apology for the way we conducted the search at your home. Rest assured we've taken our conduct into consideration and will be more discrete in future proceedings."

It wasn't much, but the Chief's apology did mollify much of my earlier resentment I had directed toward Jake. Smiling, I turned to Jake. "Sorry, I blew my top, but it was a helluva greeting to come home to. Friends?" I asked holding out my hand.

"Friends," he replied taking my hand, a bit embarrassed by my small show of affection in front of his boss.

"Why don't you swing by the house when you're done for the day—we can catch up," I offered. Then I considered how my statement must have sounded. My face flushed as I stammered, "I m-mean—well, you know—t-to talk about the investigation."

The chief looked at Jake with a quizzical grin and arched an eyebrow as if to ask, *you and Ms. Carson?*

Jake's ears reddened as he quickly replied, "Maybe tomorrow. I believe we have everything we need from you right now and it's probably going to be a long day with Ms. Comings. It may take us all night, but if she knows where Kurt Manners is, we're going to get it out of her."

They both stood up when I went to leave. Chief Andersen shook my hand and thanked me again for my cooperation.

The rain had lightened as I drove home. Inky and Dinky raced to the back door when they heard my key snick the lock. I was happy the earlier invasion of their territory didn't seem to faze them in the slightest. At least it had no long-lasting effect to judge by their frenzy over the salmon I dished out for them. I gave them each another tablespoonful exclaiming, "You two are eating me out of house and home," and stooped over to lovingly stroke each one's silky fur.

Watching the kitties devour their food made me hungry, too. Humbly, I looked at the dress I had hung in the kitchen for inspiration. It was of the size I used to wear before I married Richard and I was determined to fit into it again before summer was over—just three more weeks. It was going to be close. Grabbing a low-fat cheese stick, I sliced one of Mr. Campezi's tomatoes onto a plate, added a few raw baby carrots and retired to the living room. The tomato was sweetly delicious, so much better than store-bought. I made a mental note to thank Mr. Campezi again for the fresh vegetables. Sitting back on my sofa, I reviewed the day's events.

Lucky for me Jake and his co-workers hadn't searched my purse for the murder weapon because they would have found Carole's iPad. As soon as I took her iPad out of my purse, the nagging feeling returned to me that a vital clue lay within the data.

I went over all her notes and e-mails again with slow, methodical care. Finished, I then perused her pictures, studying all the details, settings, people, and events associated with each photo. If there was something I missed during my previous inspection, it again escaped my awareness. Nothing stood out, yet, I knew something of vital importance existed in her information.

Then I had an idea. The police undoubtedly searched the phone records associated with Carole. In doing so, they would have discovered the existence of her tablet, and henceforth, its nonexistence amongst the belongings at her house. Knowing it was missing, Jake had to have figured out that either the murderer or someone else had taken it— me.

Was the search of my premises really a way to gain entry into my home to search for Carole's missing iPad? Was the tip they received about the murder weapon only a pretense on the police department's part?

I've heard stories where they've set people up before. While deceit was a possibility, I ruled it out because no questions had arisen in connection with my iPad that was lying in the open at the time of their search while the dagger *had* been planted in my basement.

I know I should, but how can I safely return Carole's iPad? It's not like I can walk over, break into her house, and leave it where I had found it.

The police had undoubtedly scoured every inch of her house looking for clues. Even if I could surreptitiously gain entry into Carole's house, no matter where I left it, the police would know something funny had occurred. They would have even searched her car. I could make up some excuse to Jake about picking it up by mistake, thinking it was mine, and just now discovering my error. It sounded lame, but after my cooperation with them in regards to

Cyndi, he might let me skate with a slap on the hand. No, I couldn't risk it. Not in a small community where my name, reputation, and welfare were at stake.

There were no two ways about it, I'd keep the iPad and destroy it or return it to Carole's place after the case was solved. With renewed determination, I redoubled my efforts to discern anything I missed during my earlier checks. I felt it imperative that I solve the crimes to atone for taking Carole's iPad and disposing of the murder weapon, and to clear my own name.

By the time ten o'clock rolled around, I was mentally drained. Going around in circles wasn't getting me anywhere. I fed the kitties their last meal for the day after pulling one of their favorite toys, a string, around the sofa as they played, attempting to retrieve it from between and under the cushions. Every so often either Inky or Dinky managed to snag the elastic string between their teeth and I'd tug or pluck the string to animate it to their delight. They'd try to eliminate the string from coming loose by increasing their hold on it between their front paws. Eventually, they'd ease their grip, I'd pull the string loose, and we'd begin all over again. They never tired of the game.

Discomforted by my lack of finding answers, I changed into my jammies and stayed up for another hour and read. I lay awake a long time after I turned my bedside light off. I had finally fallen asleep, when I suddenly awoke with an inspiration. Excited, I picked up Carole's iPad from my side table and looked at her e-mails again. *How many times had I read Kurt's e-mail without paying attention to the time he had sent it?* My subconscious must have assimilated all the information I had previously examined, because my sudden hunch was right. Kurt had sent the message to Carole during the Peterson auction, only an hour or so before I discovered Ken's body.

Suddenly, everything began to fall into place. I knew I had the answers this time, maybe not all of them, but enough to feel confident I knew who had killed Ken. My heart raced as I considered everything I had learned regarding the various players in the murder drama. Now I had to work out how to tell Jake what I had discovered without implicating my own culpability in taking the iPad and hiding the murder weapon. I needn't have worried because my problem immediately took a back seat to a more pressing need.

Actually, Inky heard the noise before I did, but I had been so busy thinking about my revelation that I didn't take heed of her sudden animation. Maybe it was the way her body moved across the bedroom floor that caught my eye and made me take notice. Before she rounded the bedroom door, I saw her tail, twice its normal size, sticking out rigidly from her tensed body.

It wasn't until Dinky jumped off the bed, hissed, and slouched along the floor to follow Inky that I knew something was definitely amiss. That's when I heard a muffled thumping noise that filtered through the house. I immediately thought of the intruder I had previously seen outside and panicked. I grabbed my robe, made my way to the kitchen in the dark, fished my phone out of my purse, and shakily dialed 911.

"Someone is breaking into my house," I said as soon as a responder answered. Hastily rattling off my name and home address, I repeated that I needed help, hung up, and searched for a weapon. I thought of fetching a knife, but dismissed the idea as I remembered Jake telling me how attackers often turn weapons against their victims. Then too, I irrationally found the notion too repulsive based on the fact a dagger had been the murderer's choice of weapon in both slayings.

A quick glance out the kitchen window proved my suspicions correct. A dark shape, huddled over the cellar doors, was attempting to gain entry. I thanked my lucky stars Brett had installed the boards to prevent egress. The intruder, slight in build and dressed entirely in black, pulled and pulled on the handles until the rotting doors began to buckle from the strain. From the person's garb, I immediately thought of Traci North until the brittle snapping of wood breaking stirred me to action.

I quickly switched on the kitchen lights thinking if the intruder realized I was aware of their presence, he or she would be scared off, but to my stunned amazement, my action elicited the opposite effect. Instead of fleeing, the person worked more frantically at the doors. I watched in horrified fascination as the dark form jumped on the doors, bringing their full weight down on the weakened slats. The rotted wood gave way, and a few moments later the person flipped back one of the doors and disappeared down the cellar stairs into the basement.

The kitchen chair was still propped under the door knob where I had placed it to prevent the kitties from having access to the basement according to Brett's earlier suggestion. I desperately scanned the kitchen for a weapon and my eyes fell on a large bottle of olive oil sitting on the counter. Nearly full, its heft gave me a fleeting notion of satisfaction as I picked it up, listening intently towards the basement door. I positioned myself to the side of the door and waited, my heart beating furiously.

My intruder didn't waste time, and my heart leapt into my throat when I heard one of my mousetraps trip. *A critter bigger than a mouse is in my basement—a few silly mouse traps won't stop it. A bottle of olive oil won't either. What am I thinking? And now it's too late to find another weapon. Run! Run out the front door!* I thought and then an irrational boldness swept over me.

Footsteps sounded heavily on the wooden stairs leading up from the basement to the kitchen. Whoever it was, they were throwing caution to the wind, not caring to hide their presence in the least. I knew I was dead if my intruder had a gun, and in some weird twisted way during the next precious moments, I rationalized and accepted my life's short duration.

My resignation was fleeting, replaced by a growing anger. I became mad—fighting mad. From somewhere within, a voice spoke to me. It was my voice and I was reiterating what I had told Annie earlier, how I was determined to make it on my own. An inner strength flowed through me.

How dare someone enter my house and threaten me and my kitties!

Grasping the bottle of oil tighter, I waited, ready to defend my loved ones at all cost. I heard a low growl. Inky was standing alert by my feet, slouching low to the floor as if to leap on her prey. Dinky suddenly jumped down from the counter and huddled near Inky, her tail swishing back and forth in agitation.

"Shoo," I whispered to them, but they were not to be put off by my bidding. Sucking in my breath, I stood stock-still, trying not to give my position away. Suddenly, Inky hissed and flung herself at the door, shook herself off, and crouched low again, near me. I still remained motionless. I watched the door handle turn, and as the door slowly opened, I saw the chair propped under the doorknob skid a few inches back until its legs caught hold in a line of tile grout.

It's now or never. I tensed my body in readiness. An arm appeared through the opening in an attempt to remove the obstruction and I swung the bottle down on my invader's wrist as hard as I could. A man's voice howled in pain seconds before he heaved his body at the door and broke the chair into splinters. Amid more hisses and spitting from Inky, or maybe it was Dinky, the kitties ran helter-skelter, scared by the din. An arm shoved the door fully open and a body sidled around the door. I raised the bottle again and swung it at the intruder's form with all the force I could muster.

With a sickening crunch the bottle shattered against his collarbone, splattering oil everywhere. My invader's agonized scream echoed off the walls in the kitchen. I stood frozen in place, unable to move. He lurched towards me, holding his right arm to his side. Momentarily stunned, I stared at his sweat soaked, ashen face. Blinking rapidly, perspiration running down his forehead and nose, Barry looked at me with wild, desperate eyes.

He's insane! I took a step back and bumped into the counter. Time slowed to a crawl and I observed what ensued during the next few seconds as if I was another person—invisible and watching two people face each other in a bizarre struggle to the death.

"I have to do it, Nicole. You know I do. You know too much," he said almost apologetically as he closed the distance between us, his good hand reaching into his back pocket and withdrawing one of the daggers from the auction.

"The police know what I know, Barry, and they're on their way," I replied shakily.

"If the police know, then why did you put the box with the knife back in my garage?" he asked with a maniacal laugh.

"Because you put it in my basement to set me up," I said and moved a little to my left. "Why did you kill Ken?" I countered to keep him talking, while I desperately tried to think of some way out of my predicament.

He shifted to his right to cut off my means of escape around the counter. Cocking his head to one side, he peered at me curiously as if I had asked him why he walked upright. "I didn't kill Ken."

"But you did kill Carole."

"Of course, I killed Carole for killing Ken," he replied matter-of-factly and lunged at me.

The spilled olive oil probably saved my life. The foot he used as leverage slipped from under him and he fell forward, hard on his face. Seizing my moment of opportunity, I picked up a slat from the broken chair and hit him over the head for good measure. Then I jumped up and came down on his back with both feet, the breath escaping from his lungs with a loud whoosh. Without hesitating, I clamored over his prostrate body toward the front door.

I had the door open and was fumbling with the slide lock on the screen door. "The hell with it," I cried and hysterically kicked the screen out of the door. Pushing myself through the gaping hole, I raced down the front stairs in time to see a squad car, its lights swirling, lurch to a halt in front of me.

Jake jumped out of the car, gun in his right hand, and asked, "Are you okay?"

"Barry's inside with a knife. He murdered Carole," I rasped as I doubled over, fell to my knees on the front lawn, and tried to steady my nerves. Suddenly a wave of biliousness swept over me. I fought the nausea and began to tremble. Blood rushed from my head and I shook it vigorously to ward off unconsciousness, but to no avail. Blackness enveloped my vision and I collapsed on the sidewalk to the diminishing sound of sirens.

My eyesight returned slowly. A small window, blurry around the edges, grew larger until I took in the scene around me. If I thought my earlier visit by the police posed an extravagant light show, it was nothing compared to the multitude of town and county squads that now surrounded my house. An emergency medical staffer stared intently at equipment next to me. My upper arm felt uncomfortably tight and a quick glance revealed a pressure cuff. The EMT read my blood pressure while I lay prone on a stretcher— one of those trolley carts used to wheel patients in and out of ambulances.

Jake leaned over me with a concerned look. "How are you feeling?"

"I'm fine," I said and struggled to sit up.

"Ma'am, you need to lie down and keep still," the EMT told me. "You're suffering from shock."

"Do as the woman says," Jake seconded.

I felt lousy, my head ached, and the taste in my mouth defied description. "I'm fine, I tell you." I pushed myself into a sitting position, tightly wrapping the blanket around my pajamas an EMT had covered me with while I was unconscious.

"You need to lie down, ma'am. Shock is nothing to fool with. You might feel alright now, but later you can experience serious repercussions," the EMT said and gently tried to push me back.

Resisting her efforts, I said, "All I need is to brush my teeth, gargle, and take a couple aspirin," I declared resolutely. Shakily, I managed to climb off the trolley and unsteadily walk up the sidewalk to my house.

Jake grabbed my elbow to steady me. "Don't touch anything in the kitchen or living room, Nikki."

"Why? You didn't kill Barry, did you?"

"No, he gave himself up without a fight. A couple of officers took him to the hospital. We need to finish up gathering evidence. When you feel up to it, we'll go to the station."

"Yeah, only after I first answer a zillion questions," I replied with a wan smile. "I'll be ready to go after I wash up and get dressed."

"No rush, but the news hounds will be here soon."

As I brushed my teeth and rinsed the awful taste out of my mouth, a figure appeared in my bathroom doorway. It was Sergeant Reilly. "There's someone who insists on seeing you, Ms. Carson."

Actually, it was three someone's; Mr. Campezi, Annie, and Burton. They all wanted to know if I was alright. Jake immediately intervened on my behalf. Seems he had given Sergeant Reilly instructions to call Burton if any calls from me came into the station. Mr. Campezi, seeing all the flashing lights, was concerned for me and had run over, just before Burton and Annie arrived. Jake handled them all with ease, saying I was okay, but couldn't speak with anyone until the police did their questioning, and by the time they left the premises, the reporters had begun to arrive.

The street looked as though the carnival had come into town and was setting up for business in front of my house. Assorted vehicles were lined up and down the block. Jake must have read my mind because he said, "Hurry up. We can go out the back way and I'll have one of the men pick us up in the alleyway."

"No, my kitties. I can't leave my kitties," I said resolutely, thinking of my darlings huddled, frightened without me, under the bed or couch. "Can you station one of your men at the door to keep everyone outside?"

"Yeah, but the reporters won't give up from trying to get inside."

"All right, then give me a minute to put Inky and Dinky in their carriers and I'll bring them with me."

Jake helped me put reluctant Inky into her carrier after I had Dinky safely ensconced within hers. He carried Inky and I grabbed my pocketbook and Dinky as we scooted out the back. We had to dash the last twenty yards to the waiting squad car to avoid reporters who ran around the side of my house in hot pursuit.

At the station, we adjourned to the Chief's office and I resumed my old seat setting Inky and Dinky beside me on the floor. Resignedly, they accepted their temporary confinement and quietly curled up in their carriers for a nap. Chief Andersen greeted us and solicitously asked how I was feeling. After telling him I was fine, he said with a big satisfied smile, "He's confessed to killing Carole Winker and trying to kill you, Ms. Carson."

"That should make the D.A.'s job easier."

"Unless his lawyer pleads insanity—they usually do in crimes of passion that involve a loved one," he explained.

"Odd isn't it? Ken was an overbearing bully. He treated Barry like dirt in public. And yet Barry goes off his rocker when Ken is murdered."

"It isn't odd at all. It's commonplace," Jake averred. "More cops get hurt trying to break up domestic disturbances than you can shake a stick at. A wife reports her husband is beating her. We show up and when we try to subdue the husband, who's usually blotto, the wife goes after us with a gun, knife—you name it—whatever's handy."

"A bottle of oil," I chimed in.

He nodded his head in recognition of my defense weapon. "I witnessed it at least a hundred times when I worked for the city."

"Is Barry locked up?" I asked fretfully, looking about nervously, half expecting him to make an appearance at any moment.

"No, he's still at the hospital to fix his collarbone and a few ribs," Dwayne said.

"Yeah, I thought I broke something."

"Better that than your life," Jake said.

"Do you feel like talking, Ms. Carson?" Dwayne asked.

"Yeah, might as well. I don't think I'm going to get any sleep tonight. Can I get a cup of coffee?"

An officer brought in cups of coffee and I settled back. A heavy weariness enveloped me as all my pent up emotion slowly released its grip on my body. The coffee was scalding hot and tasted bitter, as if the pot had sat on a warmer for hours, which it probably had. "I'll make a fresh pot," Jake graciously offered when he saw me grimace after sipping some of the gooey brew.

The Chief and I waited until he returned with fresh coffee. I slipped my shoes off, curled my feet up under me in the chair, and obediently answered their questions.

Chief Andersen asked me to recite everything that had happened from the moment I had become aware of Barry breaking into my house. I began my monologue as a feeling of déjà vu swept over me.

"Did he say why he came to kill you?" Jake asked when I was finished.

"He said I knew too much."

"Do you?" Jake asked bluntly.

"I didn't, until earlier tonight. It was then I figured out what was going on, although I may be wrong. But everything fits."

"Tell us what you figured out, Ms. Carson," urged Dwayne.

"It all began with the auction, or auctions," I amended. Turning my attention toward Jake, I continued, "Remember when I told you I had seen Carole arguing with Ken, and that Barry was there, too?"

"Yeah," Jake acknowledged.

"Carole was hard up for money and I believe she and Kurt concocted a scheme involving Ken. We'll probably never know for certain whose idea it was originally. The three of them were in on it, but I don't know about Barry. Barry told my boss recently how Ken was very secretive in regards to their business dealings. Ken did all the bookkeeping and never allowed Barry to see the books. He kept a tight rein on their purse strings, too. But after Ken was killed I think Barry found out about what Ken had been up to."

"What was the scheme you're alluding to?" the chief asked impatiently.

"I'm getting to that," I replied, and glanced at Jake, a stifled grin on his face. He knew me well enough by now to know I had to do things my way, at my own pace. "I

216

checked with Woody, the auctioneer, about the Peterson auction where Ken was killed. Woody told me Ken performed appraiser duties for most of his auctions and was solely in charge of cataloging all the items during the appraisal process," I said, and sipped my coffee with self-satisfaction, relishing my momentary position of superiority over the two professionals. "He gave Ken free reign as Woody detested performing those tedious functions."

Dwayne gave me a frown and screwed up his forehead until it resembled an old wash board. He gave Jake a questioning look, but Jake didn't seem to notice. He was preoccupied in thought, fitting my information into his own logical pathways. Dwayne eventually broke the silence by saying, "Obviously, I'm missing something."

"Don't you see? Ken was in the perfect position to steal." I patiently explained, "Nobody would know if he omitted any of an estate's items from an appraisal catalogue. Woody wouldn't know since he gave Ken carte blanche for listing and appraising the items. Unless it was a large item or very expensive, the only people who might notice a discrepancy would be any surviving descendants or individuals named in the decease's will, someone extremely familiar with the estate property. I'm sure Ken was clever enough not to pull any hijinks in those instances. He knew when there were no surviving claimants, or if there were individuals bequeathed in the will who could check on whether or not certain items made it to auction. An auction like Clint Peterson's, a lifelong bachelor, would be a perfect target."

"I see," said Dwayne. "But how do Carole and Kurt tie into it?"

"Mind you, this is all speculation on my part, but when I saw Carole arguing with Ken, I think she was confronting him with cheating her and Kurt. I'm guessing they found out Ken was holding out on them. Remember the brooch that was by her dead body?"

"Yeah," Jake replied.

"When I saw it lying there I recalled thinking it was odd because I didn't remember Carole bidding on any jewelry at the auction. And I didn't think the piece had come up for bid. I think it was one of the pieces Ken had stolen—a piece he didn't report to Carole and Kurt. She may have showed it to Barry, or simply had it with her, when he showed up. Possibly she tried to explain to Barry what had occurred at the auction and showed him the brooch as proof to back up her claim."

"When she told what Ken was up to, Barry may have feared he would be drawn into the fray and lashed out at Carol."

"If Ken stole the brooch, how did it come to be in her possession?" Dwayne asked.

"My guess is Kurt retrieved it from Ken's storage shed when he broke into it. Or Carole may have been arguing about it with Ken when she killed him and she took it from him afterwards. Who knows? We won't know for sure unless Kurt knows and tells all, which isn't likely."

Dwayne gave me an expectant look. "You see, I think the three of them divided up the responsibility to sell the stolen goods and split the monies."

"And possibly Traci North," Jake added as much to himself as to the chief and me.

"Possibly," I agreed, "but I don't think so. If you remember, I told you how I saw her confront Ken and basically accuse him of stealing auction items from one of the cases. Her actions didn't speak of familiarity and it would have been a foolish move on her part if she was part of the theft ring to publicize the thefts in public. From what I observed of her, she's no fool. She had complained when Ken pulled a fast one at the auction by buying items added to those being auctioned after the bidding had begun. Remember?"

"Yeah," Jake reluctantly agreed.

"Plus, her behavior wasn't friendly toward Ken. Certainly not what you'd expect if they were business confederates. I think Carole suspected Traci might be involved in some way, though," I added thinking how Carole had tracked Traci's auction purchases along with those of Ken.

"Yeah, it fits," Jake said dourly.

"Ken, Carole, and Kurt probably agreed to split everything," I continued. "Somehow, Carole and Kurt became suspicious and thought Ken was not accounting for everything. No, scratch that—not revealing everything he stole. He was selling items on the side, on the sly. Carole and Kurt suspected the truth and Kurt broke into Ken's storage unit to find evidence to back up their suspicions— to find what stolen items he had hidden away."

Dwayne stared at me. "How do you know this?" he asked in disbelief.

"I sat down and reviewed everything I knew from the start of the Peterson auction up to the present. I was sure there was an explanation that tied all I knew together. I remembered something from a course in sociology I attended in college—what one of the theorists had said: 'All behavior is goal-oriented.' So I asked myself, what did the different individuals have to gain from their behavior?

"Let's start with Kurt. He wasn't accused of stealing anything from Ken's storage unit, only breaking into it. Why break into a unit if you don't want to steal something? Or, if he did steal something, why didn't Ken report what was stolen?"

"Makes sense, Chief," Jake said.

"But Ken reported the break-in," Dwayne objected. "Why did he do that if Kurt was his partner in crime?"

"To keep Kurt and Carole in check. Remember what Nikki, I mean, Ms. Carson said, Chief." Jake hastily amended. "Carole and Kurt were on to him, so Ken held a possible B&E charge over Kurt's head as a stalemate item."

"Uh-huh," I agreed. "Carole probably suspected Ken was also not accurately reporting what he sold items for—holding out money they were supposed to pool and split. She confronted him once on the first day of the Peterson auction as I told you. My suspicion is that Kurt communicated with Carole during Saturday, the second day of the auction, and informed her about what he had discovered in Ken's storage unit—evidence to prove Ken was cheating them. Carole confronted Ken again in the shed and ended up killing him—probably unintentionally during a heated confrontation."

"Except if Carole killed him, it was premeditated," asserted Andersen. "She had to steal the daggers from Traci North's car first."

"She stole the daggers but not necessarily for that reason, though. I'll get to that in a minute," I replied.

Jake didn't let my declaration stop his flow of logic. "If Barry didn't know what Ken was up to, he probably figured it out afterward."

"Right, because he would have gained access to Ken's books and storage units. Barry asked me a couple of times how well I knew Carol. I think he suspected what had been transpiring. Recently, Barry's been unloading items in our shop, selling them dirt cheap. He must have suspicioned they were stolen by Ken. And he was most interested in my relationship with Carole. Unawares, I slipped up and told him we were going to do some business together. I only meant I was considering using Carole's artwork in my room ensembles at Annie's Attic to help her out financially.

I also mentioned how Carole had asked about prices of certain items in the shop. Barry must have twisted my remarks around to his way of thinking to mean something different, possibly thinking I was involved in some way as well, and that's why he accused me of knowing too much. I also asked him if he had been married to Denise Barrington when he came to the store. He asked me from whom I had found that out, and unwittingly I again put my foot into my mouth by telling him I learned it from Carole. I'm sure he twisted that around in some warped way to come to the conclusions he did."

"What about Cyndi Comings? Was she involved?" Dwayne asked.

"Only as one of Kurt's love interests," Jake pitched in.

"One? How many did he have?" Dwayne asked in disbelief.

"At least three that we know of," Jake replied.

"Wait till my wife hears about this. She's always telling me how boring my job is and how our cases couldn't be any duller. Okay, so how does Traci North tie in?" he pursued.

Jake looked at me expectantly. "I'm not sure she does," I replied. "I suspect she's a shrewd business woman running a respectable shop. She certainly knew the worth of the daggers she bought. Unfortunately for her, they were used in the murders."

"That brings us back to my earlier question," Dwayne declared. "If Traci North won the auction for the daggers, how did Carole get one?"

"This is pure conjecture, again, but I think Carole stole the daggers because she discovered their true worth after Traci North had won them. Either that or she knew in advance what the daggers were worth, but lacked sufficient funds to buy them so she waited until they sold and seized the first opportunity that came along to steal them. I didn't know Carole well, but I find it hard to believe she had premeditated murder on her mind when she stole the daggers. I think she stole them for the money they would bring. Everybody knew Carole was hard up for money.

Being part of the theft ring, we know she was a thief, so it's not a stretch of imagination to figure she stole them from Traci North's car. The theft fits in with how North claimed they had been stolen. Carole must have had the daggers on her when she had her big blowout with Ken. In the heat of the moment, she used one to kill him. Maybe Ken strong-armed her and it was reflex. He had laid hands on her the first day of the auction. Who knows if she was defending herself from him or meant to kill him? It's now all water over the damn."

"And subsequently Barry confronted Carole. Knowing she had killed his partner, he used one of the daggers she had stolen to kill her—his way of enacting poetic justice." Jake added, nodding to himself. "But how did he obtain one?"

"Carole may have dropped them in the shed—maybe Ken accosted her and she reached in her purse and they spilled out. Or maybe taking them from North's car was part of their plan, and when she showed Ken she had them, they got into an argument about something and Carole struck. Who knows? Oh yeah, I forgot until tonight that I saw Barry rushing from the shed earlier, about the time of Ken's death. He may have even seen Carole stab Ken. If she had dropped the daggers, it would explain how he obtained one. I grant you it's a stretch, but I'm sure he got one from Carole somehow. Another possibility is that Carole had them in her studio at the time Barry broke in, or was let in, since there was no sign of a break-in. He saw them and in his deranged frame-of-mind used one to stab her and then kept it."

"Or maybe she tried to defend herself with one of the daggers and Barry wrestled it away from her—used it to kill her," Jake offered.

"Something like that, but it wasn't much of a fight to judge from her studio, and don't forget the brooch. The brooch has to fit in somehow."

"Yeah,' Jake agreed. "They must have exchanged words about what went down between Ken and her and Kurt. That would explain why she had the brooch in her hand, because she was showing it to Barry as proof of Ken's thievery. And a guy can easily overcome a woman."

"Then again, Barry isn't exactly a brawny type," I returned. "Carole was stabbed from behind."

Jake gave me a nod. "You don't miss much do you?"

He should know the half of it. Ignoring his remark, I said with fingers crossed, "You'll probably find the third dagger somewhere in Barry's stuff."

Then the chilling thought occurred to me. *What if Barry tells them about planting the dagger at my house that he used to kill Carole? No use worrying about maybes. Who is going to believe a deranged murderer over sweet little ol' me?*

"So Barry was the one who called in and reported the murder weapon at your house," Jake said, as if reading my mind. "Why did he do that if he knew the dagger wasn't there?"

"Got me. I learned long ago not to attempt to figure out how crazy people think," I replied nonchalantly as the hairs on the back of my neck tingled. "Possibly he decided he needed a fall guy, or woman in this instance, and intended to plant the dagger at my house, but never had the opportunity. I forgot to mention that I disturbed a prowler the other night. He ran off when I turned the lights on so I didn't report it. I bet it was Barry."

Jake gave me one of his scrutinizing looks. I simply returned his look with one of Dinky's tricks, giving him my best big-eyed innocent shrug.

The remaining early hours of the morning were filled with me giving another statement. As I walked out of the station, Jake stopped me and said, "It's a funny thing. We searched Carole's phone records and discovered she had an iPad, but it never turned up."

"That *is* odd."

"Yeah, isn't it? It wouldn't look too good if somebody walked off with it. Well, you take care, Nikki. Be seeing you around."

"You too," I said, and departed carrying Inky and Dinky nestled in their cases. In unison, they meowed in anticipation when I set the carriers on the back seat of the squad car for the ride home.

Chapter Seventeen

Thursday

Yesterday's rain glistened heavy in the trees as the sun rose. Annie was sitting up watching TV in my living room when I arrived home. She doted over me like an old mother hen, tucked me in, and told me she was determined to stay with me the rest of the day to handle things as they arose. She insisted I take the rest of the week off while Burton tended to the shop. Feeling safer and more relaxed than I had felt since Ken's murder, I quickly dozed off into a deep slumber.

When I awoke, Annie brought in a tray of fresh croissants with strawberry preserves, coffee, and the latest edition of the paper. Emblazoned across the front page was the headline, *Police Capture Killer.* "Looks like the mayor and Anderson are going to keep their jobs," Annie proclaimed as she set the tray on my lap.

Jake, too.

She carried in a kitchen chair, and sat down by my bedside. "Burton said Barry was kept in the hospital for observation last night and released into police custody this morning. He's been charged with first degree homicide for killing Carole and another charge of attempted murder."

"Somehow I never envisioned Barry capable of murder. He was always so docile and submissive while Ken was alive. Did you have any idea Barry could be a murderer, Annie?"

"Are you kidding? No way," Annie cried. "But remember it was a crime of passion, sweetie."

"He didn't act like he was crazy, did he? I mean, look how he was when he brought the articles to sell into the shop. He was all business as usual."

"That brings up a rather unfortunate circumstance for us," she said. "The police have confiscated all the goods I purchased from Barry until they can determine whether they were stolen or not."

With a moan, I said, "Oh well, easy come, easy go. I suspect Barry sold them cheaply because he knew Ken had stolen them."

"Yeah, I should have known it was too good to be true," Annie replied mournfully. "Even Brett, your handyman, may have some stolen goods. Apparently he told the police this morning that Carole had dropped a glass showcase off at his place. Remember when you asked about his character? He sounds like a stand-up kind of guy to me. But whatever! Let's just hope not all of what we bought is stolen.

"Want to hear the best part, Nikki? Burton says Barry's attorney is already making overtures regarding an insanity defense for his client."

"Oh, great. Do you have any more good news?"

She grinned. "Jake stopped by around noontime to see how you were doing."

"Probably wants me to come to the station for more questioning."

"Uh-uh, sweetie," Annie disagreed with a twinkle in her eyes. "His concern for your well-being goes a bit beyond professionalism."

"Oh, I don't know, Annie. He's a nice guy, but we get on each other's nerves."

"Yeah, like I do with Burton," she said all-knowingly. "You'll grow on each other."

"I'm not ready for another relationship. I'm still getting used to being divorced."

She patted me on the arm. "All in good time, sweetie, all in good time. I'm going to leave you alone for a while and go out to dinner with my husband. I'll stop back later."

After she left, I reviewed the events of the past few days in my mind. *What a whirlwind of craziness. What would happen to Barry and Cyndi and Kurt? And what did my future hold?*

As I pondered the possibilities, Inky jumped into my lap and began to purr—her not-so-subtle hint for me to part with a piece of croissant sitting on my plate. Dinky stretched toward me for a piece, too, not wanting to be left out.

"You're right, girls," I told them. "Why worry?" *Let it go. Concentrate on today, tomorrow will take care of itself. After all, if I made it through confronting a killer and solving two murders, I can get through anything.* With renewed optimism, I felt confident I could make a go of it on my own. Well, maybe with a little help from good friends like Annie, Burton, and Mr. Campezi—and of course, my Inky and Dinky.

Epilogue

One month later . . .

As predicted, Barry's attorney entered a plea of insanity to the murder and attempted murder charges. The D.A, out to make a name for himself, knew the publicity to be had from the high profile case, so he was prepared to take the case to trial. No plea bargaining was offered. Burton told me the D.A. *had* offered Cyndi a deal for her testimony against Kurt, but she refused to cooperate. Instead, she pled guilty to a couple of lesser charges and received community service time and a year's probation for her misguided allegiance to her lover.

Kurt was picked up and held by the police about a week after Barry was apprehended, but the authorities had to let him go. No one remained to press charges against him for the storage unit break-in and the police lacked sufficient evidence to proceed with charging him for burglary and the other crimes they suspected him of committing. None of the stolen goods were ever traced to him. He had made certain Carole handled all their sales transactions. The police conjectured it was a primary reason why Carole had become so angry with Ken—because she was doing all the risky dirty work. The sales of stolen goods were traced only back to her and Ken. Kurt left Hickory Grove to parts unknown immediately following his release.

After the reality that Kurt had abandoned her had sunk in, Cyndi received the court's permission and moved to California to live with her parents. She opted to have her baby at last reporting.

Life at Annie's continued as usual, but without Denise. She never again reported to work and left town after her involvement with Kurt, in addition to her former marriage to Barry, was reported in the newspaper. She never even contacted Annie with an address of where to forward her final paycheck. Rumors had it she went to Texas where a childhood girlfriend resided.

After the attempt on my life, Mr. Campezi made it a point to diligently watch out for me. He made every excuse to stop by and check on my well-being which was fine by me because he usually brought a fresh supply of veggies and fruit—not to mention a plethora of uplifting comments. He felt somewhat responsible for Barry's attack on me; for not taking more of a stance when he had first seen who he thought might have been a prowler.

Brett turned out to be everything I had hoped for, and more, as both a carpenter and friend. Eagle-eye Annie says he has an interest in me beyond friendship. She is a hoot!

I stopped hearing from Richard, thank goodness. I guess the rumors about him having a new love interest were true.

Carole's iPad mysteriously took a swim with the fish in Lake Michigan.

And Jake? We'll see . . .

If you enjoyed this Nikki Carson mystery,
visit the authors' web-sites for more fun
reading:

NICKVERRIET.COM
SOCKMONKEYLADY.COM

Made in the USA
Charleston, SC
17 February 2017